SUZETTE A. HILL was born in East Sussex, and spent much
of her childhood playing spies and smugglers on Beachy
Head and picnicking at the foot of the Long Man of
Wilmington. Hill worked as a teacher in both public school
and adult education before retiring in 1999. She now lives
in Ledbury, Herefordshire. At the age of sixty-four and
on a whim, she took up a pen and began writing. Hill
has since published nine novels, including the Reverend
Oughterard series.

suzetteahill.co.uk

By Suzette A. Hill

A Little Murder
The Venetian Venture
A Southwold Mystery

The Primrose Pursuit

A Southwold Mystery

SUZETTE A. HILL

Allison & Busby Limited
12 Fitzroy Mews
London W1T 6DW
allisonandbusby.com

First published in Great Britain by Allison & Busby in 2015.
This paperback edition published by Allison & Busby in 2016.

Copyright © 2015 by SUZETTE A. HILL

The moral right of the author is hereby asserted in accordance with
the Copyright, Designs and Patents Act 1988.

A CIP catalogue record for this book is available from
the British Library.

10 9 8 7 6 5 4 3 2 1

ISBN 978-0-7490-1749-1

Typeset in 10.5/15.5 pt Sabon by
Allison & Busby Ltd.

The paper used for this Allison & Busby publication
has been produced from trees that have been legally sourced
from well-managed and credibly certified forests.

Printed and bound by
CPI Group (UK) Ltd, Croydon, CR0 4YY

CHAPTER ONE

'But it will probably be an awful affair,' Professor Cedric Dillworthy protested. 'I mean does one really want to spend a whole fortnight being charming to florists and old ladies on the east coast? Not exactly my idea of fun. Besides I am rather busy preparing notes for my new book *Runes and Reminiscences*; the publishers are hounding me already.'

Felix Smythe, proprietor and creator of Smythe's Bountiful Blooms in Knightsbridge, sniffed and replied tartly that while he fully realised that his friend had the utmost difficulty with florists he rather thought old ladies might be just up his street. 'Such instinctive empathy,' he beamed.

Cedric scowled but ignored the jibe. 'So what do they want you to do exactly – talk to the plants?'

'I have *told* you: judge the bouquets and displays, award

prizes and give two talks entitled "My Days amid the Daisies".'

'But you hate daisies.'

'That's neither here nor there; it needn't stop one rambling on about them. The point is that now I have my royal warrant I must expect to be approached for this sort of event and where necessary pander to the public's foibles . . . It's the regal association: people like being addressed by one who has the ear of the Queen Mother.' Felix flashed a modest smile, and picking up his embroidery inserted a few neat stitches. 'Besides,' he added, 'their fee is quite decent. Such little emoluments are always welcome.'

'Even if it means going to Southend?'

Felix gave a pained sigh. 'I do not envisage myself in Southend. The invitation comes from *Southwold*, an understated but rather more distinguished resort if I may say so. Its Plant and Garden Fiesta is renowned throughout East Anglia; I am surprised you don't know that. In any case my time there will be a useful rehearsal for next year.'

'Really? What happens next year?'

Felix shrugged. 'Well Chelsea of course, they are bound to ask me before long.'

'Hmm. Perhaps. But in the meanwhile I take it we are to brave the bath chairs, the hard pebbles and that cutting east wind. I was stationed there temporarily in the war and remember it vividly – especially the barbed wire entanglement on the seafront.'

'Since we are now in 1955 it is *just* conceivable that the municipal authorities will have had both the time and wit to remove such impedimenta. As to the pebbles: it is customary to use a deck chair – or it is for those of a certain age, dear boy.' Felix gave a broad wink.

'Which leaves the wind.'

'Well naturally you will take that superb Crombie coat which I so generously produced for your birthday. High time it had an outing, so now's your chance to slay 'em on the promenade!'

Cedric replied that he was beginning to feel a trifle slain himself and that unless he was offered a reviving dry martini the idea of accompanying his friend anywhere was out of the question.

Felix mixed a treble, with copious gin and a single olive but no ice; after which the professor seemed curiously malleable.

Elsewhere in London Lady Fawcett, widow of Sir Gregory, was also exerting pressure.

'You see, Rosy, it is all very tiresome. I was specifically relying on Amy to accompany me on my visit to Suffolk. After all, except for a brief sighting across a crowded room, I haven't seen Delia Dovedale for over thirty years. I may not like her any more – not that I ever did really – so should I suddenly feel the need to *escape* at least Amy could have given me moral support . . . well, in a roundabout way I suppose.'

Lady Fawcett frowned, while Rosy Gilchrist considered Amy's qualities as a potential aide-de-camp. Roundabout or direct, she suspected that the girl's supportive role in her mother's problem would be minimal – hearty zeal being no substitute for usefulness. Rosy had been drawn into the older woman's orbit two years previously, when, burdened by the scandal of her aunt's murder, she had found the Fawcett family's blend of worldly nous and airy indifference perversely reassuring.[1] The Fawcetts had been a mild diversion from darker matters. However, did she now really want to be Lady Fawcett's companion on her jaunt to visit the questionable Delia in her rambling Edwardian villa on the outskirts of a sedate seaside town? No, not especially.

Playing for time she cleared her throat and asked if her hostess was sure that Amy couldn't be persuaded.

'Oh I've tried incessantly but she is hell-bent on this *camping* nonsense. Admittedly the campsite is near Deauville, but even so I hardly think that bivouacking in the corner of some foreign field is going to improve her marriage chances. She ought to be *here* in London going to concerts and summer parties – or at least be with me at Delia Dovedale's.'

'But would East Anglia provide such entertainment?'

'Probably not; but there's bound to be something going on however modest. And besides, there's a son: not much brain I suspect, but plenty of money. An ideal match for Amy I should say.'

'But perhaps she will marry one of her camping chums.'

'Not if I can help it,' Lady Fawcett replied grimly.

With a little more cajoling, appeals to Rosy's nobler nature, delicate bribes and flattery – 'my dear you are *so* good at dealing with people!' – Rosy finally succumbed to the Fawcett charm and found herself accepting the proposal.

[1] See *A Little Murder*

'Wonderful,' the arm-twister cried. 'You won't regret it – we'll have so much fun!'

Rosy gave an uncertain smile.

The principal problem was Dr Stanley, Rosy's boss at the British Museum. After her recent mission in Venice to procure the coveted Horace volume she was unsure whether he would be prepared to grant her long leave to go gadding off to Suffolk with Angela Fawcett. It rather depended on his current mood. Buoyed up with plaudits for his latest lecture and still mildly grateful for the Horace acquisition, he might prove magnanimously agreeable; but enraged by criticism from a rival academic he would swear she was indispensable and refuse point blank. The betting was even-stevens.

Thus picking Friday evening as a good time and with diffident calculation, Rosy made her approach. She caught him under the portico en route to the Museum Tavern opposite. What would he be: benign at the prospect of a beer and a whisky chaser, or irritable to be waylaid? She would find out.

'You don't mean you will be staying with that Dovedale woman do you?' he had exclaimed.

'Er, well yes so I gather. Do you know her?'

Dr Stanley's features contorted into a grimace of startling intensity. 'Once was enough,' was the acid response.

There was a silence as Rosy waited for him to enlarge, and as he didn't she asked curiously whether the acquaintance had been a long time ago.

'Not long enough,' he said curtly. 'We had a little walkout

just before the war. She behaved abominably.' He fixed Rosy with a baleful eye: 'Do you know, among other things she had the nerve to call me a desiccated museum piece. *Me* for God's sake. Scourge of the Bloomsbury maidens I was in those days, and then some! Huh! I can tell you she was quite frightful.' He scowled into the distance.

'Must have been,' Rosy earnestly agreed. 'But, uhm, does that mean that you don't want me to go?'

'What? Oh yes, you can go all right. We've nothing lined up immediately – or at least nothing that I can't off-load onto young Rawlings.' He paused and then leered. 'Besides you can act as my emissary – tell her what a superlative boss you have: a model of manly charm, sharp intellect and fine sensibility. Lay it on thick and stress how lucky you are to be working for such a decent fellow. Make sure you do that, now.' He seemed about to sweep on resolute for the Tavern; but then checked his stride and said sternly, 'But there is one condition, Rosy, a condition which I insist you respect: I shall require my full quota of Southwold Rock; at least two sticks. Do not return without it.'

En route to her flat off Baker Street and thinking further of the coming trip, Rosy was not sure whether she had triumphed or blundered. Some victories were decidedly pyrrhic.

CHAPTER TWO

Lady Fawcett did not drive – something which in Rosy's view was no bad thing. Given the woman's vagueness and at times startling caprice, her presence on the open road would surely have presented an even greater hazard than it already did within the cloistered drawing rooms of Mayfair. Thus to be designated chauffeur on their Suffolk expedition suited Rosy well. However, she had rather assumed that her passenger might have some modest capacity for map-reading. She did not.

'I don't know what all these numbers are,' Angela Fawcett grumbled, 'I mean why can't they just print the *names* of the roads as they do in London such as Curzon Street, St James's Street, Sloane Avenue? All these letters and figures are so confusing. It would be so much clearer if they just put "The Southwold Road" or "Woodbridge

Junction" for example. As it is the whole thing seems to be in code. And why are some lines coloured red and others green? Rather bad luck if one were colour-blind I should think!'

There were a number of answers Rosy could have given but it was simpler to say patiently, 'Yes, I agree; it is all a bit tricky. But don't worry: just sit back and enjoy the scenery. We're bound to get there all right.' Of course she knew that they *would*, but thought ruefully that progress could have been considerably eased had her companion possessed the modicum of navigation skills.

The suggestion to enjoy the scenery was taken to heart. Once out of London and moving into the unchartered territory of the Essex–Suffolk borders Lady Fawcett was clearly captivated by the rural vista and set up a running commentary on the delights of the newfound landscape, eagerly prompting Rosy to look to right and left to admire the groups of ruminating cattle and po-faced sheep. Failure to react would stimulate more insistent gesturing. After a while Rosy's responses of 'Uhm' and 'Ah' and 'Charming' began to flag and she wondered if she could divert her companion's attention to something less likely to bring the car off the road.

'It will be fascinating to meet your friend after all these years,' she said. 'What with all the water under the bridge you will have masses to talk about.'

'Possibly,' was the slightly doubtful reply. 'From what I can recall of Delia she was one of the *heartier* girls. You know the sort – always leaping over wooden horses and spraining her wrist slamming tennis balls. Perfectly pleasant of course but a trifle *loud*. For one term I had to share a dormitory with her – rather a harrowing experience I seem to remember.' From the corner of her eye Rosy noted her passenger wince, presumably in recollection.

'Well I expect she has quietened down by now. Who knows, you may find her the essence of seemly reserve.'

'Perhaps,' said Lady Fawcett. She didn't sound entirely convinced. There was a pause, and then she added, 'I did meet the husband once . . . well it was at their wedding actually. He was loud too. He had a penchant for playing the trumpet.'

'But did he do that at the wedding?' Rosy asked.

Lady Fawcett sighed. 'Incessantly.'

There was a further silence as the passenger seemed to be brooding, though whether about the deafening notes of the trumpet or on other matters Rosy couldn't be sure. However, she quickly learnt.

'As a matter of fact, Rosy dear, I find it rather odd that she should have wanted to get in touch with me at all. Admittedly both our husbands were in the diplomatic service but our paths had long since diverged – she with her husband to Switzerland – he was an attaché there – and me to embassy life with Gregory in Paris and London. Although now I come to think of it, we did overlap for a brief period. He was assigned some temporary post in Paris but I think I only saw her once there and that was in the distance . . . she had grown rather stout I recall. Anyway we returned to England and I think they stayed on for a time. Of course we are now both widowed but that hardly constitutes a common bond. I can think of several widows who are daggers drawn . . . In fact,' and she giggled, 'Elsie Granchester's last cocktail party was virtually torn apart by the row between her and the widowed cousin. Simply *torn* apart!' She lapsed into merry mirth while Rosy took the chance to grab the map and swiftly check the route. So far so good: they were still on course.

With both eyes returned the road, she said, 'But didn't she give any indication? Perhaps she is just lonely and wants to renew old acquaintances.'

'I very much doubt that Delia Dovedale would ever be lonely whatever her circumstances. She certainly wasn't at school – always involved in things and bossing the pants off everyone. And from what I hear via the grapevine she is still at it. I gather the latest project is the big flower festival in that area – queen bee apparently. It is going on at the moment so I daresay we shall be dragged there to admire the exhibits, applaud the water gardens and wilt in airless tents.'

Angela Fawcett sounded quite fatigued at the prospect and it was Rosy's turn to giggle. 'Oh I am sure you will love it once you are there. After all you always attend Chelsea.'

'Of course, but that's only once a year: attending two displays in the same season is excessive I consider. And I gather this lasts considerably longer.' She paused, and then added 'But you are right about Delia giving an indication. In her letter she said that she was very eager to show me something, something she was rather proud of and which was really very exciting but that I wasn't to say a word. How I could say any word before learning of the topic, I have no idea. Still, if she wants to show whatever it is to me I shall naturally be the soul of discretion.' Rosy very much doubted this, Lady Fawcett being known neither for her tact nor her silence.

By this stage the landscape was flattening out and the wide Suffolk skies beginning to swirl above them. 'All very beautiful but not much shelter,' Lady Fawcett observed. 'Just as well Amy didn't come after all. She prefers the challenge of mountains; gets skittish like horses on the South Downs. Still,' she added grimly, 'I daresay she is enduring quite sufficient challenges on that awful campsite in France.' She sniffed disdainfully. 'Well she would insist . . .'

Another hour passed. And after a couple of false turns in the vicinity of Blythburgh, they eventually arrived at Laurel Lodge, Delia's residence, a mile or so out of the town, and, as described, a sprawling Edwardian house of mansion proportions secluded by trees and dense shrubs.

As they alighted Lady Fawcett said, 'Oh yes I remember: Delia says there is some sort of manservant called Hawkins who is old with a black patch over one eye. She insists he is not a pirate and that apart from the afflictions of patch and age he is perfectly all right.' Armed with this information Rosy hauled the suitcases up the steps and rang the bell.

They were indeed greeted by the elderly Hawkins,

mildly dashing in a black eyepatch and magenta bow tie. With a formal bow he relieved them of their luggage and ushered them into an empty drawing room. Evidently expecting to be faced by her hostess Lady Fawcett looked disappointed.

'Oh,' she said vaguely, 'I suppose Mrs Dovedale is still powdering her nose. She was always one for taking her time.' She gave a light laugh.

Hawkins hesitated and cleared his throat. 'Er, well,' he muttered, and then paused, scanning the room as if seeking another voice or inspiration; but then returning his good eye to Lady Fawcett said firmly, 'you see, madam, as a matter of fact she is not at home.'

'Really? How strange. She was most insistent that she would be here to greet us.'

'Ye – es I am sure she was; but she can't do that now I am afraid. She's, uhm . . . elsewhere.' He looked uncomfortable.

'Evidently. But where exactly?'

'The mortuary.'

Lady Fawcett looked mildly surprised. 'Goodness gracious, whatever is she doing there? Some kind of charity work, I suppose, although I don't quite know what sort of . . . still I remember from school, she always did have a morbid cast of mind . . .' Her voice trailed off and she gasped. 'Oh my God, you don't mean that she is—'

'Yes,' he said gravely, 'I am afraid she is.'

At that moment there was a commotion from the hall and in rushed a couple of bouncing pugs followed by a youngish man in glasses and sports jacket.

Seeing the visitors he stopped and exclaimed, 'Oh lor, you're here already! Thought I would just have time to give Peep and Bo their exercise before you arrived. But these creatures are so pernickety about where they squat that it slows everything down.' He put out his hand to the older woman. 'I am Hugh Dovedale and you must be Lady Fawcett. Mother was talking about you only the other day; she had been *so* looking forward to your visit.' And looking at Rosy he added, 'and of course to yours too Miss Gilchrist. I am just so sorry that circumstances are not of the best – it's all been rather sudden you might say. Still I expect you would like some tea after your journey.' He signalled to Hawkins.

His words had been delivered at speed and volume; and what with that and the cavorting of the dogs both women felt distinctly dazed. Mechanically they removed their hats, and muttering vague condolences sat on the sofa and awaited the tea. They gazed quizzically at their host who was busy with the pugs and intent on retrieving a recessed marrowbone from the fireplace. His efforts were cut short by the rattle of cups, and as Hawkins re-entered he straightened up and said, 'Yes, rather a frightful business I'm afraid; all very unfortunate – particularly just now of course.' Dismissing the tray-bearer he seized the teapot and started to splash the contents into their cups.

Why particularly 'now of course' rather than at any other time, Rosy wondered. Death was death wasn't it? She glanced at the tea which was pale grey and decided against it.

Lady Fawcett ventured a sip, winced slightly and sighed heavily. 'But it's so difficult to take in,' she said, 'I mean the idea of Delia being dead is just extraordinary. After all she was always so *healthy* on the hockey field; it used to make me worn out just watching . . .' She put a hand over her eyes, and Rosy was not quite sure whether this was to blot out the thought of her friend's death or the image of her being healthy with a hockey stick. She rather suspected the latter.

'Had she been ill?' she ventured.

'No, certainly not, fit as a fiddle,' Hugh replied. He stopped and frowned. 'Hasn't Hawkins explained?'

'Explained what?' asked Lady Fawcett lowering her hand.

'Mother has been murdered,' he said briskly, 'poisoned actually.'

Rosy gasped, and then whispered, 'Oh my God how dreadful!' She stared at Hugh in horror.

Lady Fawcett also stared; but at her teacup not Hugh. And then in a faint voice she said, 'I don't think I really want this tea. On the whole I would prefer to lie down.' She turned to Hawkins who was hovering by the door. 'Could you show me to my room please – and then perhaps you would be so kind as to bring me a large brandy? You needn't bother with ice.' So saying she rose, and collecting her gloves and handbag walked from the room.

Left alone with the man whose mother had been murdered, Rosy felt awkward to say the least. She studied the bereaved son with a mixture of pity and baffled curiosity. It must be ghastly for him – but what the hell was it all about! Her mind whirled with questions which she was hesitant to raise. Having only just been introduced this hardly seemed the moment. Nevertheless it was the *method* of dispatch that had most shocked her, chilled her really: it was suggestive of careful premeditation. What on earth had Delia Dovedale done to cause such stealthy disposal? From Lady Fawcett's remarks in the car the woman had sounded perfectly innocuous. Tiresomely loud perhaps but hardly murder material. Thus blending sympathy with tactful enquiry, she said, 'I am so terribly sorry, it must be agony for you – especially since, as you say, she has been poisoned.'

'I daresay there are worse ways of being dealt with,' he replied carelessly. 'I gather it was pretty quick, or so the quack says.' He gave a lopsided grimace and added, 'My apologies, it must be rather a shock learning like this, especially for your friend. We had tried to contact her to say not to come but the telephone line was temporarily down and then what with one thing and another . . .'

'Oh please don't apologise,' Rosy said hastily, 'you must have so much to deal with. Besides we'll be gone tomorrow. I am sure Angela would hate to intrude.'

'Oh you are not intruding – could be very useful in fact. Peep adores being surrounded by crowds, and having one less in the house is beginning to make her shirty. Bound to adapt, but for the time being you will fill a void in her life. Stay as long as you like, you will be most welcome.' He paused, took off his glasses, and polishing them on his tie added earnestly, 'Bo is much more robust and doesn't care a damn. Funny little creatures, aren't they?'

19

Rosy nodded but was somewhat nettled to think that she was being marked down as a handy hole-filler for a dog – or plug for a pug one might say. She also rather wondered if Bo and Hugh didn't share a similar temperament. Glancing at the two of them she saw the same amiable but slightly empty expressions, the only difference being that one set of eyes was bulging, the other a startling blue.

After an awkward silence Rosy cleared her throat and asked boldly. 'So when did you last see your mother?'

He shrugged. 'About a couple of days ago. As I told the police chap, she was being busy at the flower festival down the road and last seen was enjoying a cup of tea with a fellow judge. I was in a hurry to catch the train to London so wasn't really listening but I think she introduced him as Frederick somebody . . . oh no perhaps it was Felix. Yes, I remember now: Felix Bountiful, that was the name. Sounds a bit strange if you ask me – probably slipped her a Mickey Finn.' Hugh emitted a spluttering guffaw, and even as Rosy digested the news it passed through her mind that Lady Fawcett hadn't been far out in seeing him as a potential match for Amy.

'I think you may possibly mean Felix Smythe,' she said slowly. 'He has a flower shop called Bountiful Blooms in Knightsbridge but I've no idea what he is doing here.'

'Obvious,' replied Hugh, 'if he is indeed your floral friend then presumably he is here to judge the *blooming* flowers – just like mother. One trusts he doesn't meet the same fate,' he added darkly, and snorted again.

Rosy winced and wondered how one so crass could handle such wealth; paid a good advisor presumably.

However, she was less concerned with Hugh than with the news that Felix was in the area. And where there was Felix there was also likely to be Cedric. She sighed inwardly. It was odd that she seemed fated to confront violent death whenever she encountered that pair. Perhaps she was being dogged by a malevolent jinx that had a penchant for ill-assorted trios . . .

CHAPTER THREE

A few days earlier Cedric and Felix were also en route from London to Suffolk. With Cedric at the wheel their journey had been fast and largely silent; his companion, unlike Lady Fawcett, being less concerned with the changing scenery and ruminating cattle than with visualising his next encounter with the Queen Mother and his current appearance at the Southwold festival.

For both occasions Felix was considering his sartorial options. For the latter event he had taken the precaution of bringing two suitcases (ready for any eventuality, as he had insisted to Cedric); and in the case of the former he was firmly persuading himself that another visit to Savile Row was more than justified. Yes, he would see to that the very moment they returned to London. He smiled in anticipation. And then having decided that his aubergine smoking jacket would be eminently suitable for the hotel that evening – subtly raffish for the old ladies – he settled back, and closing his eyes slipped into a contented doze.

When he awoke they were on the outskirts of Aldeburgh; and as the evening sun began to wane they drove with ease, and for Cedric nostalgic pleasure, into the sleepy little town.

'Charming though Southwold is,' Cedric observed, 'in my view it is wise to be slightly detached from the hurly-burly; that way one is not being constantly approached or inveigled into things not entirely of one's choosing. Wouldn't you agree?'

Felix had replied that on principle he did agree although it rather depended on who was doing the approaching. He winked. 'But yes, you are right; I am sure Aldeburgh will be a most suitable bolthole, somewhere safe to collect one's breath after the rigours of the day.'

'You mean after intemperate questions about compost and how to parry the garden slug?'

'No. I mean their insatiable questions regarding my illustrious patron and her floral preferences, not to mention the endless cups of well-meant tea that one will be required to imbibe. And frankly having twice spoken with one of the major-domos on the telephone – a Delia Dovedale I think – a little distance might well be expedient. She sounded rather loud.'

Cedric nodded, pleased that his friend had been so cooperative. It was not always so. 'And of course,' he had added, 'we shall have the benefit of the sea immediately on our doorstep. The hotel stands only a few yards back from the beach and I have made sure that both our rooms overlook the front: thus we shall be woken by the sun and braced by the swirling of the waves. What could be more congenial?'

'I think I would rather be braced by a dry martini,' Felix had replied. 'I assume the hotel does have a bar.'

'But of course. This is The Sandworth not some rustic hostelry! We shall be most comfortable.'

And thus with peace and comfort in prospect the two friends drove into the hotel car park, hauled out the luggage – most of it Felix's – and prepared themselves to enjoy a restful evening before confronting the forthcoming busy events. That one of the busier events would be murder was not something they had envisaged.

The following day was bright but blowy, a condition not unknown in Suffolk, and after breakfast Cedric and Felix battled their way to the shelter of their car and set off for Southwold and the scent of flowers.

Here they were met by Delia Dovedale and other committee members and hustled into the organisers' tent for coffee and briefings about the day's programme.

'Such a pleasure to meet you, Mr Smythe,' cried Delia, gripping his arm firmly and steering him through the throng. 'Your articles in the *Tatler* give constant delight and thus to meet you in the *flesh* is a real bonus!' She squeezed the flesh of his arm tightly and he winced. Then addressing Cedric she said, 'And you must be the renowned Professor Dillworthy; how fortunate we are to have two such worthies in our midst!'

Cedric returned the toothy smile but felt a little peeved

to be so called. A 'notable' yes, but the term worthy was not one he associated with himself – least of all with Felix. It suited neither the Cambridge cloister nor the drawing rooms of Mayfair. However, he murmured something suitably self-deprecating.

'So what exactly is your line?' enquired an earnest looking woman at his side.

'Er – well at its simplest, rocks I suppose.'

He was about to explain that he was basically a geologist but with an extended interest in Cappadocian landscape and its monastic caves, but wasn't given the chance as at the next moment the woman gasped, 'What an extraordinary coincidence! A rockery expert, such luck! I've been meaning to talk to someone like you for ages. You see I am having the greatest problems in choosing the right kind of rocks for my front garden. I intend on growing alpines but cannot decide whether I should order slabs or the rounder rough-hewn variety. The latter might be the more attractive but slabs the more *striking*, more modern. What do you think, professor?' Without waiting for an answer she beckoned her companion: 'Eileen dear, this nice gentleman is going to give me expert advice on designing my rockery. Isn't that wonderful!' She turned back to Cedric. 'And then you see there is the whole question of *drainage* . . .'

Cedric thought about the afternoon and wondered if he could retreat to Minsmere. Wasn't it supposed to be a bird sanctuary? Any sort would do.

In fact escaping to Minsmere was not an option, Cedric's idea being met with strong disapproval from his friend.

'But they have reserved you a seat at the front,' Felix protested. 'There is to be some sort of prize-giving followed immediately by my lecture. I shall be there on the platform among the judges all poised to give my inaugural address the moment the last recipient has returned to the audience. Since it's my opening appearance I think at least you might be present to lend moral support and to lead the applause.' He twitched his nose and ran agitated fingers through his spikey hair. The effect was that of a disgruntled rabbit.

'My dear chap,' Cedric said quickly, 'I shall be only too pleased to take my place at your feet. I merely thought that you might feel hampered by my presence. Some speakers are sensitive that way.'

Felix sniffed. 'Not this one.'

And thus by three o'clock that afternoon Cedric had taken his allotted seat and Felix was ensconced on the platform with Delia Dovedale, Councillor Ruskin chairman of the judging panel, some man in a bow tie called Floyd de Lisle and two other festival VIPs. There was polite clapping as prize-winners for some of the kitchen–garden events trooped up to receive their accolades and brandish examples of their exhibits. One or two were asked to reveal the secrets of their success, which they did with varying degrees of lacklustre animation.

The leading contestant – or *chef de la classe* as Delia Dovedale insisted on bellowing – was a small woman cradling a gigantic parsnip. Apart from success in growing these vegetables she was evidently renowned locally as an expert soup maker, her speciality being iced parsnip consommé. Asked if she could offer any tips for its making she replied earnestly that the great thing was to use plenty of salt and margarine and a good sufficiency of the root itself. 'One cannot afford to be parsimonious with a parsnip,' she announced gaily – or at least that is what Cedric thought she had said. But since she spoke with a pronounced lisp he couldn't be sure; nor presumably could anyone else as her advice was received in puzzled silence.

However, that was not the end of the matter, for in gratitude for her prize she had brought along libations of the soup for the panel to sample. This had obviously been something prearranged, for at a signal from the chairman a pinafored lackey stepped forward bearing a tray of china cups which were then distributed to those on the platform. Cedric knew that Felix hated parsnips; and he also knew that by now his friend would be itching to take the floor himself and embark on his own carefully prepared topic. Thus it was with wry amusement that he observed Felix's stony face and fidgeting left foot. At the point when cups were raised he diplomatically dropped his pen and ducked under the table to retrieve it. As he emerged others were already sipping and dutifully nodding their approval . . . including Delia Dovedale whose lips seemed already forming the compliment of 'delicious!'

However, the plaudit got lost in a sudden grimace of horror, a grimace which in turn became a rictus of agonised contortion. Mrs Dovedale's eyes rolled wildly, her hands clawed at her throat from which came the most awful gasps of animal gagging. She half turned to her right: 'Felix!' she choked apoplectically. She tried to rise to her feet, but puce in the face keeled over and crashed to the floor where for a few dreadful seconds she writhed about beneath the pall of crumpled cloth and parsnip soup. And then all sounds ceased, and the creature she had become was stilled.

The audience too was stilled, frozen in stunned disbelief at what they had just witnessed. The first reaction came from the soup-maker. 'It has never had that effect before,' she said in a pained voice, and promptly passed out.

'I know nothing about vegetable marrows,' said Felix testily to the police officer, 'or begonias for that matter. I just happened to be on the platform prior to giving my talk on the structural complexities of floral pillars – something particularly close to the Queen Mother's heart. We were required to raise our glasses to the vegetable and begonia winners and the next moment the lady had turned scarlet in the face, cried "Oh Felix", choked and disappeared beneath the table. Why she should have called my name like that I cannot think; we barely knew each other and it was all very embarrassing.'

'Hmm,' said the inspector, 'and doubtless distressing too, sir.'

'What? Oh well yes, yes of course . . . very distressing. I mean it's not what you expect is it?' Felix fiddled with his left cufflink, a sure sign of his agitation and Cedric felt sorry for him. It was hard for Felix to be put through this sort of thing when he had been so looking forward to instructing a rapt audience in the niceties of floral architecture and narrating his more piquant anecdotes about the royal patron. To be upstaged by a case of spectacular poisoning was really rather bad luck. The anecdotes could of course be slotted in elsewhere but meanwhile he had to suffer the tiresome attentions of the local constabulary. The professor flashed his friend a sympathetic smile.

'You find it funny, sir?' asked the inspector politely.

'Certainly not,' Cedric replied stiffly, 'I was merely giving Mr Smythe my support. Being of a creative nature he is naturally sensitive and unused to such interrogations, especially in these sorry circumstances.'

'Oh this isn't an interrogation,' cut in the young constable cheerfully. 'These are just a few general enquiries. I mean if you want an *interrogation* you would have to come down to the station and—'

'Be quiet, Jennings,' snapped his superior, 'I've told you before.' He turned back to Cedric. 'And I gather you were among the audience sir, in the front row I believe; a good vantage point from which to observe anything unusual. Did anything strike you?'

Cedric informed him that, alas, he had not been struck since at that moment he had been busy perusing his programme and had only looked up when he heard the victim utter his friend's name. 'And there she was choking and spluttering and clawing at the table cloth . . . oh, and then her hat fell off and she slumped to the floor. I remember that vividly because the hat was rather attractive, wasn't it Felix?'

'One has seen far worse,' the other agreed doubtfully.

The inspector cleared his throat. 'But hats apart, there is nothing else that you recall? For instance, in what tone did the lady call out "Oh Felix"?'

As the witnesses frowned and considered, Jennings again gave tongue. 'What the inspector is asking,' he explained eagerly, 'is whether it was a tone of enquiry or of shock, of appeal, incredulity, fear . . . or,' he added darkly, '*accusation*.'

'Well it certainly wasn't the last,' Felix retorted indignantly. 'I trust you are not suggesting—'

'No, no Mr Smythe,' the inspector interrupted, 'DC Jennings wasn't suggesting anything, just seeking information. It's his way: gets overcome by zeal sometimes.' He smiled indulgently at the youth. Felix did not.

'I should say it was definitely a tone of appeal,' announced Cedric firmly, 'an instinctive cry for help to a kindly colleague. Alas it was too late and no such help could be given.'

The inspector nodded and shut his notebook. 'Thank you, gentlemen. That will be all for now. But I should be grateful if you do not return to London just yet as there could be some further questions we may need to put.'

'Further questions?' Felix exclaimed. 'I can't see that—'

'Oh we have no intention of returning to London,' Cedric said smoothly. 'We have barely arrived and the area is so lovely with much to explore. And in any case naturally we want to do all we can to assist the police in this ghastly business . . . Call us whenever you wish.' He added magnanimously.

After they had gone the two friends regarded each other in some dismay. 'That's all we need,' Felix lamented, 'an appalling killing literally under our noses, both of my talks rescheduled and the police hovering in the wings busily devising fresh questions. It's too bad!'

'Most unsettling,' Cedric agreed, 'but I suppose they

might have cancelled the whole festival; and at least you will still be judging the lilies and giving your talk on Sir William Walton's Ischian estate . . . Oh and by the way, there is something I was going to tell you, something Delia Dovedale mentioned just before her unfortunate event. It may brighten your day.' He gave a sly smile.

'I doubt it; but go on.'

'A bit of a coincidence really. Considerable in fact.' Cedric smiled again.

'Well hurry up!'

'I am told she had been expecting two house guests; she was going to introduce them to the delights of Southwold and immerse them in the pleasures of the fragrant marquees on the Common. It just so happens that we know them.'

'You don't mean the Mercoli brothers? I thought they were visiting the mad sister in Norfolk.'

'Still are presumably. No, these are Angela Fawcett and Rosy Gilchrist. They are supposed to be arriving on Sunday I believe – though of course the current situation may have deterred them. Still, worth an enquiry perhaps. You may recall that Angela owes us a luncheon. I am told that The Swan in Southwold is very good.'

Felix was startled and wasn't sure whether to be pleased or annoyed. As with most people his view of Lady Fawcett was mixed: she could both charm and infuriate; enrage and disarm – frequently at the same time. Undoubtedly possessed of a worldly shrewdness, she would nevertheless display a vagueness bordering on the miraculous. Most people walk through life; some plod and others amble. Lady Fawcett wafted. It was a motion which Felix found both endearing and perplexing; and given the current perplexity he was not sure that he could manage any more. And as for Rosy Gilchrist – well, pleasant enough of course but a bit too sharp for his taste, overly alert. Their relations were cordial but not what you would call close. Besides, did he really want to be reminded quite so soon of that troublesome Venetian experience? Only a few months ago the three of them had been caught up in a most unsavoury debacle – largely of her making he considered – and from which he had barely recovered.

'Ah well, I'm not sure—' he began.

'Good,' said Cedric briskly. 'If those two do appear at the Dovedale place then possibly they may learn something of what's going on. They could be a source of useful information and hear something we haven't. It's as well to be ahead of the field.'

What blithering field? Felix thought morosely. All one wants is to do the judging, deliver the lectures, collect the fee and get the hell out back to the safety of London . . . What had that wretched police youth said – *accusation*? The cheek of it! He gasped as a thought suddenly struck him: 'My God,' he exclaimed, 'you don't think they were intending to poison *me* do you – not Delia at all, and somehow she got the wrong cup!' He stared at Cedric in wide-eyed consternation.

'Oh I shouldn't think anyone would want to do that to you,' his friend reassured him, 'or at least only on very rare occasions.'

33

CHAPTER FOUR

Dinner that night wasn't quite as awkward as Rosy had feared. To her relief they were joined by Hugh's cousin Mark and his wife Iris. Living close by at Blythburgh they were frequent visitors at the house and obviously fully familiar with the Dovedale ménage. They seemed an amiable pair, and despite the shocking nature of events their presence conferred an air of normality which somehow helped soften the blow of the stark news.

Introductions were made, cocktails taken and generalities pursued. But inevitably by the time dinner was served the talk had turned to the deceased.

'But how was the poison planted?' Rosy asked. 'I mean obviously that soup she was sampling had been doctored, but when and how? There must have been a number of people wandering about in that kitchen and it's unlikely that you could take out a phial of poison and squirt it into the soup without somebody saying "steady on!"'

'Easier than you might think. The kitchen is open-ended; it's a glorified passage really and people are scurrying back and forth all the time carrying pots of tea and whatnot. Being busy makes one less observant. And according to Hawkins who was there helping, the cups containing the cold soup had been laid out on the tray for ages – at least forty minutes before they were wanted, so it needn't have been a rush job. You would just have to casually bide your time and take a calculated risk.'

'But you would hardly take a calculated risk regarding the right cup. How on earth did they select Delia's?'

Mark shrugged and they looked at one another in some puzzlement.

'Couldn't be easier,' said Hugh. 'As I told the police, mother was very pernickety about what she drank out of. At public events like that she resolutely refused to use the communal tea cups and always supplied her own. It was always the same one – Worcester porcelain with birds on. Nobody else would have had the temerity to touch it. She had a number of little fetishes of that kind; harmless but irritating.'

'Well that would be in keeping,' Lady Fawcett remarked. 'Now you mention it, I seem to remember her having a number of funny little habits at school. In fact I think I'm right in thinking that one of them did indeed have some connection with crockery: she couldn't abide the pottery mugs we were given and always had to have her own porcelain tea cup. *That* didn't go down with matron at all

36

well. Just shows how right they are about old habits dying hard!' She smiled brightly.

'Hmm,' said Hugh dryly, 'in this case the death was not so much hard as adamantine I should say.'

There was an awkward silence during which Lady Fawcett continued to smile blandly and stooped to tickle the comatose pug.

'Well, I can tell you,' Hugh continued, 'such jolly larks tomorrow. We are faced with the advent of the vicar and the undertaker to discuss the format of mother's obsequies – whenever they are likely to be; rather depends on the whim of the police I suppose . . . Do you think I should offer them sherry or would that simply retard proceedings?'

'Mr Snelgrove is very partial to milk chocolate – Cadbury's preferably,' Iris said.

'My dear Iris,' Hugh replied mildly, 'even I draw the line at having to watch the undertaker scoff chocolate while discussing the measurements of mother's corpse.' He looked at Mark: 'What do you think?'

'A small cup of black tea; they will decline but you will have made the gesture.'

Hugh nodded. 'That's it.'

'You know,' said Lady Fawcett changing the subject, 'as I was telling Rosy in the car, Delia said she had something rather special to tell me but that I wasn't supposed to breathe a word. Since I hadn't a clue what it was about the matter didn't arise. However, one rather wonders what it might have been . . .' She smiled vaguely at the round-eyed pug which had seated itself heavily at her feet. They exchanged appreciative glances.

'Hmm,' said Hugh, 'Mother was always telling people not to say a word. It didn't make much difference whether it was the vicar's verruca or the state of the nation, the topic was invariably under wraps – well, that is until she got bored and decided to broadcast it to all and sundry.'

'And did she?' enquired Rosy.

'Did she what?'

'Broadcast whatever it was she warned Angela not to.'

He shrugged. 'Difficult to say. I'm afraid I didn't always pay attention to Mother's confidences – there were so many.'

Rosy was about to laugh politely but was interrupted by Iris. 'Oh I bet I know what that was: the wretched *book* that she has been writing. It was top secret; in principle at any rate. Though she let it be known that the topic was broadly horticultural; in fact I rather gathered it was something to do with her days as an aspiring lady gardener imagining herself as Gertrude Jekyll – sort of floral reminiscences, I suppose. She did tell me the title once.' Iris paused, frowning in recollection. 'Something about violets I think – which was odd really as I don't think she liked them terribly; described them once as being puny common little things. Delia liked the big effects, such as massed gladioli laced with hydrangeas! . . . Oh yes that was it, *Violets and Other Vicissitudes*. I think it was a sort of plantswoman's journal or whatever it is these flower people write.'

'And I suppose the vicissitudes were the snares of groundsel and creeping elder,' added her husband.

'I've no idea, she never divulged. But I think she rather enjoyed it – the secrecy, I mean. There was what she called her "violet hour", i.e. six o'clock when she would mix a

38

large gin and Dubonnet, take it up to her bedroom and apparently scribble away until dinner.'

'Huh,' Hugh snorted, 'I don't know about that – not so much writing as napping, I should say.' He turned to Mark. 'Don't you remember that time we came back from fishing and the house was quaking under the sound of mother's snores. Even the pugs had taken cover!'

Iris laughed. 'Oh come on Hugh, that was only once; you do exaggerate. No, she was definitely writing this garden thing – or at least she *was*. But actually, now I come to think of it, for the last couple of months there had been no mention of it at all, not a word . . . probably gone off the idea. You know how she used to get these sudden crazes. Still, at one time there had been some talk of getting it published, though I don't know whether there was anyone who—'

'What about illustrations?' Lady Fawcett enquired, 'I don't recall Delia being good at art – what one might call a trifle unfocused; used to give Miss Spinks apoplexy. Maybe she had someone in mind – a local artist perhaps?'

'Hmm. I doubt it. I did ask her once and she replied rather grandly that her prose was sufficiently graphic in itself and didn't need extraneous embellishment . . . Delia could be awfully pompous at times!'

'I remember,' replied Lady Fawcett dryly, 'and loud with it.'

Rosy winced in embarrassment. But her companion sailed on smoothly: 'Ah well, no such little vagaries now I fear; those days are gone . . .' She sighed heavily and stared at her plate. Absence of tears did not prevent her from assuming an expression of lachrymose pain.

There was an awkward silence. And then Mark coughed and said, 'I know we've gone over this endlessly, but I really cannot imagine *why* it should have happened. I mean what on earth was to be gained by Delia's death?'

'Well it certainly wasn't money,' Hugh said gloomily. 'Under the terms of the trust I don't get anything for another ten years – when I am forty-five. And it's only when I reach seventy that the big stuff comes in.'

'Ah, just in time to fund a really good funeral,' his cousin observed; 'should be quite a show. But that's rather rare isn't it – to stagger things in that way. Is that what Delia wanted?'

Hugh shrugged. 'It was Pa's idea. He always did like making difficulties.'

'Well it hardly matters,' Iris said. 'I mean what with your grandpa's legacy and your own investments doubtless you can manage to hang on till the splendours of old age.'

'Oh doubtless. But I do think Ma might have provided for Peep and Bo; they are very high maintenance – aren't you my darlings?' Hugh addressed the pugs who snuffled rapturously.

'Perhaps she was going to but hadn't reckoned on the potency of poison,' Mark said soberly.

'Which brings one back to the original question,' ventured Rosy. 'Who would benefit?' As a stranger to the household and not of the family she was hesitant to intrude on such speculations, but having been largely silent on the topic felt social duty required some comment.

'Exactly,' chimed Lady Fawcett, '*cui bono*?' She spread

her hands and gazed quizzically around the table.

Goodness, Rosy thought, wherever did she pick that up? Jury service presumably. But she was even more surprised when the questioner answered her own query. 'You see,' Lady Fawcett continued in a confidential tone, 'it is my belief that this dreadful event benefits no one. For all we know it was merely a form of practice.'

'Whatever do you mean – practice for what?' Iris exclaimed.

'For someone else presumably . . . a sort of dress rehearsal for the real thing.' There was a silence as cutlery was laid down and the diners regarded her blankly.

'You are not suggesting there was something *un*real about mother's death are you?' asked Hugh. He sounded puzzled as well he might.

'Oh not unreal,' Lady Fawcett replied mildly, 'just unwarranted. Perhaps dear Delia was simply being used as target practice – a sort of handy guinea pig.'

Hugh looked startled. 'A handy guinea pig? I don't think Mother would have liked that – puts her in a rather secondary position: functional merely.'

'There's only one position Delia is in and that's under the turf – or she will be shortly,' Iris remarked grimly. 'She's dead poor woman, and it's appalling!'

'Appalling,' her husband repeated. And then leaning towards Lady Fawcett said, 'But I'm interested in your theory. Why do you say this?'

Lady Fawcett shrugged. 'Well you have said yourself the matter has been endlessly discussed and that you can think of no obvious reason for anyone wanting to do away with her. Thus it strikes me that whoever was responsible was using the situation as a kind of dummy run – that is the term, isn't it? After all, unless one is a practised poisoner I imagine that the prospect of administrating it must be quite daunting. It would certainly daunt me . . . I mean, just think, one could make the most frightful hash of things! Yes, if it were me I'd certainly want a couple of goes first – or one at any rate.' She smiled helpfully across the table before returning to her shepherd's pie which she pronounced as being awfully good.

Glimpsing Hawkins' sudden smirk in the sideboard mirror, Rosy assumed the concoction to have been his. Angela was right: the shepherd's pie was indeed excellent . . . though whether she was right in her idea of Delia as guinea pig was definitely more questionable. What a curious notion! But it held a sort of rough logic she supposed. Rosy regarded her companion with curiosity. What an odd mixture the Fawcetts were: a perplexing blend of vacuous inanity and worldly nous; even Amy and her cousin, the kindly chump Edward, had been known to show flashes of clarity . . . Besides if Angela Fawcett could throw such masterly parties, as she most certainly did, there had to be some acumen at work behind the placid veil.

'Well that's a new one all right,' Hugh observed, 'and it's certainly not anything the police have come up with. Perhaps you ought to suggest it to them Lady Fawcett, they could do with a clue,' he laughed; and then looking more serious added quietly, 'I wonder what Mother would have thought of it. She'd certainly have had *something* to say;

always did.' For a moment he looked mildly wistful.

Iris shook her head. 'Oh it's bound to be something much simpler: I bet it's to do with the mythical garden book; probably a case of jealously – some rival horticulturist also writing their floral memoirs got wind of her literary aims and in a moment of toxic spleen organised a quick disposal. It happens all the time,' she added airily, and then frowned. 'I'm so sorry; I'm being rather flippant . . . a sort of escape mechanism, I suppose.' Her voice faltered. 'God, it's all so dreadful.' She bit her lip and stared out of the window.

Mark flashed his wife a sympathetic smile. 'Well,' he said easily, 'you might just be right, I suppose. But I can't think of anyone else locally who is engaged on such a project.'

She smiled back, grateful for his support. 'There's always Claude Huggins with that huge garden at Dunwich.'

'But he has been at it for years. I hardly think—'

'*Precisely*,' Hugh interjected, 'it is because he has been doing it for so long that it has become sort of second nature. It's his life's work and he's damned if he is going to be pipped at the literary post by some gardening parvenu!'

Rosy felt sorry for Mr Huggins, and had visions of him toiling over his 'life's work' earnestly ranking varieties of fuchsia and lavender, unaware that he was being assigned the role of rage-wracked poisoner of snobbish bent. 'Poor man,' she murmured smiling, 'he's probably perfectly harmless.'

'Not entirely,' replied Hugh shortly. 'But he's not the type – too earnest for that kind of thing.'

'They're the worst,' Lady Fawcett observed.

* * *

43

There was a pause in the proceedings as shepherd's pie was ceremoniously replaced with rhubarb crumble, the rhubarb's acidity palliated by a globular custard of vicious sweetness. Clearly Hawkins' culinary talent was for mince and potato, and Rosy rather hoped there might be a concluding morsel of Cheddar to sharpen the sugared palate. 'Will there be an announcement in the newspapers?' she enquired.

'Oh yes, *The Times* and *The Telegraph*,' replied Mark. 'But if we want anyone to come to the funeral it had better be pronto. What do you suggest, Hugh?'

Hugh made a face. 'Not very good at this sort of thing – but we don't want anything too elaborate, it's bound to be costly.' He looked at Iris. 'What do you think?'

'Oh something like: "Delia Dovedale: passed prematurely on 19th June—"'

'Passed where?'

'*On* of course!'

'Hmm, sounds a bit lyrical,' remarked Mark, 'I think we need something snappier; and besides it makes it sound too leisurely.'

'Ah,' said Hugh, 'you mean like "Delia Dovedale on 19th June: settled with poison". Nothing leisurely about that!'

'Oh don't be such an ass, Hugh. Be serious,' Iris snapped. She turned to Rosy. 'Have you any idea?'

'Well if you want something to denote speed without drama I should think, "Suddenly in Suffolk" would do. It's a conventional phrase and hides a multitude of causes.'

'Excellent,' Hugh said, 'just the ticket: "Suddenly in Suffolk on 19th June: Delia Dovedale, beloved mother of

Hugh. Funeral at St Edmund's Church, Southwold on such and such a date. No flowers by request".'

'Whose request?' Iris exclaimed, 'certainly not your mother's. Considering she was the doyenne of the flower festival, not to have flowers would look perverse. In fact, when one comes to think of it the coffin should be smothered in them. It's only fitting.'

Hugh gave a pained sigh and muttered something to that effect that one could have too much of a good thing. What exactly he meant by that Rosy wasn't sure – no surer than she was of 'beloved mother' . . . a somewhat questionable declaration, she suspected. However, fortunately, it was none of her business. After all, her role was simply that of chauffeur and, according to Hugh, to fill a passing void for the bereaved pugs. She glanced down at the pair busily wrangling over an eviscerated toy and was struck by a grisly thought: if Angela Fawcett was right in her surmise that Delia had simply been used as 'target practice' for some more pressing disposal, perhaps the pugs were destined for the same fate as their mistress . . . after all they did rather resemble fattened guinea pigs!

After coffee and less sensitive topics the cousins departed, promising to return the next day in time for the vicar's visit, and the bereaved son announced it was time he gave the pugs their evening canter. On being asked if she would care to witness the event, Lady Fawcett declined saying that, delightful though the little dogs were, the prospect of the undertaker's visit the following day, not to mention the vicar's, necessitated an early night. 'One needs to be fighting fit with these people,' she confided to her host, 'otherwise they'll ride roughshod over your proposals and pull a fast one before you can say "knife".'

Hugh looked slightly taken aback but thanked her for the warning and muttered something about curtailing the pugs' nightly rampage.

Later when Rosy went to bid Angela goodnight it was to find her seated at the dressing table in curlers and a billowing peignoir. She enquired about the guinea pig theory. 'Do you really believe that?'

Lady Fawcett did not answer at first, being too intent on rubbing cold cream onto a surprisingly unlined face. 'I am not sure if this stuff is any good,' she mused, 'but then if one *didn't* do it the worst might occur sooner rather than later . . . What do you think, Rosy?'

'Er, what sort of worst?'

'Disintegration, of course.'

Rosy laughed. 'Oh I'm sure you don't need to bother about that.'

'Oh but one does bother! You'll learn that soon enough my dear.' (Thanks a lot! Rosy thought.) 'However,' she continued, 'I suppose the main thing is to try to parry the ravages while you can. Rather like people really: if you don't fend them off firmly they'll take you over, and then . . .'

'And then you are in the soup!' Rosy giggled.

Lady Fawcett beamed. '*Exactly*.' And she applied a further scoop of cream.

'So what about your idea at dinner?' Rosy persisted. 'Did you mean it?'

'As good a suggestion as any others I daresay. As said, from what I recall of Delia although she could be exceedingly tiresome I cannot see her actually posing a threat to anyone – other than to induce fatigue or deafness of course. But I should have thought that poison as an antidote was a little excessive . . .' She tightened one of the curlers. 'Oh and talking of excessive, tomorrow is going to be a *very* heavy day. Apparently in addition to the vicar and undertaker, the day after we are also to be faced with the Brightwells. They live quite near and are – or were – close friends of Delia. We used to know him years ago in Paris but I've never met the wife. Gregory quite liked Lucas but personally I always found him rather dull. Of course people can improve but I rather suspect that is not so in this particular case. I am told he has become rather high-minded . . . Oh dear, the cloth, the sexton and Lucas – not the most enlivening of trios.' Lady Fawcett sighed and looked genuinely weary.

'We don't *have* to stay,' Rosy said brightly, 'as you said yourself, we could always find an excuse and escape back to London.'

'Oh but I think we *should* stay. Or at least it would quite interesting to do so, don't you think? In fact,' and she dropped her voice, 'things are more intriguing than I had expected. And Hugh seems most eager that we should remain until at least after the funeral. Seemed to think his mother would have wished it . . . well I don't know about that, but I suppose if that's what he wants it would be churlish not to, though goodness knows when they are likely to release the body for burial. Don't they have to do *tests* or something? Poor Delia, she was awfully squeamish you know.' For a moment Lady Fawcett looked pensive; but then giving a final rub with the cold cream, added, 'And you see if I am still up here in Suffolk when Amy returns from her camping trip it means I shall be spared the brunt of the initial onslaught.' She closed her eyes in painful prospect; and taking her cue Rosy slipped from the room.

CHAPTER FIVE

'But Hugh,' Iris protested the next day, 'you must provide some sort of sustenance if only tea and cake. After all many will have travelled some distance. And whatever the distance, enduring a funeral is always hard work, it sort of takes the stuffing out of you.'

'Yes, but we don't want the thing to drag on do we,' her cousin replied. 'It's not as if this is Ireland where their wakes persist for days.'

'A cup of tea and a slice of seed cake is hardly a wake! Do be realistic. And a few cucumber sandwiches wouldn't hurt, otherwise it looks so mean; I'll make them myself if you like.'

'All right,' Hugh conceded gloomily, 'but I draw the line at jelly and cream. I suppose you'll be suggesting that next.'

Such culinary wranglings were interrupted by a voice from the doorway. 'Rosy dear,' said Lady Fawcett benignly, 'would you mind awfully if we drove into Southwold? I think a little outing might clear my mind of this wretched business. I hardly slept a wink last night and I am sure a touch of sea air would help enormously. Besides, I really must try to find a good black hat – I can hardly wear my pink one.'

'Good idea,' Hugh said, 'I wish I could accompany you but there is the delightful prospect of the undertaker's visit, not to mention the vicar's to discuss the order of service . . . whenever that's likely to be. I wish to God the police would hurry up, we can't hang about for ever. Oh by the way, you don't have any suggestions regarding hymns do you? He is sure to ask.'

Lady Fawcett paused, apparently deep in thought; and then said brightly, '"Fight the Good Fight" is very popular, it has a rousing swing and gets things off to a good start. Yes, one can't go wrong with that, it fits most things,' she added helpfully.

Even murder? Rosy wondered.

Hugh nodded. 'Most suitable,' he declared.

'Well at least we have outmanoeuvred the undertaker,' Lady Fawcett remarked once they were in the car, 'and if we stay away long enough we shall miss the vicar too.' She smiled in satisfaction. 'Both very worthy I am sure, but one needs a little uplift at such times and I cannot see it coming from that direction . . . I suggest we have some coffee before we embark for the milliners, there's bound to be somewhere nice. Hawkins may make a good shepherd's pie but his coffee is *most* disagreeable.'

They set off for the town; and as Rosy drove slowly up the High Street and into the Market Place she tried not to be distracted by her passenger's cries of approval as she urged the chauffeur to take note of the passing scene: 'Oh *look*, what a gem of a façade – it's pure Georgian. Quick Rosy or you'll miss it! . . . Oh, and just look up at that lovely painted lady! It must be a ship's prow; what do you think? She must be a mermaid . . . And my goodness, is that a lighthouse looming over there? It's as if it's in the very next street. Do turn your head!'

And thus the commentary continued; but luckily Rosy soon found a parking place and she drew up in sight of Gun Hill, the sweep of turf graced by the six heavy guns guarding the little town from the French or other maritime marauders.

'Most picturesque,' Lady Fawcett observed as she gazed at the view, 'and it's reassuring to think we are protected by the artillery, but cannons are not much use against this wind. All very invigorating but I shall be quite blown away! Coffee calls I think.' They turned back in search of elevenses and hats.

Meanwhile Cedric had detached himself from Felix (being lionised in a tea tent) and was wandering around those parts of the town familiar to him from wartime. He had spent some time there in the months leading up to D-Day, and, although by then the worst of the bombing had ceased, the little town was badly battle-scarred and still forlornly alert to enemy bombardment. With the evacuation of a large bulk of the population – children, the elderly, mothers and other non-combatants – its centre had been relatively quiet, busy but hardly bustling; the residual inhabitants, such as military personnel, stubborn stalwarts, firefighters, fisherfolk and those in clerical and executive positions, discharging their duties with a stoical sobriety.

And yet, Cedric mused, despite such denuding of the normal populace – or perhaps because of it – there had been an extraordinary sense of unity, an intimate camaraderie which, for all the tensions and threats of war, had been curiously pleasurable. Southwold then had been a tiny microcosm: a world in miniature tough and watchful; echoing the mood of London, Liverpool, Coventry and countless other parts of the British Isles, cussed and unbowed.

In a reminiscent mood he walked slowly along Pier Avenue, into Marlborough Road, recalling the devastation of the then bombed-out houses and marvelling at the strangeness of their restoration. Some of course had never been renewed, the old Grand Hotel at the bottom of Field Stile for instance. Even now he could visualise its gutted rooms, the scattered tiles and debris, gaping windows from which no guest would ever gaze again. It had been like that when he had arrived and remained so until his leaving . . . And now twelve years hence spruce bungalows were being built and the ravages of incendiary in turn obliterated.

At the corner of Stradbrooke Road, just in sight of the lighthouse, he stopped abruptly, seeing the fire watcher Bertie Simmonds sprawled bizarrely on the pavement. Two colleagues had lain there with him, idly strafed by a Jerry bomber returning from Lowestoft. They had stood up; Bertie Simmonds never did.

He continued towards the lighthouse, as upstanding now as miraculously it had been through the bombing; and as he reached St James's Green, graced by its flagpole and the reinstated pair of guns, his mood lightened as he suddenly recalled the night he and the others had staggered from the corner pub bellowing some scurrilous song from the earlier war, and then linking arms had done an absurd capering cancan across the little triangle.

He gazed quizzically at the pub: not much change there it would seem. Should he go in? He hesitated but decided not. 'You can never recapture the moment,' a woman's voice echoed. 'You can try but it never works and then you're buggered.' Cedric gave a wry smile. It was the voice of a woman he had once known yet never loved. But she was right of course, and instead he turned to stare at the sea and listen to the plaintive notes of crying gulls . . .

Enough of nostalgia! Cedric pulled himself back to the present. Roaming around rekindling wartime memories made thirsty work; a cup of Lapsang beckoned. Would he find such? Probably not but coffee would be welcome. He made his way to the High Street trying to find the tea shop he had once patronised. It wasn't there of course, but something similar and smarter stood two doors down, a sign outside proclaiming 'Mammoth scones straight from the oven.' He wasn't sure about the mammoth part but a warm scone did sound inviting – perhaps he could order a mere half. He entered, and as he hovered looking for a suitable table heard a familiar voice.

'But it's so tiresome having to buy a black hat,' Lady Fawcett exclaimed. 'I mean one has masses at home – what I call my death collection – but I hardly came *here* expecting a funeral. Perhaps that marvellous woman in Knightsbridge can jazz it up in time for Ascot . . .' she broke off, suddenly seeing Cedric poised by the entrance, and beckoned imperiously. 'We gathered you were here,' she said gaily. 'Do sit down. Rosy and I were just talking about you both.'

'No you weren't,' said Cedric, taking the third chair, 'you were talking about hats and funerals.'

'Oh well, much the same – I mean you *are* coming aren't you? You must have known her quite well.'

'Far from it,' he replied, 'we had met her twice, that's all.'

'Yes, but the last time was rather shocking. I should have thought that—'

'Angela means that having been in at the kill – front row one hears – you would presumably also have a prominent seat at the funeral,' Rosy interposed dryly.

'My goodness, Miss Gilchrist,' Cedric said in not entirely mock surprise, 'you don't mince your words! It must be this invigorating Southwold air – it sharpens the tongue. I must remind Felix to wear a thick muffler.'

'And where is Felix?' Rosy asked.

'Being loquacious among lilies. It helps him to keep his mind off things, especially the prospect of more questions from the police. He's convinced that he is their prime suspect. But he is equally convinced that he was the intended target.'

'Pure paranoia,' she laughed. 'Would you like the other half of this scone? It's too mammoth for me.'

Cedric graciously accepted the offering, spread it carefully with a thin layer of jam and ordered some coffee. As he did so a man wearing a trilby and a raincoat with a turned up collar entered the café. He had a small moustache.

'Do you think he's a detective?' breathed Lady Fawcett.

'Either that or a tax inspector,' Rosy replied.

Cedric looked up. 'He is neither. His name is Floyd de Lisle.'

'There you are, you see, straight out of *Casablanca*! But how do you know his name?' Lady Fawcett asked.

'Because he was one of the judges on the platform when Mrs Dovedale collapsed. He was among those interviewed with Felix.'

'Really?' asked Rosy. 'He doesn't look very horticultural. I shouldn't have thought he would know a hoe from a turnip.' She watched as the man strode over to a far table where a young woman was sitting on her own, removed his hat with a flourish and planted lavish kisses on her outstretched hand. She simpered and knocked over her tea cup.

'Hmm,' murmured Cedric, 'not quite in the Bogart

and Bergman style I should say.' The other two nodded agreement and returned to the more interesting subjects of hats and homicide.

'I wonder if they know yet what sort of poison was used,' Rosy mused.

'I believe cyanide has been mentioned,' Cedric replied. 'Apparently one of the other panellists told a reporter he had heard her mutter the word "almonds" just before crying out Felix's name. One gathers that some victims have an acuter sense of smell than others. Still, people tell the press a lot of things that aren't strictly true . . .'

'Such a ghastly way to go,' Rosy said with feeling.

'Oh putrid,' Lady Fawcett agreed with slightly less feeling, 'especially as she hated it.'

Cedric was startled. 'What on earth do you mean? Surely you are not suggesting she had some familiarity with the stuff?'

'Oh no. It was simply that she had an aversion to the taste of almonds. I remember at school, matron tried to give her an aspirin dissolved in some almond milk and she spat it out all over her gym shoes.'

'An example of age retarding reaction,' observed Cedric. 'A few seconds quicker and she might have survived . . .' He glanced at his watch. 'Now,' he said briskly, 'I'll get the bill and then I propose we go and book a table at The Swan for two days hence. We haven't dined together for some time, not since you were our guest at Covent Garden. What a pleasant evening that was!' He flashed Angela an encouraging smile.

She blinked and after a fractional pause, said, 'Yes, simply delightful – and now I can return the favour.'

'How kind,' Cedric murmured.

Afterwards in the car going back to Laurel Lodge, Lady Fawcett remarked to Rosy that in her view Cedric Dillworthy was getting too sharp by half and it was just as well she had remembered to bring her cheque book.

CHAPTER SIX

Like a number of others in Southwold, Floyd de Lisle, proprietor and sole representative of The Select Publishing Co., was more than puzzled by the horrific nature of Delia Dovedale's death . . . it had been shocking, grisly and so appallingly public. When she had begged him to appear on the platform as a replacement for Claude Huggins (laid low with one of his usual footling colds) he had been quite amused, flattered really; after all, his knowledge of gardening was nil and the only vegetables he ever ate were spuds. But presumably the organisers had felt he might add panache to the panel – a touch of wit and colour notably lacking in old Huggins. Still, had he known that *this* was going to happen he would have stayed well away – as presumably would she!

He frowned and brooded on the victim: a nice enough

woman, but too gushing and intense; being patronised by assertive females was not to Floyd's taste, and the generational difference had added to the social gap. Thus on the whole he had had little in common with the deceased – except of course until recently when he certainly did.

It had been the blessed novel, or, as she would coyly describe it, 'my naughty bit of nonsense'. When she had first approached him with the preliminary chapters he had been dubious (debut novels by elderly ladies of a certain ilk not being noted for their commercial value), but since the thing was relatively literate and she had not flinched when he had mentioned his considerable fee he had graciously accepted her proposal and mooted a print run of one thousand.

'You won't regret it,' she had cried eagerly. 'I assure you, there is more in this than meets the eye!' (A claim he had firmly doubted). And swearing him to secrecy, she had rushed from the office threatening to deliver fresh material the instant it was penned.

By and by such deliveries were made and Floyd had grown moderately interested. The thing was less bland than he had expected, indeed in places was surprisingly risqué; and the setting – largely Paris – was well established. At one point he had enquired if she wanted her own name on the cover. 'Oh I think not,' she had replied, 'it mightn't be wise.' She had paused, and then with a little smirk added, 'You see, speaking *confidentially*, Mr de Lisle, it is not entirely of my *own* devising.'

He had been disappointed and immediately revised his idea of offering the old trout a small fee reduction.

Why should he lose money to some collaborator or ghost-writing crony? 'Ah,' he said coolly, 'so a friend has written it with you, has she? What one might call a shared muse, I suppose.'

Delia Dovedale had looked indignant. 'Nothing shared about my book, I can assure you,' she retorted. 'Barely a word or thought touches these pages that is not my own!' She had looked rather fierce, and Floyd had smiled in swift apology. 'My point is that this is only partially fiction: a great deal of it is material that I have *transmuted* into the fictional mode. I believe "faction" is the term your trade uses.'

Floyd was impressed that she should know the term; it was only just coming into vogue. 'I see,' he said slowly, 'so these characters, these events, have been part of your own life – part of your life in Paris after the war?'

'Precisely. And with luck I'll have another two chapters for you in the next fortnight. Now I can't stay any longer – the pugs are in the car and they'll get fractious and cause a riot. So tiresome.'

Other than her welcoming speech on the festival platform those were the last words Floyd heard the authoress utter, and he certainly never received the promised new chapters.

Nevertheless, after that last encounter he had reread the manuscript more carefully and done a lot of thinking. Current business was not all that marvellous – there being a limit to how much effete poetry and 'fascinating' life stories readers were prepared to swallow, or, more to the point, purchase. Admittedly he charged enough up front for producing the damn things, but the real kudos lay with the subsequent sales, a handy fifty per cent of the takings. Of such sales, latterly there had been precious few and the local bookshop owner was becoming bored with his clients' mediocre 'vanity' offerings. The section the shop allocated to the Select Publishing Co. was becoming irritatingly sparse. Something new was required – something original, racy and of sound commercial value; a book whose obvious success would bring would-be authors pounding to his door, would please the bank manager and earn him a nice little vacation . . . skiing in Austria would be fun, he hadn't done that for ages. He saw himself begoggled on the slopes, ski-sticks slung casually over his shoulder and a pretty Fräulein on his arm. Yes, he mused, it was time he had a bit more of that . . . after all he wasn't getting any younger.

The old girl's tale was intriguing, not simply because of its risqué element, but because he got the distinct impression that it was based on someone she had known well – indeed she had hinted as much – someone quite likely still alive: after all Paris just after the war was not so long ago. Delia had moved in high circles so whoever it was could presumably be of some standing or distinction. Never having been to Paris nor moved in such circles Floyd hadn't a clue (though presumably de Gaulle could be ruled out!) but he knew people who might have: publishing chums in London. It was amazing what could be picked up via the Soho and Fitzrovian grapevines. Admittedly she had sworn him to secrecy – as so many of his aspiring authors did – too shy to reveal their dreams until the thing was a glossy reality – but it was hardly an immutable embargo. Besides, she was bound to have confided in one or two cronies, they always did. Indeed for all he knew sly gossip was already insidiously doing the rounds – gossip that he could certainly exploit when the time for publication arrived. A few discreetly worded phrases on the back cover and a well-judged press release might net invaluable returns. Meanwhile he would make subtle enquiries. The ski slopes and the pretty Fräulein beckoned.

Thus with such a rosy prospect in mind the news of Delia's fate had initially hit Floyd hard. Certainly he had come to quite like the lady and was genuinely upset by her fate, but on the whole his feelings were more acutely engaged by his own loss: barely half of the thing being in his possession and its author now dead. Frustratingly the golden goose had turned a delicate shade of grey . . . It was only later that he recognised the platinum potential.

Later that day Rosy came across Hugh in the greenhouse – not contemplating his late mother's plants but sprawled in a deckchair reading a book. She noted its title: *Bulldog Drummond Strikes Again*.

'Ah,' she said diffidently, 'I expect you can do with some relaxation. It must be awful having to deal with all the police enquiries.'

'Not half as bad as having to cope with Snelgrove,' he informed her.

'Who?'

'Reginald Snelgrove, our esteemed undertaker. I thought I would never get rid of him. Kept wanting to know what I thought Mother's wishes would have been. "Wishes?" I said. "To be left in peace presumably and the sooner the better."' Hugh frowned. 'I got the impression that wasn't the right answer. He kept hovering around and mumbling something about did I want a Grade One or a Grade Two interment and did I have any destination in mind for the wreaths after the ceremony . . . Frankly it was all quite bothersome.' Hugh put the book down and heaved a sigh.

'I can imagine,' Rosy said sympathetically. 'You've so much to cope with. Are you really sure you want Angela and me to remain? We could slip away quite easily you know.'

'Oh no,' he said startled, 'you must stay at least for the funeral. After all, Mother needs all the support she can muster! She approved of people rallying round in time of need.'

Rosy nodded slightly nonplussed. 'Well, if you are sure—' she began.

'Oh absolutely. Besides I'm going to go to London shortly for a couple days. Got one or two things to sort out. You can hold the fort with Peep and Bo and make sure that old Hawkins doesn't play the giddy goat,' he emitted a snort of mirth.

The picture of Hawkins playing the giddy goat was difficult to envisage, but Rosy smiled and then said something to the effect that she was glad the police weren't being unduly restrictive about the movements of witnesses. 'One hears they can be quite pernickety in such matters.'

'You forget, Miss Gilchrist,' Hugh replied coolly, 'I was elsewhere when it happened and thus not a witness – although possibly that does not preclude me from being a suspect.' He tapped the book. 'After all according to this chap, killers quite often mastermind disposals from afar – though rarely of their mothers it seems. Still, I am sure the police are aware of that. Thus should they – or indeed anyone else – want me I shall be at my club.' He flashed a formal smile and returned to his book, while Rosy cursed herself for being so inept.

She returned to the house vaguely disconcerted. Hugh's seeming insouciance in the face of his mother's shocking demise was puzzling. Was he as indifferent as he appeared, or was the flippant exterior simply the product of tight schooling and emotional discretion? Either was possible. But it wasn't just that that nagged her, there was something else. Much of the time he appeared the genial buffoon, shallowly good natured. Yet very occasionally – as just now for instance – she detected a hint of hardness and a flinty intelligence he seemed at pains to conceal. It was strange, and on the whole she felt she would be glad when the funeral was over and they could return to London.

CHAPTER SEVEN

Rosy did not dislike the Brightwells, in fact she found Freda Brightwell quite engaging in a limited way. Her bulky figure was not especially enhanced by the expensive coat and skirt and stylish brogues, but she exuded a brisk benevolence which, given the situation, Rosy found cheering. And compared with the languorous Angela her personality verged on the almost bubbly.

No such bubbles, latent or actual, could be detected in her husband. Lucas Brightwell had the look and demeanour of a man who knew what he was worth – and according to Iris he was worth quite a lot. In his youth he had made a substantial killing on the stock exchange, and following a briefly successful spell at the Paris Bourse after the war had returned to London to make more money in the City. But Lucas's talent for spotting a good deal did not make him a mere city slicker, for he had combined his financial acumen with sound public service – being occasional financial advisor to the government, sitting on a couple of hospital boards and supporting a number of high-profiled charities. Worthy, able and respected, he was destined for higher things – a permanent post as government advisor, and, it was whispered, a possible recipient of a newly created baronetcy. The previous evening Hugh had made a comment in questionable taste to the effect that Brightwell had better get his smug act together before the rug of elevation was pulled from under his feet. 'You'll see,' he had said darkly, 'the days of the hereditary system are numbered and they are already docking mere knighthoods. Old Lucas may just slip through the closing door, but he had better be quick about it otherwise he'll be left without a handle to his name. No perks for jerks!' He had roared with laughter and passed rapidly on to something else.

Sitting next to Lucas at lunch it had certainly not struck Rosy that her neighbour was a jerk, nor indeed that he was smug – or at least not in any crude sense: there was assurance most definitely, and, as Lady Fawcett had hinted, a whiff of self-regard . . . but then many people had that. Some sign of leavening humour would have been welcome, but she could not detect any. Still, he was pleasant enough and his descriptions of his charitable activities interesting. She couldn't help thinking that her host's observation had been uncalled for – but perhaps Hugh's disparagement of his guests was customary. She wondered wryly what he might have to say about herself and Angela once they had departed.

The conversation at lunch had been bland and general – hard to be otherwise given the shattering absence of the hostess. The air hung heavy with unspoken comment and question; but an aura of practised normality prevailed and food and drink consumed with pleasure and compliments.

After the coffee Lucas Brightwell murmured an excuse and took himself off, leaving his wife to accompany Iris to Delia's bedroom to sort the dead woman's personal belongings. Turning to Lady Fawcett, Freda Brightwell observed, 'Such a sad task but needs must, I fear. Should we save you some small memento, a reminder of happier days perhaps? A little knick-knack to keep on your desk or a handkerchief sachet?' She gave a kindly smile.

Lady Fawcett looked startled. 'Er . . . well,' she replied doubtfully, 'I am not sure whether – I mean, well it was nearly forty years ago . . .' And then in a firmer voice and with equally firm smile, she said quickly, 'How thoughtful! Any little trinket would be most welcome.'

When they had left the room, she said to Rosy sotto voce: 'I cannot imagine why it should be supposed I might want one of Delia's bits and pieces. Anyone would think we had been bosom pals; and why I should be interested in her handkerchief case I cannot imagine! She had one at school I recall – badly embroidered and always grubby.'

Rosy suppressed a smile. 'Oh I am sure Mrs Brightwell meant well.'

'Oh doubtless . . . just like Amy.' Lady Fawcett sighed. 'I do hope that girl is all right. She has never been camping before and I can hardly telephone her in a *tent*.'

'But she is bound to be fine,' said Rosy encouragingly, 'after all wasn't she in the Girl Guides?'

'Hmm, but not for long. She wasn't suited – kept unravelling all those knots they would insist on tying. I thought it showed dexterity, but they called it sabotage. Ridiculous! Her father was most indignant, but they stood their ground and she had to go.' She frowned in bemused recollection.

An hour or so later when Rosy had returned from her ramble with Peep and Bo she encountered Iris and Freda Brightwell coming down the stairs burdened with holdalls and loaded carrier bags.

'Well that's broken the back of it at any rate,' Iris announced triumphantly. 'Most of the clothes can be collected by the Red Cross and much of this can go to the Mothers' Union, they are always glad to get good stuff for their bazaars. I think we've had a pretty good sort-out, don't you Freda? We deserve some tea. I'll ask Hawkins to bring a tray.'

Freda, who now looked rather less soignée than when she had arrived, agreed eagerly. 'Oh yes a cuppa, as they say, would be most restorative! You're right, we do seem to have dealt with most of it.' She paused, frowning slightly. 'But I am rather surprised that we didn't come across her book.'

'Which book?'

'That one she was writing.'

Iris laughed. 'Oh you mean the precious nature notes or whatever they were. Probably thrown in the dustbin ages ago. Delia was a creature of whim and passing fad. Something would occupy her for a while and then she would lose interest and rush on to something else. Mind you, this latest fad did seem to be occupying her rather longer than usual, but it was probably jettisoned . . . Come on, let's go and sit down. I need a cigarette.'

She led the way into the drawing room and the two women followed. Rosy noted that Freda still looked preoccupied and was not surprised when she pursued the matter by asking if anyone had searched the writing desk. Iris assured her that this had already been done by Hugh and that nothing of interest had emerged least of all a literary manuscript.

Freda had looked slightly disappointed and seemed about to take the subject further but was forestalled by Iris. 'Actually,' she said apologetically, 'do you mind awfully if we move on to something else? I think I have had rather enough of poor Delia for one afternoon. Sifting through those things upstairs was quite difficult.' She suddenly looked tired and drawn, and Rosy was reminded of her link to the murdered woman. Being the cousin's wife and living so near, she must have known her in-law quite well. Despite the outward calm, she was probably finding the whole affair excruciating. Tactfully Rosy started to ask about the garden festival and other matters of local interest.

Later, with Lady Fawcett retired to her room – assiduously resting – and Iris and Freda departed for Blythburgh, Rosy was left to her own devices. She scanned the large bookcase, and, taking down a copy of *Punch* and a volume of short stories by W. Somerset Maugham, decided also to spend a quiet hour in her bedroom.

She went into the hall en route for the stairs, pausing to confront a large portrait of Delia hanging above the banisters. The sitter, wearing a filmy grey cocktail dress and assertive pearls, gazed down benignly. The picture was likely to have been painted at least a decade earlier for the carefully waved hair was still a resolute brown, and on her lap sat not a pug, but a small cairn terrier – probably the beloved 'Arthur' of yesteryear that Hugh had mentioned in passing.

Rosy gazed at the face with its placid innocuous expression, and wondered how on earth such a one had been fated for murder. Admittedly, Angela Fawcett's recollection of her school friend had been one of loudness and robust vigour – so perhaps Delia had been more aggressive than the portrait implied; and certainly from what hints Rosy had gleaned from Mark and Iris it would seem that she had been no shrinking violet. Had the artist deliberately softened the features to give a milder countenance? Or conceivably he had discerned something in his subject not generally apparent, some aspect fundamentally mellow and kindly and to which he was stirred to pay tribute . . . Well whatever it was, the poor lady had hardly deserved that sort of fate. For the first time since her arrival Rosy felt a surge of indignant anger on behalf of her deceased hostess, a feeling not of conventional pity, but a raw stab of pain and a sense of loss for one she had never known.

She resumed the stairs, curiously troubled. And then

just as she was about to enter her room she sensed a slight movement from the other side of the landing. 'I see you were appraising madam's picture,' Hawkins said. 'It's quite well hung there, just catches the light from the transom.'

'Er – yes, yes I was . . . and it does,' Rosy replied startled. She had been completely oblivious of his presence. Crikey, he crept about like an ageing centipede!

'It's quite good, isn't it?' he murmured politely.

Rosy agreed that it was most effective; and still ruffled by his sudden appearance she smiled vaguely and quickly turned the handle of her door.

CHAPTER EIGHT

That night Rosy had difficulty in sleeping. It wasn't just the details of Delia's dreadful end that haunted her, nor indeed the questions of motive and perpetrator – disturbing though these certainly were. It was Hawkins' confident assertion about the novel that intrigued and kept her frowning into the darkness. Dinner over and Hugh and Lady Fawcett retired to the drawing room, Rosy had remained behind for a few minutes indulging the pugs' insistent overtures. She had asked Hawkins if he knew anything of Delia's gardening book: 'I gather she was terribly enthusiastic about it.'

'Oh no, miss,' he had replied casually, 'nothing about *flowers*, she was writing a novel; been at it for months.' When Rosy had asked what sort of novel he had seemed not to hear and had made great play and clatter with stacking the plates onto the trolley. Further diffident enquiries had been met with an impassive countenance and mild shrug. 'That's all madam told me,' he had said, and clearly had no intention of being drawn further.

Rosy was puzzled. Hawkins may have known his employer had been writing a novel but nobody else in the family seemed to. Certainly they had been aware she was engaged on some sort of literary project but from what had been said they clearly assumed it to be something horticultural. Why should they have thought that unless it was what Delia had deliberately implied? Still, flowers and fiction were not mutually exclusive – as Frances H. Burnett's *The Secret Garden* had so brilliantly shown. Perhaps Delia's efforts were intended as something comparable; or a fantasy perhaps in which rhododendrons masqueraded as queens, evil gnomes lurked in the rhubarb patch and lilies took tea with the lilac . . .

Absorbed by such images and lulled by imagined twitters of robins in hidden gardens, Rosy's restless mind drifted into reverie and thence into the realms of sleep where questions of murder and motive held no place.

She awoke shortly before dawn and got up to close the window. The night had turned surprisingly chilly, and pretty though the eiderdown was it lacked the insulation effect of a thick service greatcoat. Yes, she thought wryly, being in the ATS had certainly had its uses. Her present coat had been left downstairs, and in any case was hardly of the bed-slinging kind. With shivering optimism she thought there might be a spare blanket in the wardrobe. She recalled her mother's advice to always keep a blanket in the guest room; candles too, she had said. 'You can never tell when the next power cut will be. It's the government – they enjoy the element of surprise.' At the time Rosy had been indifferent to such adult concerns; but now standing in the chilly dawn she just hoped that her late hostess had shared her mother's foresight.

She went to the wardrobe and investigated the top shelf. Nothing. Blast! She looked down at the drawer at the base and began to pull it open. It jammed – impeded by a rough plaid blanket. Gratefully she dragged it out and spread it on the bed, and turned to close the drawer. A small white folder lay on the floor which must have come out with the blanket. As she went to replace it in the drawer some pages fell out. Several were blank, but a few were covered in a heavy scrawl. She slipped them back and replacing the folder closed the drawer. It seemed an odd place to store stationery but there was no accounting for people's domestic arrangements – she had had an uncle once who regularly stored jam in his medicine cupboard.

Eager to make the most of the refurbished bed and with only three hours till breakfast she thought no more of it; and drawing the bedclothes over her head closed her eyes.

'You know I can't help thinking about what poor Delia was going to tell me,' mused Lady Fawcett as she and Rosy sat in the morning room perusing the newspapers. 'I wonder whether I would have been interested.' (Not unless it concerned the runners at Ascot or which caterers to engage for her forthcoming party, Rosy surmised.) 'After all,' Lady Fawcett added, 'the son seems to think it was nothing.'

'From what I can make out he seems to think most things are nothing,' Rosy said. 'Very pleasant, of course, but I can't see that the loss of his mother has been much of a blow – unless he has an unusually resilient upper lip.'

'Hmm perhaps . . . It makes me wonder how Amy will react to *my* death when it comes – though I trust not in such circumstances. I do hope the dear girl will cope all right and not cause a rumpus. It would be really too bad.' Lady Fawcett's placid brows creased slightly, presumably visualising her daughter haranguing the vicar or incommoding the pall-bearers.

Rosy laughed. 'Amy will rise to the occasion with élan – just as I must to tidy my room; apart from Hawkins I don't think there's any domestic help and I am sure he is far too busy in the kitchen.' She rose and left her companion gazing pensively out of the window.

Upstairs Rosy tidied the dressing table, removed the plaid rug and made the bed. It was only when she went to replace the blanket in the wardrobe that she was reminded of the folder. Mentally more alert than during the night, she opened it up and glanced at the few pages. Her eye was caught by what appeared to be a heading: *The Proposition (Ch.3)*. Rosy smiled. Could this perhaps be bits of the mythical novel!

The pencilled untidy script gave the impression of being part of a hastily composed rough draft, and intrigued Rosy sat on the bed and started to read:

Lucian Lightspring had had some difficulty in persuading the young man to accompany him. It wasn't that the youth was nervous or hostile, merely indifferent and seemed in a hurry to be elsewhere. However, with the offer of a Turkish cigarette and exercising the usual charm and blandishments Lucian succeeded in awakening Ralph's interest, and together they walked down the embassy steps and set off along the Faubourg in the direction of the Rue du Bac. As they went he apprised his companion of the plan. 'It couldn't be simpler,' he explained, 'all your sister will have to do is be nice to the fellow – you know what I mean,' he winked and squeezed Ralph's arm, 'and after that it'll be plain sailing. Peters is susceptible and will hand over the file without a murmur, and your delightful sister will receive our undying gratitude and a little emolument.' He paused, and then added, 'As a matter of fact quite a large one . . . as will you if you can spare the time to amuse a homesick banker.' He gave a soft laugh.

Ralph said nothing and they walked on in silence broken only by an occasional tap from the older man's cane as he casually flicked a kerbstone or railing. By this time they had reached the door of Lucian's flat; but before inserting the key Lucian removed his grey homburg, and turning directly to face Ralph fixed him with a clear gaze. 'You have made rather a good choice,' he said easily, 'what one might call a sound investment. You won't regret it I assure you. My credentials are excellent, you won't be bored. Besides, there are the parties – very select with the most charming boys and girls. And if you can persuade your sister to act further on our behalf then things could go very well for you . . .' Ralph nodded and they went in.

Later that evening sitting with Klaus in the bar of the Crillon he ordered a bottle of Taittinger to celebrate his success. 'It couldn't have been easier,' he laughed, 'the boy is not the brightest and luckily very fond of his wallet, as is the sister. Once she has acquired the file and we have made a copy you can approach Andreski. Tell him our terms and don't budge an inch; any concession and he'll assume you are a fool.'

'Oh you can rely on me,' Klaus replied, 'I make few concessions to anyone – ever.' He spoke with a smug assurance.

Lucian nodded and sipped his champagne. Inwardly he reflected: deluded little toad, typical of that prosaic mentality – mistakes intransigence for strength! Outwardly he said, 'Yes, things are proceeding well and I have had good reports from our special clients regarding your choice of "material" for them . . . very discerning they tell me.' He raised his glass. 'Let us drink a twofold toast to venality and venery: a most felicitous union!' They clinked their glasses.

At that point the narrative ceased and Rosy slowly reread the passage, taken aback by what seemed to be its theme. Somehow the topic did not fit her picture of the murdered woman as conveyed by Angela! She flicked to the second page but this displayed merely random jottings of dates (Jan. '46, May '47 etc.) and places: Neuilly, Brasserie Lipp, Les Tuileries. There was a short list of pencilled notes and queries:

1) *Tie pin – otter's head too obvious, change to fox.*
2) *R's accent? Keep but omit the stammer.*
3) *Include name of bridge.*
4) *Substitute bank for Bourse.*
5) *K's embassy job? Keep vague but describe room overlooking Seine.*

Never having written a novel (nor wanted to!) Rosy found such disjointed jottings of little account but assumed they were something to do with the 'emerging muse'. She turned to the third page. Ah, at least another snippet of proper prose and also with a heading – *Ch. 25: Finale.*

He contemplated the young man draped on the parapet, irritated by the cool defiance and the smile which no longer charmed. 'On the whole I think not,' he replied softly, 'I have other plans. Besides I make it a rule never to succumb to blackmail – it makes everything so crude. Don't you think?' He stepped forward, firmly pressing the other against the broken rail. It collapsed immediately, and with a cry of terror Ralph fell back and plunged into the swirling icy waters.

For a moment Lucian gazed thoughtfully down at the pathetically floundering person who had

never learnt to swim; and then lighting the inevitable
Abdulla, turned on his heel and walked in the
opposite direction. 'Fearful bad luck,' he murmured
to himself.

You can say that again, Rosy thought. What a nasty end! Herself a poor swimmer and hating the cold she felt a stab of empathy for the hapless Ralph. But whether it was the end of the novel itself one couldn't tell. As indicated, the lines were obviously from the last chapter, but there was nothing to suggest that they were necessarily the concluding ones. Absurdly Rosy felt a pang of frustration; she had become quite intrigued. But what intrigued her even more was that such scenes had presumably come from Delia Dovedale's pen. So was this the thing she had been so busily concocting during her 'violet hours'? Nothing to do with plants, but all to do with murder and other unsavoury matters! She wondered where the rest of it was and what Angela would say on the subject.

Returning to the morning room eager to tell Lady Fawcett of her find she found the bird had flown. In her place was Hawkins busily dusting and plumping the cushions. Rosy cleared her throat: 'It was very interesting what you said last night about Mrs Dovedale's novel. I wonder where it could be. I mean if she had kept it in her desk or bedroom presumably it would have been found by now. I gather that Mr Dovedale has already dealt with the papers in her desk, and neither Mrs Stannard nor Mrs Brightwell found anything of that sort when they came to deal with the personal things in her bedroom. Curious really; I mean if

I had the energy to write a novel I would make jolly good sure to put it somewhere safe!'

There was a silence as Hawkins continued to smooth the cushion he was holding and then replaced it carefully on the sofa. 'Perhaps it was destroyed,' he said, picking up the other one.

Rosy was about to ask why on earth that would have happened, when he added quietly, 'Or sent off to a publisher.'

'Oh – yes, that's quite a possibility! Do you think so?'

'I wouldn't know, madam; but I understand that is what writers tend to do.' If Hawkins was interested in the matter he certainly didn't show it, and straightening a pile of *Country Life*s enquired whether Rosy would like tomato or mushroom soup at luncheon. 'Mr Dovedale collects the fungi from the woods,' he volunteered.

Rosy told him that on the whole she would prefer tomato, a choice Hawkins seemed to approve. He nodded. 'Safer,' he said sepulchrally and left the room.

CHAPTER NINE

'Do you think Felix Smythe would notice if I absented myself from his talk this afternoon?' Lady Fawcett asked Rosy. 'He gave one of similar title in London only two weeks ago. Fascinating though the subject is, one *can* have too much of a good thing . . . I mean I know the dear Queen Mother has impeccable taste, but I think I have heard rather enough of her floral preferences for the time being. It doesn't do to gild the lily, does it?'

Rosy laughed. 'I doubt if Felix would agree – but no I am sure he won't mind if you're not there. After all it was pure coincidence that we happened to be in the area at all. And knowing Felix he will be so enraptured by his own anecdotes that he'll notice nothing except the applause at the end.'

Lady Fawcett smiled evidently pleased with Rosy's

response. 'Mind you,' she observed, 'I am a little surprised that the organisers haven't cancelled the whole thing. Delia's tragedy will surely have deterred so many from attending.'

'Hmm. Rather the opposite I should think,' Rosy remarked dryly. 'Doubtless the murder will be an added attraction. Besides, it must be a pretty costly business mounting a festival like this; to close it down could be ruinous.'

'Yes, I suppose so – and I daresay Delia would be all for it continuing. She was like that, always thrusting on. Unstoppable really . . .' She heaved a sigh – whether from regret or fatigue Rosy wasn't sure but suspected the latter. 'Anyway,' she continued 'I propose retiring to the conservatory with my library book, *Rajahs I Have Known* by Hermione Fitz-Hartington. She was our head girl – *much* quieter than Delia. Had an obsession with elephants, I remember; and judging from the size of her husband, still has . . . So what are you going to do? Write some letters?'

Rosy said that actually she might go back into Southwold to visit one of the festival tents to pick up some ideas for her apartment balcony. 'Apparently there's some woman who makes a speciality of that sort of thing. And then I *may* just drop in to catch the tail end of Felix's lecture,' she grinned.

'Oh what it is to have energy,' exclaimed Lady Fawcett, 'but I do advise you to take a coat. That east wind on the Common could be bitter!' She shuddered and gathered herself to retire with the rajahs.

* * *

Rosy's principal reason for returning to Southwold that afternoon was less to do with Felix or ideas for her balcony than to simply enjoy the chance of having a pleasant wander in the town on her own. Constant companionship was all very well, but it had its drawbacks, and just occasionally one did rather enjoy the luxury of solitude in which to do one's exploring.

Unlike Cedric she had no nostalgic recollection of the area and instead indulged herself in its novelty. For half an hour or so she pottered happily in the vicinity of South Green with its gracious Regency houses, quaint side lanes, broad sweeps of turf with bounding dogs; and a little further on of course, the magnificent naval guns. Passing these Rosy walked on towards the windswept sand dunes, where among the dry grass tussocks she gazed out to sea studying the gulls and distant fishing smacks. Apart from the cries of the gulls there was total silence.

She felt both soothed and then strangely moved. Some words of an Ulster poet came to her mind: *The dazzle on the sea, my darling, reminds me of you.* There was only one person she would have wished to have at her side at that moment – and that could never be again: Johnnie, shot down just before Dresden a decade ago. For an electric moment she heard his bantering laugh, sensed his hand on her shoulder, could feel the texture of the uniformed sleeve and even caught a whiff of his favourite tobacco . . . She shrugged. Christ Almighty let it go, let it go! But she knew that it never would.

Abruptly she turned from the sea and looked inland surveying the spread of the town, its rearing lighthouse, and to the far left the white tops of the festival marquees on the Common. Seeing these brought to mind another tragedy – less noble perhaps, and more shocking. She shivered. Who on earth could have done that to the woman – and why for God's sake! Slowly she made her way back to the Market Place, and despite her grim thoughts she continued to absorb the charm of her surroundings. She recalled Mark mentioning something about the Sailors' Reading Room – apparently a small building on the East Cliff originally established as a sort of recreation space for the local mariners to divert them from the demon drink. It was, she understood, still going strong and was not only a secluded spot for reading and relaxation, but also housed a remarkable display of nautical memorabilia, photographs and other items of local interest. 'Well worth a visit,' Mark had said, 'and somewhere to shelter from that persistent wind: it's a real little bolthole.'

Intrigued by his description she enquired the way, and five minutes later was standing beside its flagpole and reading the inscription over the gabled portico. She had just set her foot on the lower step when the door opened and she nearly bumped into two people coming out. 'Oh, I'm so sorry,' exclaimed the man raising his hat, 'not looking where we're—' He broke off and stared in surprise. 'Oh, it's Miss Gilchrist isn't? We met at the Dovedale's the other afternoon . . . Doing a bit of exploring are you? You'll find it fascinating.'

Rosy nodded and smiled politely at Lucas Brightwell, and also at his pretty companion. For some reason the girl looked vaguely familiar.

Brightwell hesitated fractionally, and then said, 'This is

Miss Morgan, the mainstay of Floyd de Lisle's publishing firm and without whom the whole thing would go down the tubes!' He gave a loud laugh, and then added, 'She has to produce a brief introduction to one of his clients' local history books, so I was just introducing her to this invaluable institution. Plenty of handy stuff here, isn't that so Betty?' He laughed again and the girl looked blank. Then glancing at his watch he exclaimed, 'My goodness, time you were back at the office, otherwise I shall have your estimable boss on my tail!' Turning to Rosy he murmured something about hoping to meet her again, and briskly hustled the girl into the road and round the corner.

In the normal way Rosy would have immediately reflected upon the encounter. But as she entered the Reading Room she was so taken by the scene that met her eyes that all other thoughts vanished. She gazed around in delight at the plethora of things nautical and maritime: the walls plastered with old photographs of grizzled coastguards and fisher folk, glass-fronted cabinets of intricately modelled vessels, brightly painted ships' figureheads, shelves of books and magazines, an obviously much used chess board, worn comfortable chairs, a table strewn with newspapers – and everywhere the soothing smell of books, tobacco and the past. It was an ancient toy shop, a haven, a magical rabbit hole of the quaint and unexpected.

For twenty minutes or so she wandered around reading this, examining that; until seduced by a battered arm chair she sat down and closed her eyes. It was only then that the image of Lucas Brightwell and Betty Morgan came back to mind.

She remembered the girl of course: it had been the one in the teashop the other day, the girl Floyd de Lisle had approached. Presumably, and as just indicated by Lucas, Betty Morgan was his secretary. What had her companion said? That she was compiling an introduction to one of de Lisle's publications? Rosy couldn't help feeling a little dubious. Certainly the girl was very pretty and doubtless very nice – but bright enough to compose an introduction? It seemed a little unlikely. Immediately Rosy felt ashamed by her own snobbish cynicism, but it persisted all the same.

They struck her as an unlikely duo – the suave, middle-aged Brightwell and the gauche teenage secretary (not even his own). She couldn't imagine that they had much in common . . . well, other than the age-old and obvious! She recalled Mark's description – 'a nice little bolthole'. Was that really what they had been doing in the Reading Room: conducting a cosy little tête-à-tête surrounded by photos of the knowing old salts and the roguish eyes of ships' figureheads? An odd venue perhaps, but it certainly had the merit of warmth and seclusion. One could think of less convenient places.

As she prepared to go she noticed something propped against the table leg, a smart attaché case. It didn't look like a permanent fixture to the Reading Room and in all probability it had been left by someone – though not, she assumed, by one of the regular denizens. A visitor like herself perhaps; maybe even Lucas Brightwell . . . If he had been busy chatting up the girl something as prosaic as an attaché case could easily have slipped his mind.

She picked it up and inspected the contents. At first all she saw was a copy of that day's *Financial Times* and a spectacle case. Not much of a clue there. She withdrew the newspaper hoping to find something more indicative of the owner. Ah, that was better – a small folder holding a few bits and pieces: a couple of London theatre tickets, a newspaper cutting about some tin mines in Bolivia . . . And yes confirmation: three cheques made out to local tradesmen signed Lucas Brightwell. He would be glad to get those back – as no doubt would the recipients. What else? Nothing much – an invitation to one of the Buckingham Palace garden parties later in the season marked 'accepted' and a small Basildon Bond writing pad.

Without thinking she casually flipped open its cover to see a half page of pencilled notes or what might be the draft of a letter. Indifferently she ran her eye down the page. When she reached the bottom she muttered something a trifle unladylike: 'Blithering hell!'

The contents struck her as singular especially the penultimate sentence. There was no salutation.

I consider your action to have been precipitate to say the least: a monumental blunder and one you may live to regret. When you made the proposal naturally I thought it was said in jest. Never for one moment did I think you would pursue such an idiotic scheme. Yes, the initial problem is now disposed of – but

oh my God at what likely cost! If it backfires, as it
may well do, the consequences could be mutually
disastrous.

Let us hope that the powers that be are too inept
to draw conclusions. However, should they begin to
I shall have no hesitation in stopping your mouth.
Meanwhile if you take my advice you will decamp
for a 'well-earned' holiday.

There was no signature or date and the words fizzled out
into squiggles and asterisks. Rosy assumed that its writer
(Brightwell?) had run out of steam – or spleen. There had
been plenty of the latter all right! She wondered whether the
edited text had ever been posted and whether its despised
recipient had taken the advice about a holiday. But who
was the recipient? A business colleague who had been less
than prudent? Some collaborator in a scheme that had gone
wrong? Or more sinisterly perhaps Brightwell had been
engaged in something illicit or fraudulent even, and which
was now jeopardised by the man's action. Well whatever
it was the writer was certainly very angry – and distinctly
threatening. The coarse note struck by 'I shall have no
hesitation in stopping your mouth' was as unexpected as it
was crude. Could this this really be from the pen of Lucas
Brightwell?

She thought of the man's slightly starchy dignity, his
bland courtesies and complacent pronouncements on
the government's mishandling of the markets. It seemed
unlikely. But then she also recalled Hugh Dovedale's acid
observation – 'no perks for jerks!' Perhaps he was less

upright than his formal manner would suggest. And what about the wife, Freda? Rather a wholesome sort of woman she had thought. Did she know of her husband's financial affairs? Possibly not – although she might know more of the other sort. (Assuming of course that there *was* another sort: after all just because she had bumped into the pair coming from the Reading Room porch hardly meant they were conducting a torrid liaison.)

Rosy grinned and told herself she was turning into a regular old woman; snooping all over the place and drawing the most scurrilous conclusions. Doubtless Lucas and the girl had been earnestly discussing Southwold's maritime past and the Battle of Sole Bay. And as for the contents of the note pad – well perhaps he was writing a part for the local drama society's next production. That was it. *Obviously!*

She hesitated wondering if he had already missed the thing . . . perhaps he was about to return to the Reading Room. Oh well, she couldn't hang about on the off-chance. She would telephone that evening.

Making her way back to the car she inspected a couple of sweet shop windows in the vague hope of glimpsing some of Dr Stanley's required peppermint rock. There seemed plenty of toffees and pear drops, but no rock, unless one counted the thin barley-sugar sticks. Well he would just have to settle for a couple of bottles of Adnams special brew – bound to be more sustaining in any case. Knowing him the yen for pink rock was probably just another of the pre-war fantasies that he so readily indulged . . . She also decided to give Felix Smythe's lecture a miss – as Angela had earlier remarked, one could have too much of a good thing.

As she drove, her thoughts went back briefly to the two on the East Cliff; and she reflected that when returning Brightwell's property it would be best to keep a discreet silence regarding Betty Morgan, especially if Freda happened to be with him. No point in mentioning his companion unless he did first. She heard her late father's voice: 'Foot in mouth, that's what my girl!'

Back in her room she heard a tap on the door and Lady Fawcett appeared looking unusually animated.

'How were the rajahs?' Rosy asked.

'Very dark,' she replied. 'But much more entertaining have been the police: they arrived about an hour after you left and started asking Hugh questions all over again about Delia's friends and whether he know of any new acquaintances she may have made in the last six months; or indeed was he sure that she had no enemies or someone with whom she had any recent altercation. I can't say that Hugh was in the most cooperative of moods and he told them that he wasn't one for monitoring his mother's social contacts, and as for enemies – well didn't we all have those . . . As a matter of fact judging from that inspector's rather sour expression I suspect Hugh has just made a new one! He wasn't exactly what I believe the newspapers call a sympathetic witness.' She paused and then said pensively, 'In fact in some ways that young man reminds me of Amy: stubbornly difficult. Except of course the dear girl *means* well. I am not entirely sure that Hugh always does.' She paused again, and then with a bright smile added, 'fortunately I was able to be of help.'

'Really?' Rosy asked in some surprise. 'In what way?'

'I told them my theory of Delia being of no account to anyone.'

'You said what? That was a bit harsh wasn't it?'

'Oh I don't mean of no *value*, simply – as I've said before – that she was being used for practice fodder or as a decoy. Indeed I told the inspector I thought he was barking up the wrong tree and that if I were in his shoes I would be marching up and down the east coast looking for other instances of sudden poisoning. "There's bound to be a pattern," I told him, and "Mrs Dovedale was just a random factor".'

'Er, and how did he react?' Rosy enquired, trying to imagine Lady Fawcett marching anywhere.

'He didn't: just stood and scratched his head. But the young constable seemed very impressed. Kept nodding and making notes. And then as they were going I heard him say to the inspector, "You know sir, I think that lady may have something".'

'What did the inspector say?'

Lady Fawcett shrugged. 'Grunted, I think. But frankly in my experience our law officers are not always the most articulate . . .'

'I don't suppose by any chance they gave a clue as to when the body might be released did they?'

'Oh *yes* I knew there was something important! It seems that panellist who Cedric mentioned may have been telling the truth after all and that he really did hear her say "almonds". The laboratory people have finished their tests and established cyanide as the cause. Disgraceful! Still, the inspector said the body can be released for burial, so at least that's an achievement if nothing else.' She paused and then said, 'And another might be if we could prise some sherry out of Hawkins. Do you think he might serve some in the drawing room? All this police work is really quite exhausting.'

Later, with supper over, Rosy went into the hall and picking up the telephone dialled the Brightwells' number. Needless to say it was Freda, not Lucas, who answered; and slightly wrong-footed she hesitated before explaining who she was and why she was calling.

'You see,' she said, 'I was in the Sailors' Reading Room this afternoon and came across a briefcase. I think it may belong to your husband and I imagine he may be looking for it.'

'Not to my knowledge,' Freda answered. 'But why do you think it's his?'

Rosy explained that she had found the cheques and the Royal Garden Party invitation, but made no mention of the scribbled letter – or indeed of Betty Morgan.

'Well I suppose it must be his,' Freda said doubtfully, 'but what an odd place to find it. I don't think we have been there since about five years ago when they were holding some commemorative thing for perished sailors. Are you sure it is his?'

'Well that's what the cheques say – Coutts, and his name and signature. The cheques are just made out to local firms.'

'Oh well, it must be his then – how strange.'

At that moment Rosy heard the faint noise of a door opening and then the sound of movements, followed by voices. 'It's that Rosy Gilchrist,' she heard Freda say, 'something about your briefcase . . .'

The next voice was not Freda's, but that of Lucas himself. 'Ah, he said, 'I was wondering where that had got to. How kind of you to call. I'm not in a position to pick it up just now – I have some urgent business in London and we are about to take off immediately. It's not essential but I should be most obliged if you could guard it safely. Naturally we shall be back for Delia's funeral. I'll see you there.' The next moment he had put the phone down.

It wasn't the most gracious of responses, Rosy felt. And feeling slightly peeved at his perfunctory manner, when she returned to her room she opened the case and had another look at the letter. Huh! Whoever the recipient was he had certainly had a dressing down! Not at all the thing one would like to receive. She wondered about him and what his response had been – assuming of course that the thing had ever been sent. But even if a mere draft written in the heat of the moment it did rather suggest that Lucas Brightwell was not a man to be trifled with . . . She had better watch her p's and q's when she saw him at the funeral!

As she pushed the thing back into an inside pocket her fingers touched what seemed like a stiff piece of cardboard. She pulled it out. It was a photograph of a young man: head and shoulders and obviously posed, like a studio portrait. The youth was rather good-looking with dark lazy eyes and an ironic mouth . . . Brightwell's son? No, they didn't have any children. She remembered Freda making a joke saying that was one less thing to worry about. The photo wasn't exactly pristine – in fact it looked quite old, taken about ten, fifteen years ago? She turned it over looking for a date. There was nothing except the letter R written in slightly faded black ink.

CHAPTER TEN

While Rosy was acquainting herself with the charms of Southwold, her host had been receiving the attentions of Detective Inspector Rawson and his assistant DC Jennings. Their visit to Laurel Lodge had not been especially productive.

As they walked back to the car, Jennings observed, 'Rum sort of fellow isn't he, sir? I mean you'd have thought that what with his mum being done in like that he'd have shown a bit more interest. If you ask me he was more concerned with those blooming dogs than our questions.' He shot a sly look at the inspector. 'Actually from what I could make out the only time he showed any real reaction was when you put your hat down on top of that china vase thing. He didn't seem too pleased about that, not pleased at all!' He grinned.

The inspector grunted. 'Typical of that sort – dogs and *objets d'art*, that's what they like; human beings take a back seat in their priorities.'

'But do you still think he may have done it?'

'Never thought he did. I've told you before, no motive. Plenty of money and doesn't inherit any more for another few years regardless of whether Mummy is dead or not. Nothing to be gained.'

Jennings let in the clutch thoughtfully. 'But there could be something else, something *psychological* – I mean money isn't the only factor, is it sir?'

'Isn't it?' said the inspector curtly. He had just been baulked of a handy payrise and was in no mood to listen to Master Freud chuntering on about psycho this and psycho that.

'You see,' Jennings continued, 'it's my belief it could be a case of blackmail. It often is, you know.'

His boss emitted a billow of pipe smoke into the car which fogged the driving mirror. 'I see. So you have the deceased marked down as putting the frighteners on the vicar for some misdemeanour in the vestry, and being none too pleased with her curiosity he gives her a lethal dose . . . Yes, yes, Jennings, good thinking; I am sure you are getting close.'

'Oh much simpler than that, sir,' explained the detective constable undeterred by the other's jibe, 'I think she could have been putting the frighteners on her son.'

His boss looked mildly shocked. 'As a general rule, Jennings, mothers don't do that.'

'Oh mine does,' replied Jennings cheerfully, 'all the time.'

'Hmm. So you think that Mrs Dovedale had uncovered something dubious about her son's past or present activities, cut up rough and threatened to expose him. Or was she perhaps milking him dry and saving up for a mammoth world cruise? Could have been either, I suppose.'

The other frowned and gripped the steering wheel more tightly. The problem with one's superior officers was that the bastards thought they knew it all.

When they reached the station the inspector was about to alight when his colleague suddenly said, 'And what about that other lady, sir?'

'What other lady?'

'The one with the title and long nose.'

'What about her?'

'Well like I said, I think her theory about the deceased being used as a sort of decoy was not necessarily all that daft. She might just have something there.'

'Ah, so we have discounted the son theory, have we?'

'It's as well to keep an open mind, sir,' replied Jennings primly.

A little later the inspector sat at his desk nursing a cup of cocoa and brooding on their not very satisfactory visit to Laurel Lodge. A funny lot really: a po-faced one-eyed butler – or whatever it was these people employed – a pair of squinting canines, the victim's son sardonic and testy, and the thin languid woman from London who claimed she had known Delia Dovedale at school.

He thought he might have got a lead there, some clue from the past perhaps. It had been a long shot but he needn't have bothered. When pressed all she could do was rattle on about some school play they had been in and the hash the deceased had made of the third act. And as for her notion about the victim being just a cipher in a bigger plan – well really, you wondered where the public got their ideas from! Those Agatha Christie novels presumably that young Jennings had always got his nose stuck in.

Still, he reflected, she had also made some casual allusion to the florist person they had questioned at the time of the death. 'Frightful for poor Felix to be sitting so close,' she had lamented. Well 'poor Felix' had been a lousy witness, as had that smug friend sitting in the front row. He had put them at the bottom of his 'Try Again' list. But perhaps now was the time for another approach. One of them might suddenly remember something, such late memory flashes were not unknown . . . Besides, he was still puzzled by the victim's cry of 'Oh Felix'. Did it signify a closer relationship than the chap had acknowledged? Yes, he brooded, perhaps a closer look there was called for.

He summoned his subordinate. 'We'll have another go at that Smythe and Dillworthy pair over at Aldeburgh.'

'Good thinking, sir.' Jennings exclaimed approvingly.

The inspector sighed.

'This is too bad,' Felix protested furiously to Cedric, 'I am clearly being the victim of police persecution! Just because Delia Dovedale uttered my name like that they seem to be convinced that she and I had some dark and close connection. As it happens – as you well know – I spent much of my time trying to distance myself from that awful braying laugh! Why she should have called out my name I cannot imagine; it has put me in a very embarrassing position.' Felix gripped the arms of his chair and crossed and uncrossed his legs irritably.

'Yes,' observed his friend mildly, 'it wasn't the most tactful of remarks – though of course it was her *last*. And I daresay that in such circumstances one might not pick one's words too carefully.'

'What? Oh very funny, I'm sure . . . It's all very well for you, Cedric, but you didn't see that young constable's face when he was making his notes. Wolfish it was, positively wolfish. And when I suggested that just conceivably the poison may have been meant for me and had they thought of that, all he could do was snigger!'

'Have another martini – you'll feel better,' Cedric suggested smoothly.

Felix replied that he would have another martini but that in no respect would he feel better.

He bent forward, and lowering his voice said, 'Thank goodness they approached us in Southwold and not here.' He glanced around at The Sandworth's decorously elegant lounge and winced. 'Can you imagine the Keystone Cops blundering in here to interview me? It would have been too shaming! Frankly the sooner one gets back to London the better. I mean word does get about . . .' He nodded towards an elderly lady in the far corner. 'Take that one for instance. She may seem to be asleep, but I bet her ears are flapping all right. It's people like that who spread the gossip. You do realise that if my patron gets to hear that one of her warrant-holders has been fingered by the law they could take my plaque away!'

'Oh no,' said Cedric soothingly, 'she would probably be simply fascinated. And you could tell *such* a good tale.'

'Hmm. Perhaps.' Felix looked slightly mollified, and Cedric suspected his companion was already beginning to weave some piquant fantasy for royal ears.

Left alone he considered the situation. The interview hadn't really been as bad as Felix had made out. Routine really. Certainly the inspector had asked some searching questions about the purpose of their visit and when Felix had made the arrangements, and how well they had known the deceased before coming to Southwold. But these had not been especially provocative, just tiresome. The significance of the victim's choking exclamation had naturally been gone over again more rigorously; but Felix had clung to his view of its having no meaning, and eventually they had seemed satisfied.

Nevertheless he sympathised with his friend's agitation. The whole business was most unpalatable and not at all what they had envisaged. Once the funeral was over and Felix had done his bit at the concluding trophy ceremony they would indeed return swiftly to London. Apart from Chelsea it would be a very long time before another such flower festival would be graced by their presence!

CHAPTER ELEVEN

Floyd glanced at the front page of the evening paper and noted the brief announcement regarding Delia Dovedale's impending funeral. It was to be held a few days hence at St Edmund's church with all welcome both to the service and refreshments afterwards. Somehow it seemed only right to attend – besides it was a chance to duck out of his afternoon with Betty. The girl had covered mounds of typing recently (and with unusual accuracy) and in a moment of thoughtlessness he had offered to take her to the cinema. *The Dam Busters* was on in Ipswich, and although having seen it once he was eager to see it again. But on reflection it seemed better to go on his own: she was bound to get bored or fail to follow the plot . . .

Thus substituting the dead for the rather tiresome living,

some days later Floyd duly joined others in the magnificent medieval church to participate in Delia Dovedale's obsequies.

Although in their initial exploration of Southwold Rosy and Lady Fawcett had seen the great tower of St Edmund's looming from afar it was the first time they had been at close quarters and Rosy was enchanted with its setting of St Bartholomew Green. The afternoon was warm and sunlit, and its secluded triangle of grass and shrubs watched over by snoozing weavers' cottages held an almost fairy-tale quality. More sombre, but equally peaceful, was the adjacent churchyard with its ancient tombstones and shadowy lofty yews. Church, green and graveyard exuded an air of unruffled calm and slumbering serenity. Rosy was glad that the woman she had never met would have the benison of so graceful a resting place.

Such reassuring sentiments were rudely broken by a jarring thought. Supposing the assassin was *here* amid the mourners and well-wishers! Here, bidding an ironic farewell to the enemy (for enemy Delia must have been); here, watching and gloating, assessing . . . Assessing? Assessing what for goodness' sake? The effects of his or her handiwork? The reactions of the bereaved? Surely not. She glanced apprehensively at the knot of people standing in subdued groups by the cobbled wall chatting quietly before taking their places in the great nave. Absurd: the scene was too normal, too seemly to harbour such malevolence.

Rosy turned, and like Lady Fawcett ahead of her, walked firmly in the direction of the beckoning porch.

* * *

The service itself had been conducted with brisk efficiency by the vicar, who being ex-army was adept at managing large numbers with minimum fuss or indulgence.

'"*I am the resurrection and the life*",' rang out with sombre clarity. The two popular hymns – mercifully kept to only three verses – were discharged at a sharp tempo, and the eulogy delivered by one who clearly knew the art of public speaking: succinct, loud and lucid. Floyd had only a hazy recognition of the speaker: his name was somebody Brightwell, a friend of the family. Actually he was slightly surprised that the son Hugh hadn't assumed the task – in their late teens they had overlapped briefly at the same school where Hugh had invariably won the elocution prize. He was there in the front row all right, and from where Floyd sat, behind but well to the side, he had a clear view of his profile. The chap appeared to have his eyes shut throughout the entire ceremony. Searing grief or total boredom? It could have been either. Floyd didn't like him much – a funny bugger in his view, always had been. So his instinct was to ascribe the latter. But of course one couldn't be sure, appearances being so frequently deceptive. Take Betty for instance: looked as bright as a button, but as it was . . .

Briskly conducted though the service was, inevitably Floyd's thoughts started to drift and he found himself furtively fingering his cigarette lighter and checking his watch. And then in a trice such fidgeting stopped and he stared in rapt excitement at a piece of angelic carvery above his head. Inexplicably a marvellous possibility had struck him – a possibility that if properly handled could see him on those ski slopes yet! And at Biarritz too he shouldn't wonder!

Ever since the news of Delia's fate, Floyd had been smarting from the blow to his publishing hopes. Earlier plans to capitalise on its potential for salacious gossip were now scuppered – death had seen to that. With only half the manuscript submitted and its author in no position to complete, the project had lost all commercial value. He had felt bitterly frustrated – something he knew to be ignoble, but which dogged him all the same. Nevertheless with grim stoicism he had resigned himself to pursuing the usual spate of less lucrative submissions. The poor old girl was dead. End of story.

'Not so,' the carved angel had suddenly signalled from above. 'Not so at all!' Floyd stared upward, transfixed by the image and the ideas that were forming in his mind. Yes, the old girl was dead – but the point was she had been *murdered*. And authors who had been murdered surely had market value! Ideally of course if their novels were complete; hers was not. A slow grin spread over his face (wrong moment: the mourners had just been invited to kneel in prayer). Hardly an insuperable problem, he mused, the solution was clear: *he* would complete the novel and no one would be any the wiser!

As those around him murmured dutiful pieties, Floyd had a vision of the *Times Literary Supplement* and its headlines: DISGRACEFUL REVELATIONS FROM AUTHOR GRUESOMELY MURDERED! PUBLISHER DECLARES IT THE MOST EXTRAORDINARY DEBUT NOVEL HE HAS EVER HANDLED.

Floyd sunk to his knees with the others, and with head bowed offered up a tiny prayer of gratitude.

* * *

'I must say,' Felix Smythe was heard to whisper to his friend in the graveyard prior to the burial, 'that publisher fellow clearly imagines he's Caruso. I've never heard "Fight the good fight" bellowed with such vigour. Even from behind I was totally deafened!' He shot a baleful glance at Floyd de Lisle standing deep in thought beneath a yew tree.

'Often happens at funerals,' Cedric informed him, 'people like to let off steam.'

'Well kindly don't let it happen at mine,' Felix said, 'it was enough to wake the dead.' He clutched Cedric's arm and whispered, 'Oh my God what on earth is that werewolf thing doing tethered to the railings – look, over there by the war memorial!'

Cedric followed his gaze. 'I think it's something to do with the vicar,' he whispered. 'Apparently it's his St Bernard, Alice. She likes to come along and watch. Quite docile I gather.'

'You could have fooled me,' Felix whispered nervously. Warily he returned his eyes to the coffin in time to see it lowered into its allotted space with neither let nor hindrance.

It had been a smooth graceful disposal utterly at odds with the subject's demise. And with satisfied relief the mourners walked swiftly back to the church hall poised for cakes and gossip.

The former was rationed, the latter was not. And in low and decorous voices the congregation pursued the manner of the lady's death with discreet tenacity. Even the dullish Claude Huggins was heard to speculate about the provenance of the poison. 'I did enquire of that young

Detective Constable – Jennings I think his name is – but the youth closed one eye and said it was top secret and not for the likes of me to know. Can you imagine! One really doesn't know where they get the recruits from these days or indeed who is responsible for their training. I made a perfectly civil enquiry and I get that sort of lip!' Frowning he slid off in quest of another Chelsea bun, but from what Rosy could make out was faced with a similar rebuff as the one given him by the young constable.

'Poor old Claude,' a voice said behind her, 'takes himself too seriously. Lucas used to know him slightly years ago in Paris before we were married. He was younger then of course and apparently mildly more fun – which I don't imagine is saying a lot. But nowadays he's become awfully curmudgeonly.' Freda Brightwell beamed at Rosy and offered her a sherry.

'But I gather he has a splendid garden at Dunwich,' she replied.

'Oh yes, the garden's all right; it's just the gardener you want to watch . . . well not so much watch as avoid.' She laughed: 'I mean, ask the wrong question and he'll immediately entrap you into listening to an interminable report on the latest section in his plant treatise. Delia once asked him if it wouldn't be more sensible to condense the whole thing into six paragraphs and submit it to the *Reader's Digest*. I can tell you, that didn't go down at all well!'

Rosy smiled and enquired what Huggins had been doing in Paris.

'Oh nothing very exciting, you can be sure of that.

Some sort of minor official in the lower echelons of the British embassy there; Lucas still sometimes refers to him as "Huggins the pen-pusher". But now he's pushing his pen elsewhere – among the plants in his Dunwich conservatory, and don't we know it!'

She moved away to speak to some of Delia's festival colleagues; and at the next moment was replaced by her husband. 'Ah,' said Lucas Brightwell, 'good to see you again, but so sorry it should be in such sad circumstances.'

Rosy agreed and murmured congratulations on his moving tribute in the church.

'She deserved it,' he said earnestly, 'it was the least I could do.' He paused, and then clearing his throat said, 'So sorry I wasn't more communicative the other day when you telephoned. As said, we were on the verge of driving up to London and were in rather a hurry. However, I *would* like my briefcase back. Absurd of me to leave it like that! I could come over to Laurel Lodge tomorrow to collect it but as it's the day after her funeral I doubt if Hugh will welcome random visitors.'

Rosy agreed and said that in any case she and Angela had tickets for one of the flower events and had been invited to lunch by the organisers.

'In that case what about twelve o'clock at The Crown on Friday? I have some business in Southwold to attend to – rather tedious really – and a little break would be most welcome. Meanwhile I know it couldn't be in safer hands!' He flashed her a lavish smile and Rosy felt a twinge of guilt knowing she had already rifled the wretched thing.

* * *

Gripped by his sudden inspiration and impatient to rise to the challenge he had set himself, Floyd was poised for flight. But he was forestalled by a willowy middle-aged woman of fine features and bland expression.

'Weren't you one of poor Delia's colleagues on the judging platform?' she enquired. 'A friend of mine, Felix Smythe, was there too and he says you had been awfully distressed. It must have been a terrible shock. I do so sympathise.' She gazed at him earnestly, and added, 'Delia and I had been at school together, and it seems so strange to think of her now lying under that lovely yew tree rather than sprawled on the hockey pitch.' She sighed, 'Ah well, none of us knows when the Reaper will strike I fear . . . I say you couldn't *possibly* get me some sandwiches, could you? I find these occasions make one utterly ravenous!' She smiled sweetly.

Genuine though the woman's concern had seemed Floyd had nevertheless been annoyed by her curtailment of his flight. However, reference to the hockey pitch had instantly altered things. His manner switched from taut civility to cringing compliance. 'Of course!' he beamed. 'Which would you like, the salmon or cucumber – or how about a few of each?' Seeing a spare chair which the loitering Claude Huggins had his eye on, he thrust it towards her and elbowed his way to the refreshment trolley.

Despite grumbles from the guardians Floyd swiftly piled the plate with the requested sandwiches and hurried back to what he was now sure could be a valuable source of promotional spin. 'So you were a school chum of Delia's, were you?' he began eagerly. 'How fascinating. She must

112

have been quite a girl in those days I bet – full of jolly japes and all that!' He smiled encouragingly.

'Ye–es,' Lady Fawcett agreed hesitantly, bemused by his interest. 'She was certainly always very busy – quite inventive really: plays and things . . .' She broke off. 'Oh but aren't you a publisher? I hear you have a thriving concern on South Green. Very nice, but rather exhausting I imagine – all these aspiring authors thrusting questionable manuscripts at you. Must be difficult making the right choices; and after all some must be deadly dull!'

'Many are, but *not* all. Sometimes you get a winner – not often, just occasionally. In fact,' and Floyd lowered his voice and leered, 'between you and me, I happen to have something in hand just now which could become a bestseller, something which could cut quite a dash and make yours truly a nice little packet.' He nodded happily.

His companion, thoroughly relishing her sandwiches, appeared riveted. And such evident appreciation from his author's school friend persuaded Floyd to go further 'Actually,' he confided, 'it's something Delia gave me, something that has dynamite potential!'

'*Really?*' Lady Fawcett exclaimed, visibly impressed. 'You do surprise me. I hadn't realised that Delia had such talent . . .' she trailed off with a puzzled frown.

At that moment they were interrupted by one of the catering organisers eager to relieve Lady Fawcett of her empty plate. 'I take it you won't be wanting anything further,' she said rather pointedly.

Lady Fawcett agreed meekly that she would not, and stood up to go. Floyd too was ready to go but not before putting his finger to the side of his nose and warning his agreeable confidante to keep it all 'under that very smart hat.' He moved towards the exit making a mental note to ask the lady for more biographical snippets nearer publication. He had gathered she was a guest at the Dovedale house so renewing the contact shouldn't be too difficult. He would enquire of the Iris woman, she was generally quite helpful.

He smiled: it really had been the most productive of funerals.

CHAPTER TWELVE

'No, I am not trying to get out of it,' Cedric explained patiently, 'it is just that I feel one of my fatigues coming on and so I couldn't possibly do justice to his kind invitation. Why, I should be like the spectre at the feast all pale and wan!' He contrived to look so.

'Take a couple of aspirin,' Felix said shortly.

'Well I *would* – but you know how the combination of pills and wine plays havoc with my digestion, and it would be so unfair to our host if I just nursed a tumbler of water all evening . . . No, I fear I shall have to sacrifice the pleasure and settle for an early night.' Cedric smiled sadly, and then said, 'Besides, without my being there the two of you can rattle on endlessly about matters horticultural without fearing that I might be bored . . . not that I should be of course,' he added quickly.

'Hmm. Perhaps,' said Felix sceptically.

Cedric beamed. 'I knew you would understand. Now I really must go and have a quiet lie-down or I shall find myself literally felled by fatigue.'

'Felled by fatigue, my arse!' Felix muttered after his friend had left the room. 'He just can't face the prospect of Claude Huggins prosing on, that's what!'

They had encountered Claude during their first day at the festival, indeed had been introduced by Delia Dovedale, and while finding him perfectly pleasant had also noted his tendency to talk about few things other than his garden and the tome which had preoccupied him for the last decade, *The Huggins' Encyclopaedia of Horticultural Anomalies*. In themselves the two topics could have been entertaining, but it rapidly became clear that Claude was one of those people whose hobby horse was ridden at an unswerving plod. As an amateur his knowledge of plant life was indeed remarkable, but its delivery showed little sign of zest, merely an earnest intensity. Thus when he had pressed Cedric and Felix to dine at his Dunwich domain they had been hesitant, but taken by surprise had no ready excuse to decline. Since then, however, Cedric's nerve had clearly failed.

The prospect of being closeted with Claude Huggins without the bolstering presence of Cedric had made Felix uneasy. After all, he barely knew the fellow; and impressive though his garden had sounded, and much lauded by others, he was not entirely sure that he wanted to spend a whole evening mulling over varieties of columbine and phlox. Had Claude been a commercial florist, it might have been different. They could have spent an amicable time disparaging the egregious taste of the flower-buying public, tutting about the rising prices at Convent Garden (not to mention the increasing ill-manners of its porters) and speculating just how much longer Moyses Stevens was going to hold sway in central London. And after all, had there been a lacuna in the conversation Felix could always have filled it with the saga of his Royal Warrant and the Queen Mother's graciousness in granting it.

Unfortunately he rather suspected that Claude Huggins knew little of the flower trade and even less of Royal Warrants. Exotic grasses and coastal sub-species appeared to be his main speciality, and frankly Felix cared not a fig for either. He envisaged the likely tedium of the visit, but comforted himself with the thought that at least if things became too sticky he could always enliven matters by enquiring of his host exactly how much longer he expected his garden to survive the ravages of wave and wind before toppling into the sea to nestle with the rest of the submerged parish . . . Yes, if the worst came to the worst he could always play the Dunwich Erosion Card: a handy backstop should all else fail.

However, such mental preparation proved largely unnecessary. That morning Claude telephoned to ask if Felix would mind frightfully if there were a slight change of plan. Apparently his oven had given up the ghost and the electricity was on the blink. Thus in the circumstances it seemed sensible to switch the venue of Dunwich for his brother's house in Walberswick. This, he explained, was a much smaller residence but in the present situation *safer.* 'Of course Fabius will be there too,' he added, 'but I can assure you he's perfectly docile.' He gave a thin chuckle. It was only later that it dawned on Felix that the reference had been not to the dog but the brother . . . Oh well, so long as he is *docile* does it matter, he thought. Might even be handy.

Despite the warmth of the day Felix found himself that evening driving through Walberswick in a veil of mist. It cast a vaguely romantic aura on the clusters of cottages and partially ruined church. Aesthetic no doubt, but it didn't make finding the Huggins' place any easier. Claude's directions had been sparse. He had been told to look for a small whitewashed cottage with wooden railings (Could have been one of many!) What was its name? Oh yes, something ridiculous like Hampton Court; an attempt at irony he supposed. He drove past the two pubs, peering irritably from side to side and finally located it set back slightly at an angle to the road. Contrary to what he had heard of Claude's domain this was indeed of modest dimension – less 'bijou' than shed size, and a rather shabby shed at that. But assuming the food was edible and, as Claude had promised, the owner docile things should be all right.

He parked the car, negotiated the narrow path and rapped firmly on the door. It was opened by what at first Felix took to be a scarecrow: a gaunt ramshackle figure in carpet slippers, collarless shirt and dilapidated trousers hitched uncertainly by frayed braces; and whose straggling beard and shoulder-length hair seemed virtually indistinguishable. The figure looked at the visitor saying nothing, and it occurred to Felix that perhaps Claude's brother ran some sort of refuge for tramps.

'Er . . . I'm Smythe,' he began nervously. 'I believe I am expected for dinner.' He smiled brightly.

'So my brother tells me,' the other replied slowly, extending a tentative hand. 'You had better come inside.'

He led the guest through a low-slung hallway and then into an unexpectedly large room: a room that was not dissimilar to a minor bombsite. Books, furniture, newspapers, discarded garments and all the random debris of years lay strewn in profligate disorder. It was like confronting a sort up visual uproar. A pair of Burmese cats crouched on a bookcase like vagabond sentinels, surveying the blitz and its intruder with studied indifference.

But what riveted Felix was the vision in the centre: amid the appalling chaos stood a richly polished Georgian table resplendent with the most exquisite silver, white napery and flickering candelabra. Posies of flowers, delicate Sèvres and Meissen porcelain and glinting crystalware had been arranged with meticulous care. Such an elaborate display must have taken an age to assemble and the effect was dazzling . . . and given the context impossibly surreal.

'How beautiful,' Felix said faintly, not sure whether he was in the Ritz or a doss house.

'Hmm,' muttered Fabius. 'I like to eat decently in the

evening, puts a full stop to the day. I'm not one of those to slum it with bread and cheese and a tray on my knee. No fear! After all, one must maintain standards.' He looked rather grim and Felix nodded in hasty agreement.

There was a silence during which Felix wondered where Claude was but didn't like to ask. Instead he looked at the cats. 'Charming creatures,' he remarked vaguely.

'No, they're not, they're bloody,' the other replied. 'I only keep them because of Claude. He kept moaning that they interfered with his work. So for a bit of peace and quiet I offered to keep them here – bloody things.'

Felix cleared his throat. 'And er, is your brother coming?'

For the first time the other smiled. 'Oh yes, old Claude's here already. I've set him to work on the soufflé. He likes doing that – it's the rotating of the egg whisk, his one culinary skill. Keeps his mind off that confounded book of his . . . Still, I suppose with you being here there'll be no holding him.' He sighed. 'But at least we've got the Château Mouton Rothschild to compensate, it's a 1945.' He nodded in the direction of a rickety sideboard where there stood a pair of stylish claret jugs and a large decanter of whisky.

Crikey, Felix thought, Cedric will be wild with envy! But it serves him right for being such a traitor. He smiled, anticipating the satisfaction of telling the coward what he had missed.

The meal, including the soufflé, had been good and the claret excellent; and despite the incongruity of the dreadful surroundings – and, as Fabius had predicted, Claude's

120

lengthy discoursing on his project – Felix had found the experience not displeasing. Unlike his brother, Fabius spoke only occasionally but when he did it was to utter something mildly gnomic or unrelated to whatever it was Claude was expounding. On the whole Felix welcomed these contributions.

'You know what,' Fabius suddenly said apropos of nothing, 'I think the son did it.'

There followed a blank pause; and then Claude said, 'I take it you are referring to the tragedy of poor Delia.'

'Of course I am,' Fabius replied, 'what other topic of current interest is there?' Claude looked pained, but before he could resume his own theme the other had continued. 'You see,' he said, addressing Felix, 'if you ask me, that Hugh Dovedale has always been odd – ever since he was in short pants. A funny cove altogether; not what you would call orthodox. A bit weird I should say.'

Felix contemplated the Wild Man of Borneo sitting opposite him at the lavish dining table in its shambolic setting. 'In what way weird?' he enquired politely.

Fabius shrugged. 'What they call *psychological* – to do with his mother I suppose. Oedipus gone wrong, I shouldn't wonder.' He winked at one of the cats and took another helping of plum tart.

'Yes, well I am sure our guest doesn't want to listen to your unsavoury speculations, Fabius,' Claude intervened quickly.

As it happens Felix would have very much liked to hear some unsavoury speculations – whether about Hugh

Dovedale or anyone else. However, he didn't get the chance for at the next moment Fabius announced he would treat their visitor to a glimpse of his priceless collection of old photographs. 'You'll like them,' he said sternly.

Felix said that he was sure he would and diffidently enquired their subject.

'Suffolk shire horses circa 1900. They're my speciality; few people have so many.' He left the table and went to rummage noisily among a conglomeration of boxes in the corner of the room.

'You are privileged,' Claude remarked dryly, clearly piqued that his own obsession was being upstaged, 'he doesn't show them to everyone, only the chosen few.'

Felix was startled; and fingering his chic bow tie wondered which was preferable – to be seen as having an affinity with cart horses or to be dubbed one of Fabius Huggins' elect. Neither was especially appealing. However, before he could explore the matter further his host was at his elbow, and clearing a space on the table began to deal out the photographs in front of him like playing cards. The Chosen One gazed down at the rows of sepia beasts with their massive rumps and mop-like hooves. Apart from the fact that some had knotted manes and some did not there seemed little distinction. 'Remarkable,' he declared.

After a while and further tactful epithets, Felix managed a covert glance at his watch and was able to make suitable excuses about the lateness of the hour and the likelihood of fog. 'It was quite misty when I arrived,' he said hopefully.

The brothers concurred; and sombre valedictions over,

their guest picked his way down the unlit path wondering vaguely how long it would take Fabius to dismantle the splendour of his table. Half the night he imagined. And the following evening – would the ritual once more be so enacted? He rather thought it would.

CHAPTER THIRTEEN

Affable though his hosts had been, Felix was glad to get away. As feared, Claude did go *on* rather, especially about the niceties of indexing, and the brother's endless photographs of hulking farm horses had challenged his patience more than somewhat.

Still, the latter's comment about Hugh Dovedale had certainly been intriguing and he wished he had heard more – though whether such views could be taken seriously was hard to say. But whatever the chap's own oddity he had certainly been generous with the food and drink. Too generous really, as the latter, plus the two cups of coffee, was beginning to taunt his bladder. If he drove quickly he could surely reach the hotel without inconvenience . . . But then that was just it: what with the encroaching fog and the unfamiliar twisting road across the heath, driving quickly was more than a touch hazardous. He eased his foot from the accelerator, and to distract his mind thought about the Queen Mother.

She really had been most gracious at their last meeting and he liked to think that his suggestions about the gardenias had been appreciated. She had certainly *looked* very interested. But then one never quite knew with royalty . . . perhaps she had been mentally mixing a gin and tonic. Or was that the footman's job? Possibly. To the faint sound of bustling corgis he brooded upon the drinks protocol of the royal household. It wasn't the best of subjects; for images of gin, tonic water and flunkies wielding soda siphons rekindled thoughts of his bladder. How vexing, he really would have to stop!

He slowed seeking a suitable place to park. By now the fog had come down quite heavily and he was hard-pressed to see the side of the road – or indeed the reeded ditch running close beside it. He drew up carefully, got out and promptly slipped on a slurry of mud. Steadying himself he could just make out a small plank bridging the ditch into the nearby field. Old habits of propriety die hard, and while it was unlikely that at such an hour he would be caught in someone's headlights, instinct prompted him to move a few yards off. Gingerly he crossed the ditch, and standing in the lee of a small hedge unbuttoned his trousers.

Phew! What relief! Fog permitting he could now drive on to Aldeburgh liberated from such concerns and be greeted by a nightcap and a warm bed. He thought of the comfortable room with curtains drawn and neatly turned down covers. How restful! He started to squelch his way back over the rutted ground peering for sight of the wooden plank.

He had just put a tentative foot on it when something appalling happened. There was a sudden sloshing noise. And out from the reeds a shape reared up at him: something big and solid, with glittering eyes, monstrous orange fangs and outlandish white whiskers. He froze, paralysed with horror. 'Christ almighty!' he gasped.

The thing gasped in return – or rather made what sounded like a rasping belch, a sharp creaking noise like a rusty hinge. Felix stared transfixed by the vision. The chomping jowls loomed enormous; and for a split second he shut his eyes vainly hoping to make the figment vanish. It did not but remained only too palpable. And then – horror of horrors – it began to advance slowly, dragging a thick rope-like tail swishing in the grass with sinister rhythm.

Felix felt he was going to faint. However, instinct prevailed and he moved instead: backing hastily and then tried to leap sideways. But the creature, by now making odd grunting sounds and awaking all the terrors of childhood, also leapt; and then with a purposeful sally thrust itself towards Felix's right foot.

This was too much, and with a banshee shriek which later embarrassed him Felix hurled himself towards the road, missed the plank and slid into the ditch. Careless of the brackish water he staggered on wildly to the sanctuary of the car convinced the fiend was at his heels.

Five minutes later with breath recovered, nerves moderately under control and trousers soaked, he thought about the blithering coypu. Yes, that's what the bastard had been – one of those beaver things Claude Huggins had been talking about at supper; one of the 'fascinating fauna so typical of our Suffolk marshes.' At the time he had thought the man was exaggerating but now he had first-hand knowledge. Rotten sodding thing! Shouldn't be allowed! He drove on grimly through the fog, desire for a warm bed replaced by need for a searing brandy.

But alas, this was not to be the last of Felix's trials that night. More was in store.

What with the fog, tiredness, and his mind still addled by the features of the coypu, he had somehow taken a wrong turn; and instead of driving south to Aldeburgh had in fact been trundling in the opposite direction – indeed, had reached the approaches to Southwold. Here the fog was much thicker and it was only after he had driven over the Buss creek and recognised the vague outline of the King's Head that it dawned on him where he was. He groaned. 'That's all I bloody need. If it's not one bloody thing it's the frigging other.'

He cursed himself but also his two hosts. After all if it hadn't been for Claude Huggins' effusive insistence he could have spent the evening safely enwrapped at The Sandworth sampling their excellent cocktails and sporting his new smoking jacket. It was too bad!

He heaved a sigh and started to turn the car, but in mid-manoeuvre was struck with a thought. What with the strain of the drive and stress from the creature he could do with a fag and a short stroll, perhaps even a whiff of sea air; a calming respite before driving all the way back to Aldeburgh. Thus righting the wheel he continued slowly along Station Road and up the High Street in the direction of the sea front. By this late hour there wasn't a soul about – or if there was the enfolding murk would have made it impossible to tell.

He drew up in the Market Place now utterly deserted and without a glimmer of light even from the windows of The Swan. He got out, and lighting a cigarette wandered along the narrow alley of Church Street towards East Green. The air was still and faintly clammy, and the little houses jostling either side shrouded in mist and sleep. Despite the silence his thin shoes, now heavily caked in mud, made no noise, and he almost felt as if he were walking in a dream. A dream considerably more agreeable than the nightmare of the bloody coypu!

Emerging into the Green he was confronted by the lighthouse looming spectral in the mist and casting a pallid ray towards the sea and its sailors. He leant on the railings above the promenade hearing the mournful bittern-like calls of the fog horns far out in the bay; and below onshore the dragging slap of wave on shingle. He remained standing for some time, lulled by the sounds and savouring the merest touch of a breeze ruffling his hair. Only at this point could he have felt such a touch; a few yards inland the air stayed eerily calm.

He lit another cigarette and walked on towards South Green. This too was swathed in an enveloping mist, and the grand houses skirting its western edge utterly obscured. He hesitated, wondering whether to walk straight back along the central path to the Market Place or to take the more circuitous route past the six sentinel cannons on the cliff and then to veer inwards. He decided on the latter. What with all the festival commitments, not to mention the ghastly murder, there had been little chance for sightseeing and as yet he had only seen the artillery depicted on postcards. He would take a quick look now – as good a time as any – and then make for the car and home.

He strolled across the turf peering at the outline of the guns – or rather at their blurred dark shapes. From his current vantage they could have been anything, rocks or giant pieces of driftwood. But as he moved nearer he could just make out the long barrels and wheeled undercarriages. He went up to the first for a closer inspection and despite the dark and the mist could detect enough to be impressed by its strength, solidity and fine preservation. He ran his fingers along the hard cold metal. Even in the present gloom he felt that collectively they made an imposing, heroic effect. 'Rather good theatre,' as Cedric might have said.

For a brief moment Felix saw himself on the nursery floor sprawled out with his fort and collection of lead soldiers. Among the Howitzers and machine guns there had been a couple of grey cannons – his pride and joy and far smarter than those mouldy tin things that belonged to Robert Wilson next door. He smiled in superior recollection.

And then as he took a final look around his gaze fell on the gun at the end of the row, and smile turned to a puzzled frown. There was something on it surely, a shape of something rather big. How odd.

Curious, Felix moved closer; and then stopped abruptly

and stared, unable to believe his eyes. The shape wasn't a thing at all, it was a person. A person draped astride the barrel, arms wound round its neck and feet dangling. A trilby hat was tilted rakishly over one ear.

Again Felix experienced a mad flashback as he recalled the cowboy films of his youth, Tom Mix & Co., in which invariably there would be some poor sucker gunned down and slung lifeless astraddle the flanks of a plodding nag.

But this was no nag: it was an ancient municipal gun and with luck the poor sucker was merely drunk. But even as the hope darted through his mind he knew that was not the case. The man was dead all right. And as if to prove it, at that moment the body slowly rolled off the barrel and slumped to the ground on its back. What Felix saw sickened him: a huge splodge of viscous jammy fluid covering half the man's chest. The eyes were open, the mouth twisted in a contorted leer. Whether the wound had been inflicted by blade or bullet Felix didn't know and didn't care. All he knew was that something terrible had happened, something obscene and fearful and from which he must run. There was nothing he could do, no help he could give: the man was horribly dead, his agony done.

Sweating and terrified Felix blundered his way across the interminable stretch of grass towards the safety of the car. His stumbling flight away from the guns and back into the Market Place seemed to go on for ever. And the fog, which a little earlier he had found almost soothing now seemed to smother, and he wrenched at the car handle with panting breaths. Yet the turmoil in his mind was not reflected in the outside world: the High

Street and its alleyways being just as silent as when he had first arrived. The town continued in its placid sleep, unmoved by Felix or the horror he had seen on its docile cliff.

Whereas earlier in the night agitation had made him careless, fear now focused Felix's mind remarkably well. He gripped the steering wheel tightly, and alert to every bend and turn, and despite the poor visibility, negotiated his way back to Aldeburgh without further alarm.

Using his guest key he entered the darkened hotel and wearily climbed the stairs. But before going to his own room he slipped into Cedric's, and switching on the light approached the recumbent sleeper and shook him by the shoulder. 'I have been chased by a coypu and encountered a dead man on a cannon,' he announced.

His friend opened his eyes blearily. 'Really?' he muttered. 'Well that's nice. Now go away.' He turned over and resumed his slumber.

CHAPTER FOURTEEN

The morning following Felix's ordeal all signs of fog had dispersed and in its place Aldeburgh's seafront was sparkling with brilliant sunshine. The two friends had elected to take their breakfast in the conservatory from where they could observe the dogs bounding on the pebbles and the fishermen mending their nets . . . or at least Cedric was observing them; Felix's head was bent, preoccupied with his egg and other matters.

'No,' he said tightly, 'I did not say the corpse was fired from a cannon. I said it was sitting on the bloody thing – or it was to begin with, and then it fell off.' He sniffed and smoothed his napkin.

Cedric studied his companion for a moment and then asked mildly whether the previous evening's dinner had been convivial and if Huggins' brother kept a good cellar.

Had Felix not encountered the corpse and had Cedric been a trifle more sympathetic he would have recounted the early part of the evening's events with theatrical relish. As it was he merely shrugged, and said, 'I've no idea, but the stuff seemed all right and there was plenty of it.'

'Hmm,' Cedric murmured, 'I daresay.'

Felix looked up sharply. 'Oh that's it – I see. You think I was stoned out of my mind and seeing wild animals and dead bodies all over the damn shop. Typical!' He glowered across the table.

'Perish the thought, dear chap! I merely thought that the combination of fog, food and drink, *plus* the fact that you had omitted to take your glasses – left them in the lounge, silly boy – that just conceivably your perceptions were not entirely razor sharp.' Cedric proffered a calming smile.

But Felix was far from calmed. 'Listen,' he retorted angrily, 'there may have been fog, I may have had a few drinks, and yes, I didn't have my glasses. But I know what I saw and I can assure you that both man and beast were totally real. If you don't believe me I suggest you drive over to Southwold this very minute and see what's cooking. Something will be I can tell you! There are probably hordes of police swarming all over that cliff even as we speak. Why don't you telephone Rosy Gilchrist? She's bound to know!'

He gazed out of the window twitching irritably and Cedric's scepticism melted. 'It all sounds very distressing,' he said gently. 'Now let us withdraw to that corner over there and you can tell me more.'

Thus taking the remains of their coffee and retreating to a more secluded spot they began to discuss the more shocking of Felix's traumas and how best it might be handled.

'In practice of course one really ought to go to the police. Presumably you are what they call a "key witness" with information material to the fact,' Cedric mused.

'I don't care what I am material to,' Felix said, 'I am not going near a police station. I've had quite enough of being a key witness. Sitting on that stage and seeing Delia Dovedale keel over after shrieking my name is more than sufficient thank you very much. If the authorities now find that I was also in the proximity of that poor beggar on his gun they're bound to think that I am dodgy! And what would my clients think for God's sake? Especially Her Majesty.' He shuddered in horror gripping his coffee cup so tightly that Cedric feared it might break. The latter said nothing for a moment, and then agreed that on the whole and by and large and with all things being equal Felix was doubtless right and that the less said the better.

For the first time since getting up that morning Felix relaxed. He emitted a loud sigh of relief. 'Good. That's settled then.' And splashing more coffee into his cup he announced casually that he intended taking a little stroll along the promenade past Crag House on the off chance of getting a sighting of 'You know *who*'.

'I don't know, actually,' Cedric replied, 'unless of course you mean the composer chap – or would it be the singer?'

Felix leered. 'Either will do.' With a slow wink he stood up, selected a newspaper and stepped out through the French windows.

Cedric watched his friend's slight figure as it sauntered

casually across the strip of lawn and turned right in the direction of the Jubilee Hall. He smiled. And then reaching for his sun glasses and settling back in the wicker chair he began to give serious thought to the latest extraordinary development.

Failing to report a crime was, of course, an indictable offence . . . but by now it would most certainly have been reported by others. Felix was surely right in assuming that the Southwold constabulary would be swarming all over the place; and no doubt their forensic people would be in the process of fixing the time and the likely circumstances of the death – if they hadn't already done so. Yes, he reflected, any information that Felix could contribute would surely duplicate their own . . . and having listened to his friend's account he couldn't say it had been the most succinct. Indeed, Cedric thought wryly, Felix's version might well cloud rather than clarify. Besides, the poor fellow was right – didn't he already have enough to cope with regarding the Dovedale death? To be involved in a second would surely invite comment on the platform, as Oscar Wilde had more or less once remarked.

He settled further back in the chair and brooded. It really was the most intriguing business. Whoever could the man have been – someone with equestrian interests perhaps, he thought wryly. A jockey felled by a rival? After all Newmarket wasn't all that far! Felix had gabbled something about a hat. Well that shouldn't be too difficult to trace; and presumably the other items of clothing would betray some traces of their owner. The police were sure to pick up on those. But how remarkable for that demure little town to have two such dramatic disposals within so short a while! Perhaps there was some rabid maniac at work who specialised in bizarrely choreographed killings, but also had a penchant for sea air.

He shelved the matter and instead turned his thoughts to the crossword. Disdaining the *Daily Sketch* he looked in vain for *The Times*. Drat Felix! Why he had felt the need to take a newspaper with him on his prowls one couldn't imagine – some sort of cover he supposed.

Felix had been right about there being 'something cooking' in Southwold: the hob was hot and police and tongues were sizzling. The body had been found at five o'clock that morning by an early dog-walker and the alarm raised. And after much busyness, brisk enquiry and perusal of the wallet and garments, the victim's identity had been firmly established: the proprietor of The Select Publishing Co., Mr Floyd de Lisle. Cause of death? Shot by person or persons unknown.

'You are sure of that are you, sir?' enquired Detective Constable Jennings of his superior. 'I mean, who knows – it might have been suicide.'

The inspector regarded him coldly. '*Everyone* knows, Jennings, that it was not suicide. You don't straddle a cannon, put a bullet through your chest and then throw the offending weapon away so as nobody can find it. Use your brain, boy!'

Jennings looked mildly piqued. 'But you always say that one should never discount alternatives, and that's just what I was doing – sort of lateral thinking.'

'There's lateral and lateral,' retorted the inspector heavily, 'and yours is wide of the side. And besides, alternatives are only useful if they make sense. Yours does not.'

The young man shrugged. 'Oh well, win one lose one,' he muttered cheerfully.

The inspector returned to his notes while Jennings gazed out of the window tracking the progress of a kite being flown high above the Common. Then kite out of sight, he turned back to the inspector. 'You know what is troubling me, sir? I can't help wondering why—'

'Your troubles are no concern of mine, my lad. Now shut up and let me get on!'

Unperturbed Jennings continued, 'Well it's not that I'm *troubled* exactly but what you might call intrigued. You see it does seem a funny place to want to sit in the middle of the night, especially as there are plenty of handy seats up there. I mean why climb on a cannon? Unless of course the man was drunk; but then again we know that he—'

'That he wasn't,' his boss concluded. 'The medics have assured us of that.'

Jennings nodded. 'So what was he doing?'

'Obvious,' the inspector said, 'practising at being Don Quixote for the Reydon carnival.'

Jennings frowned. 'No. Seriously, sir, you must admit it's odd. And do you know what?'

'What?'

'*I* think he was put there; after he had been done in.'

The inspector beamed. 'Now that's what I do call a sensible alternative. My thoughts exactly.'

At that moment the telephone rang. The inspector

lifted the receiver and listened intently to the voice the other end. 'Oh yes,' he said casually, 'that's been on the cards right from the start: no other explanation . . . Behind the Casino you say? That would figure: fits our theory exactly.' He replaced the receiver and smiled complacently at his colleague. 'Nice to know they're on the job. That was the Chief Superintendent's office catching up with our analysis – about him being placed on the gun after he was dead.'

Jennings looked bemused. 'But what was that casino you were talking about? I didn't know there was one of those in Southwold. You could have fooled me!'

'Ah but then you lead a sheltered life – not at all your sort of thing I shouldn't think. Like I always say, appearances are deceptive; there's more to this town than meets the eye. You'll learn that.'

'Yes, but where on earth—' began the other.

The inspector sighed and said patiently, 'The *Casino*, Jennings, is that small octagonal building just next to the guns. Somebody or other erected it in the eighteenth century when it was used for dances and tea parties and such, but recently it's been a coastguard station. Could do with a lick of paint if you ask me . . . Anyway, according to my informant from the super's office that's where the victim was dealt with. Just behind it. It's only a few yards from the guns so I suppose the body was dragged over and then hoisted up.'

The younger man nodded eagerly, pleased that he had got something right. 'Still,' he said, 'it seems a funny thing to do after you've just shot a chap – to waste time heaving his corpse about like that. I mean it wasn't as if he was trying to conceal it! If that had been me I'd have scarpered pronto.'

'I am sure you would,' the inspector agreed.

'Well wouldn't you, sir?'

'Not if I had a perverse and warped mentality I wouldn't.'

'Ah,' Jennings replied sagely, 'that explains it of course. So we are dealing with a nutcase are we? A raver. In my opinion they're the worst kind, difficult to predict you see. It's the mental processes – up the spout. Oh yes, just mark my words sir, we're going to have our work cut out on this one, you can be sure of that!'

'Is that so? Well, well, what d'you know,' said the inspector. He reached for his pipe.

Half an hour later there was a knock on the inspector's door. 'There's been a break-in,' announced the duty officer, 'at his premises.'

'Whose premises?'

'The dead man's – Floyd de Lisle's. The team had just finished going over his rooms in Chester Road when this girl appears in tears saying that when she went to open up his office on South Green she found the side door had been forced and one of the filing cabinets ransacked. Papers and letters all over the shop. She's his typist – or was – and had gone over early to feed the cat and to retype a letter she reckoned she had messed up. When she saw the state of things she rushed to his place in Chester Road to tell him, and then of course bumped into our lot. She's here now, in an awful state wailing and moaning and saying it didn't ought to have happened.'

'Which? The break-in or the murder?'

'Both, I suppose.'

'Hmm. Give her some Jaffa cakes and an aspirin, it usually works. And then tell Jennings to talk to her. He'll like doing that – he's got a new notebook.'

The inspector reached for his hat and jacket, and rounding up an assistant prepared to visit The Select Publishing Co.

CHAPTER FIFTEEN

What the inspector found there was what might be termed controlled mess: controlled in that the main part of the premises was comparatively ordered except for a corner by the window, a corner housing a filing cabinet substantially smaller than the other three. Whereas the rest of the area was conventionally organised with a couple of desks and typewriters, a bookcase and the larger filing cabinets, the window corner had been blitzed.

The two drawers of the cabinet had been wrenched open and their contents, including several of the cardboard dividers, scattered wildly in every direction. A vase of flowers which must have been standing on its top had been dashed to the floor, its blooms still intact, but water soaked heavily into the thin cotton rug. There must originally have been a bunch of keys sticking in the lock for these, too, appeared to have fallen out or been thrown carelessly on the floor.

At first sight it seemed that it had been this area alone, with its sheaves of jumbled manuscripts that had been the focus. But on the floor at the side of the cabinet was a small cheap strongbox of the kind sold by Woolworths. Its lid was open revealing a ten shilling note and a handful of silver, while on the mat lay a saturated white fiver. The box gave the impression of having been hastily rifled and its main contents quickly pocketed.

The inspector was puzzled. What connection was there between the strewn documents and the tin of petty cash open on the floor? What had the intruder been searching for – money or goods? If the former he was unlikely to have snatched more than fifteen quid or so, a small sum you would think for all that trouble. And if the latter why would he want to snaffle a bunch of probably rather third-rate scripts from aspiring amateurs? After all The Select Publishing Co. wasn't exactly Victor Gollancz or Chatto & Windus, and he rather doubted that there was a budding Graham Greene or James Joyce on its stocks.

The inspector grinned. It was amazing how bumptious some of these creative types could be – even the third-rate ones (often the worst). Perhaps Chummy had had his submission rejected by the publisher and this was his revenge: wreck the bugger's filing cabinets. Or perhaps, cheated of a promised advance he had come to grab what little cash he could: screw the bastard! Probably both: a mixture of avarice and wounded literary pride. You never knew with 'artists', they were a sensitive lot – take that Van Gogh fellow and his severed ear. Or had that been Proust?

He checked with the young constable about the front door. Had the intruder a key? Evidently not, the lock, a flimsy one, had been forced. Any sign of mud or footprints on the stairs? Not obviously, the linoleum was grubby enough as it was. A cigarette stub had been found on the landing, a Piccadilly – a brand regularly smoked by the dead man; there had been a packet in his trouser pocket when they found him.

The inspector was puzzled. What had been the *point?* In some ways the raid seemed to have been focused – its aim the smaller cabinet by the window, the others evidently ignored. But if so why bother with the money box? Was the intruder simply a random opportunist who while intending to go on to the other cabinets had been diverted by the cash – and then losing interest had quickly scarpered? The front door might suggest that: it had been left wide open with no attempt to conceal the break-in or delay its finding. Indifference or haste?

The forensics would have to do their bit with the fingerprints, but he doubted if that would yield anything – the place was probably smothered in de Lisle's dabs and the typist's.

Thinking of the girl he wondered how Jennings was getting on and whether he had succeeded in calming her down and obtained anything useful. He picked up the telephone from the untouched desk and rang the station. 'Bring Miss Morgan over here, would you,' he said curtly.

* * *

145

Betty Morgan arrived tear-stained, but collected. She had declined the aspirin, but had enjoyed the Jaffa cakes. She had also quite enjoyed Jennings' attempts at avuncular patience. For a young man only a few years older than herself he seemed ever so wise! She wondered if he had a girlfriend.

She was less impressed with his boss. He looked a bit stern – like her father on Saturday nights when he wanted to know why she had come in so late – well if you called eleven o'clock late!

The inspector gave her a statutory smile and gestured to the disrupted filing cabinet. 'Anything special about that? What's the system here?'

'System?'

'Yes. How do you file the stuff? What goes into what?'

She hesitated; and then glancing at Jennings for reassurance, announced: 'Fiction, biography, war memoirs, cats and dogs, flowers and natural history – Mr de Lisle is very particular about the categories. I get into awful trouble if I muddle them up.' She stopped and corrected herself: 'I mean he *was* particular.' Her face started to crumple but seeing no sign of a Jaffa cake she managed to compose herself.

'So what was in that one?' the inspector asked again.

'Oh that was for the *special* submissions – there aren't too many of those which is why it's the smallest.'

'What do you mean "special"?'

'It's part of Mr de Lisle's other system – what he called "the hierarchy of quality": "Good", "Goodish", "Moderate" and "God Awful". This is for the good stuff,' she nodded towards the ransacked cabinet and its scattered papers.

The inspector beamed. Well at least something mildly useful. 'That is most helpful Miss Morgan. Now after I've had our fingerprint people here I would like you to come back this afternoon and make a list of the "good" scripts and then tell me which, if any, are missing. We'll send a car if you like.'

The prospect of having a car sent was quite appealing. Nevertheless she had arranged to meet Tina for a spot of shopping in Lowestoft; perhaps he would be happy for her to do it the following day.

He wasn't. 'Some things take precedence over shopping,' he said severely. (Hell, just like her father!) 'A man has been killed, Miss Morgan, and his office broken into. You wouldn't like it to be thought that you had obstructed the police in their enquiries, would you?'

She agreed that she wouldn't and promised to return at three o'clock. There was no further mention of a police car.

'But you know, sir,' Jennings said after she had left, 'even if she does find something missing we still shan't know if this business is connected with the murder. The fact that the office has been done over – or part of it – doesn't necessarily mean that the two events are linked. It might just have been a coincidence: that while the man was being shot and shoved on top of the cannon, someone just happened to be breaking and entering. I mean, we shouldn't discount the possibility of a temporal parallel, should we?'

'"A temporal parallel"? Certainly not,' replied the inspector, 'it's what I am always telling you.'

The lad was absolutely right, he brooded. Chance and coincidences played a far bigger role in crime – or in anything else for that matter – than was popularly supposed. Still, in this case his instinct tended to suggest otherwise – not that that got him very far. Perhaps the girl would come up with something relevant. Meanwhile a nice pint at the Red Lion might help clarify matters . . .

That afternoon Betty Morgan knelt among the papers and tried to reassemble them into some order. It wasn't easy, as although they all had page numbers few of the individual leaves bore names or titles. For example, she came across the first page of Mrs Grantham's offering, *Cats Against Castration* but had some difficulty in collating the remainder; they tended to get mixed up with Colonel Wishart's memoir *Crisis in Europe*. Even those that she had typed herself she couldn't always recognise because on the whole she tended not to bother with reading the stuff – just copying it.

Still, there had been one item that she remembered – a story about somebody in Paris called Lucian. He had had a French poodle and seemed to go about doing a lot of leering in back alleys. She didn't think she liked him very much and had only bothered to read bits of the thing because it was set in Paris, a place she hoped to visit one day . . . Anyway she could find no trace of the leering Lucian or his stupid poodle, and she had just laddered her best nylons. She sat back on her heels and sighed.

'How are we getting on?' asked the inspector emerging from the kitchenette bearing a cup of tea. 'You can probably do with this.'

The man seemed less stern than in the morning, but she still rather resented him for making her stay scrabbling about with manuscripts when she could have been shopping with Tina. After all it was her day off!

'Well,' she said, 'most things seem to be here, but there is one item I can't account for although I've found its folder tag.' She held up the small piece of cardboard with a name scrawled on it.

The inspector took it. 'So who is Millicent Merrivale?' he asked.

She shrugged. 'I don't know really.'

'What do you mean you don't *know*? That's what it's got here; it must be the name of the author, one of your boss's clients!'

Betty regarded her lengthening ladder. 'My late boss,' she said pertly.

Little madam! he thought angrily; and then fixing her with a hard stare, said quietly: 'Exactly, your *late* boss: Mr Floyd de Lisle, who only ten hours ago was found shot to pieces on the cliff top with no one to help or save him. I should be obliged if you would answer my question, Miss Morgan. Who is Millicent Merrivale?'

Betty burst into tears.

Once the sobs had abated and he had pushed some more tea in her direction, he repeated the question in a gentler tone.

'You see,' she explained, 'sometimes they use pen names. They can be a bit shy about revealing their identities – until publication that is. After that it's generally all right, they're only too happy for people to know. But one or two can be awfully secretive and hang on to their fake names for even longer. Mr de Lisle was very pernickety about respecting their wishes: sometimes he wouldn't even tell me who they were.'

'And this was such a time?'

'Yes. Mr de Lisle would hand me the chapters to type, but he would never say who had actually written them; there was just this name, Millicent Merrivale. He used to joke and say the lady had a nice sense of alliteration, or whatever it's called.' Betty blew her nose and got to her feet. 'Do you think I can go now?' she asked plaintively, 'I've got one of my heads coming on.'

The inspector nodded. 'You've done very well. Now there is just one more thing and you can do this at home. Try to think back over the last couple of months and write me a list of the people who had visited Mr de Lisle in his office. I don't suppose you will remember them all but put down as many names as you can – and I'm not talking about the cleaners or metre readers, just those who came to see him personally.'

She nodded.

'Oh, and if you like,' he added graciously, 'I'll see that DC Jennings gets over here with a police car.'

It was of course a long shot and if, after all, the thing turned out to be simply petty robbery, a wasted effort. But there was just a chance that by a process of elimination they might work out the author of the missing manuscript and thus get some clue as to what the hell was going on. He would have to grill the girl again the following day when she brought the list. Perhaps Jennings might like the task.

CHAPTER SIXTEEN

The same night that Felix was negotiating the hazards of the local marshes and of Gun Hill, Rosy was lying awake tossing and turning. She had dropped off quickly enough; but waking an hour later she lay restless, her head seething with discordant images: images of the recent funeral, the vicar's massive St Bernard meekly tethered to the church railings (would she ever encounter such a breed again without being reminded of the murdered woman's interment?), the victim's portrait gazing benignly from the stairs, the curious scribbled narrative tucked under the blanket in the wardrobe . . . and looming in the background Dr Stanley's disgruntled expression were she to return to the Museum without the promised stick of Southwold Rock. Would he really appreciate the substitute of Adnams ale?

She thought also of Hugh's insistence that they should

prolong their stay a little longer. 'Mother would have approved,' he had said, adding that in any case their presence kept Hawkins on his toes. 'We don't have many visitors these days and he is apt to get lazy,' he had joked. Rosy was slightly surprised by his attitude; it wasn't as if she and Angela were old family friends – least of all herself. But when she had said as much to Angela the latter was of the opinion that Hugh was far more affected by his mother's death than he let on and that having guests in the house, even comparative strangers, was his way of regaining normality. 'Doubtless we are being *very* therapeutic!' she had declared confidently.

Oh well, nice to be needed, Rosy thought wryly . . . diversion for the pugs, therapy for their master and a corrective to the butler's idleness, what more could a girl want. She rolled over and was about to try sleep once more when she suddenly heard the rumbling of a car coming slowly up the drive. It seemed to stall, and then with a crashing of gears and much revving re-engaged itself, only to stop again while its engine ran on.

Intrigued Rosy pushed back the bedclothes, went to the window and peered out. There was thick fog, but she could just make out the shape of a vehicle displaying only a single hazy headlamp. Abruptly it lurched forward again, seemed to veer across the drive and then with a loud rasping of gravel propelled itself into the low wall. There was a muffled crash followed by a silence.

As Rosy peered in wonder, the driver's door opened and a figure climbed out and rather in the manner of the car itself began to weave slowly up the front steps before stalling at the top. She heard a curse, followed by what sounded suspiciously like one suffering the effects of nausea.

Oh Lord! Was this their host back from the Harbour Inn after an evening carousing with cronies – or conceivably playing bridge with the vicar? There were, Rosy supposed, a number of possibilities. She was about to return to bed when there was the sound of the front door being opened; a light was switched on followed by a murmur of voices. She thought she recognised one as being Hawkins'. A figure crunched across the drive to extinguish the still glowing headlamp, and a minute later the front door was slammed shut and the light switched off. From somewhere below she could hear stumbling footfalls and the querulous bark of a pug. And then silence. Rosy returned to bed, drew the blankets over her head and went to sleep immediately.

The first thing she did the next morning was to look out of the window. The fog had vanished, as had the car . . . Indeed had it not been for the fact that the wall was no longer in its unblemished state and a heap of bricks and flints lay tumbled on the gravel, there was nothing to suggest that the episode had not been a figment of her imagination. Craning her neck Rosy could just make out the garage at the far side of the house. Its doors were firmly closed. Was that where the vehicle was? Shunted tidily away to await the repairers or until claimed by its driver? However, she more than suspected that the latter was Hugh himself. She would make tactful enquiry of Hawkins when he brought her breakfast.

'A minor mishap,' Hawkins confirmed gravely, 'a

couple of knocks and scratches, nothing that can't be soon remedied.' He cleared his throat and added quietly, 'although I fear that can't be entirely said of Master Hugh. He is not quite himself this morning, a touch under the weather, if you take my meaning.'

Rosy did take his meaning. Huh, she thought, he's got a monumental hangover that's what! She wondered if such nocturnal 'mishaps' were frequent or whether it was to do with the current situation. After all to have had a mother dispatched in such a way would be enough to make anyone overdose on alcohol and ram a wall. It occurred to her that it might be tactful if she and Angela made themselves scarce for the day: they could drive to Orford and view its castle, or have a little tour of some of the Suffolk churches: Blythburgh's was said to be especially fine, as of course further afield was Lavenham's. With luck by the time they returned in the evening their host would be fully recovered and normality restored.

Hawkins looked mildly relieved at her proposal, as was Lady Fawcett when Rosy informed her of the commotion in the night.

'Oh yes, if the young man has a head like my Gregory's in the old days he will be quite impossible and one will be required to tiptoe about and speak only in whispers. Too boring for words! The sooner we go off somewhere nice and leave him to it the better. But not *too* many churches, Rosy dear; after all one had an excellent view of St Edmund's during the funeral and it doesn't do to be excessive, does it?'

Rosy smiled and said that perhaps they could manage to squeeze in a small one between some light shopping in Woodbridge and motoring on for a leisurely lunch at Orford.

And so it was only when they returned to Southwold in the late afternoon that they heard the news of the second murder – 'the body on the gun' as it was already being dubbed – and learnt of the shocking fate of Floyd de Lisle found that morning in a parlous condition on Gun Hill.

The news was relayed by Mark and Iris, plus Hugh now moderately recovered from his earlier indisposition. 'Well,' he said caustically, 'this will give our local law officers something to muddle them further. No progress regarding my mother's death – or at least if there is they certainly haven't bothered to inform *me*. And now there's de Lisle. Extraordinary really.'

'Weren't you at school with him?' Mark asked.

'What? Oh – yes, yes I was for a short time. He arrived in my last year. Rather a tiresome type, a bit of a swot and cocky with it. He had the nerve to ask if I would like him to edit my English prep as his version would be immeasurably better than mine. Bumptious little creep.'

'But he's dead, Hugh!' Iris protested. 'You can hardly hold that against him now.'

Hugh agreed that he couldn't, but judging from his cold expression Rosy rather thought he could.

'But who on earth would want to kill the man?' enquired Lady Fawcett. 'I met him at the funeral. He seemed most affable and cheerful – well as cheerful as is suitable on such occasions I suppose.'

'Ah, so you mean he didn't know that he was due for the chop,' Hugh said lightly.

For a few seconds Lady Fawcett regarded him speculatively, and then just as lightly, replied, 'As no more did your poor mother.'

Hugh seemed nonplussed, and then turning aside bent to fondle a pug.

There was a slightly awkward silence, broken by Mark announcing that they had to be off: 'We only dropped in to see if you had heard the news, and now we must rush home before the Brightwells appear. They're picking us up to attend a concert in Aldeburgh – though frankly with all this ghastly business going on I'm not sure that I shall be all that receptive . . . By the way Lucas may have a notion or two, he's pretty chummy with the Chief Constable so just conceivably he may have picked up something from that source. I'll try to sound him out.'

'Huh,' Hugh replied carelessly, 'Lucas is chummy with anyone who might be grist to his social mill and secure him a gong. You see, the next thing he'll do is to found a charity for the protection of minor publishers! Never misses a trick that chap.'

'Oh honestly, Hugh,' Iris exclaimed, 'for goodness' sake go and mix a hair of the dog, you'll feel so much better.' Smiling apologetically at the two guests she followed her husband out to the car.

After they had gone Hugh sighed. 'I say, ladies, would you mind awfully dining alone this evening? I'm still not quite *dans mon assiette* as our French friends would say. A little penitential dry toast in my room is as about as much as I can manage. Would you mind?'

Slightly relieved they said that of course they wouldn't and was there anything they could do.

'To soothe my fevered brow?' he laughed sardonically. 'No, only sleep will do that.'

'But what about Peep and Bow?' Rosy asked. 'Would you like me to give them their bedtime run?'

He beamed. 'Oh yes, that would be most kind, a real help!' It was, Rosy felt, his one spontaneously decent response of the past half hour.

Over supper, and with Hawkins safely busy in the kitchen, Rosy suggested that perhaps it really was time that they should return to London. 'Delightful though Southwold is one must admit that two murders hardly make it the most soothing of holiday venues! And despite what he says, I am sure Hugh can't really want us hovering around much longer. Perhaps we should cut and run while we can.'

Lady Fawcett looked startled. 'While we *can*?' she echoed. 'Whatever do you mean? You are surely not expecting one of us to be the next are you?'

'No, of course not. I merely meant that this might be an opportune time to leave. We have paid our last respects to Delia, the festival is nearing its an end, and now that there is this fresh scandal it surely seems the right moment to bow out gracefully. If we pack tonight we could be on the road back to London early tomorrow.'

Lady Fawcett's response was not what Rosy had

expected. And thinking about it later she realised that she had made a tactical error in using the word 'scandal'. It must have struck a Pavlovian chord in her companion's mind which tipped the balance between languid curiosity and avid fascination.

Thus there was a pause while Angela Fawcett's mild grey eyes slowly roamed the room before coming to rest on the young woman opposite. She bent forward. 'You know, Rosy,' she said solemnly, 'I consider there is more to this than meets the eye.' You don't say, Rosy thought irritably. But irritation turned to surprise when the other added, 'And I feel it is our bounden duty to pursue the matter more fully. To leave now would be very negative, not to say slipshod . . . I mean, it is not that one is officious or vulgarly inquisitive – perish the thought! But I do feel that there are certain things incumbent upon one to *find out*. Wouldn't you agree?'

'Er, well,' Rosy replied doubtfully, 'I am intrigued, of course, but I can't quite see where bounden duty comes in; and besides presumably the police will solve things sooner or later.'

'Hmm. Later I should say – if at all. Think of all those cases that have been shelved for years with no one any the wiser. We wouldn't want that to happen with Delia, would we? Or indeed to that unfortunate publisher.'

'But you never liked her very much, or so you said.'

'Immaterial. We went to the same school and swung on the parallel bars together. That counts for something you know.'

The idea of Angela Fawcett swinging on parallel bars

was difficult to imagine but Rosy nodded politely. 'What about Floyd de Lisle?' she asked. 'We only spoke to him once and that was at the funeral. I am sorry he is dead, of course I am, but he was a virtual stranger.'

'He was most mannerly; brought me a chair and a plate of sandwiches. We had a nice little chat and he was most appreciative of my hat. I consider it disgraceful that someone should have done that to him . . . No, I can assure you Rosy that I have no intention of simply walking away. Now tomorrow we must telephone Cedric Dillworthy at The Sandworth and arrange a consultative meeting. Cedric can sometimes be useful, though what Felix will make of it all I am not so sure. He is not of the most robust.'

Rosy was amused. For one not noted for her own reserves of energy, Angela Fawcett's current resolution was distinctly atypical. But she knew that such determination was fed less by a moral imperative than by an instinct for the hunt. Indignation on behalf of the two victims was genuine enough, but the real stimulus lay surely in the prospect of unearthing some almighty scandal . . .

CHAPTER SEVENTEEN

That afternoon Rosy had the house to herself. Hugh had disappeared and Lady Fawcett had been collected by Freda Brightwell to see a friend's exhibition of watercolours in Halesworth. It was peaceful in the house with even the pugs fast asleep and Rosy took the opportunity to get on with her book, a collection of Katherine Mansfield stories.

Yet despite the writer's undoubted charm she had difficulty in concentrating. The memory of Floyd de Lisle at Delia's funeral was so insistent. Not that he had made any special impression at the time, and it was Angela with whom he had been talking so earnestly. Nevertheless she remembered him well enough, and now that he was so bizarrely dead even more so. What on earth had he done to prompt so dreadful an end?

Uneasily she tried to escape back into the book but failed.

She put it aside and contemplated the pugs snoozing fatly on the rug: they could jolly well make themselves useful by being taken for a walk! A bit of exercise might help divert her mind from the publisher's fate.

She roused the sleeping beauties, who with appreciative snorts and snuffles, eagerly sashayed towards the garden door and rollicked onto the lawn. One of them – Bo? – went haring after a baby rabbit to no effect; while the other pranced in yelping circles and then sat down to water the geraniums.

Rosy shooed them away from the flower beds and round to the side of the house into the long grass. It stretched down towards a potting shed and small shrubbery; and with Rosy in tow the two dogs scampered off in its direction.

In a small clearing some yards from the shed were the makings of a bonfire. The rubbish was well stacked and the kindling neatly laid. Whoever had made it – the gardener presumably – was obviously an expert in such matters. Rosy was about to turn away, when amongst the usual detritus she noticed a couple of crumpled hat boxes, a pair of worn bedroom slippers and a faded blue counterpane, and with a pang realised these must have been some of the things collected by Iris and Freda from the dead woman's room. She sighed and fixed her attention on a blackbird warbling lustily from a nearby sycamore.

Then out of the corner of her eye she saw Peep and Bo rampaging excitedly by the shed. They were gripping what looked like a large piece of material, each with a corner in its mouth. A tug of war was in progress with much snarling and shaking. What on earth did they think they were savaging – a half-dead coypu? As Rosy approached, a rabbit shot past and the makeshift prey was instantly dropped in favour of the real thing. With a collective shriek the pugs charged in pursuit, their stumpy little legs churning hell for leather.

Rosy went forward to examine the thing and saw that it was a raincoat, a man's by the look of it, creased and dirty. Where had it come from? The bonfire, presumably. The pugs must have tugged it out from under the rest of the debris. It looked rather murky and initially she was going to leave it where it was; but an instinct for tidiness made her stoop to throw it back on the rubbish pile. As she did so she saw clearly that its large dark patches were not dirt at all – but blood.

She stepped back. How disgusting! No wonder it had been thrown out. And then as she stared the blood seemed not so much disgusting as faintly sinister. What the hell was it doing daubed like that all over the sleeves and lapels? There were large stains, too, on parts of the hem. She continued to stare, puzzled and repelled.

And then she heard a light footfall from behind, and whirling round was confronted by Hawkins. 'I caught the pugs,' he said. 'They were about to break through the hedge, but I stopped the little varmints and they're back in the kitchen now. No need to worry.'

Rosy hadn't been worrying, being far too absorbed by the bloodstained garment at her feet. She had recognised it as being the grey raincoat worn by Hugh Dovedale to his mother's funeral. It had been considerably smarter then. She recalled he had removed it before entering the church, and then left it in the pew. Someone had handed it back to him on the way to the refreshments after the burial . . . Yes, it was definitely his all right.

Hawkins followed her gaze. He nodded: 'Master Hugh's – one of his nosebleeds, I fear. He gets them sometimes.' He picked it up and thrust it beneath the kindling at the foot of the bonfire.

'Rather a large nosebleed,' Rosy said lightly, 'though I gather some people do have that trouble.'

Hawkins must have seen and heard her scepticism for the next moment he gave an awkward cough and said, 'Yes, madam is quite right to be doubtful. I apologise – but the truth is not entirely savoury.'

Rosy shrugged and remarked that on the whole copious blood was rarely savoury.

He gave a wintry smile and said he took her point, but it was less the blood that was unsavoury than the circumstances. 'You see,' he explained, 'you may recall his returning home the other night rather the worse for wear . . . Well to tell the truth he was actually smashed out of his mind and had already had a little accident in the vicinity of Saint Felix School. Indeed not so little really. The car skidded in the fog and went straight into a flint wall and he cut himself badly when clambering out. Blood everywhere, on his mac and in the car. As you can imagine, he's not too keen on the news getting about, particularly since it is not the first time he has come off the road. It would be better if nothing were said.'

Rosy regarded the man steadily. 'Keen on walls, is

he?' she enquired. 'Two in one night is quite good going and I imagine the car is in a pretty bad state after all that buffeting – yet I noticed him drive off in it this afternoon smoothly enough. Are the Southwold mechanics generally so quick, or for that matter the Suffolk flints quite so sharp? Where did he get that gash – on the carotid artery?' She hesitated, and then to her horror heard herself adding, 'Coincidence really that he should have such an eventful time on the same night that Mr de Lisle was being shot.'

'You must think before you speak, Rosy,' her father had once admonished.

'But it's the truth!' the child had replied.

'Very possibly, but you have to couch it in a certain way otherwise there can be trouble.' He had smiled and ruffled her hair. 'Grown-ups call it tact.'

As she gazed at Hawkins shocked by her boldness she wondered what sort of trouble might be in store. What a fool she had been to blurt it out like that. Tactless, tactless idiot!

Rather to her surprise the man remained impassive. And then clearing his throat he said quietly: 'You are right: it must look very suspicious.' He glanced at the garden seat a few feet away. 'Perhaps you would care to sit down? If you don't mind I think I will.' He suddenly looked very old, and without waiting for a response walked slowly to the seat. Mechanically Rosy followed him and settled herself at the opposite end.

For a few seconds neither spoke. And then with a sigh he said: 'No, Miss Gilchrist, he didn't do it. Despite the blood and my own rather foolish lies my employer is entirely innocent of the gentleman's murder. Admittedly he did see him that night. Oh yes!' He gave a bitter laugh. 'But I can assure you he didn't gun him down.'

Well that's a relief, Rosy thought, providing it is true. But what on earth is he getting at? She scrutinised the tired features and black eye patch – an ageing pirate spinning his final yarn? Or a loyal retainer desperately covering up God's knows what. She said nothing and waited.

'Yes,' he said musingly, 'he did meet him – or at least in a manner of speaking he did.'

'What does that mean?' she asked tersely.

'He was dead already: shot through the chest behind the Casino, that little building beside the guns. Nearly tripped over him I gather.'

'Hmm. So Mr Dovedale was strolling along through the fog at midnight on the high cliff, when all of a sudden he stumbles over a body strewn in his path. I suppose he said something like, "Oh bless my soul, what have we here? A dead publisher if I am not mistaken!"'

For the first time she saw a flicker of annoyance pass over the old man's features and she instantly regretted her words. What it was to have a caustic mouth! 'I am so sorry,' she stammered, 'that was rather cheap. Please go on.'

Hawkins gave a faint smile. 'I see Mr Dovedale is not the only one given to impulsive response; he called me "a blithering dunderhead" yesterday.' He gave a pensive sigh. 'But in my opinion his insults are not a patch on his father's, not a patch. Doesn't have the same imagination . . .'

Rosy couldn't care less about her host's imagination or his father's, but she did want to know about his bloody raincoat. 'Do go on, Mr Hawkins,' she said quietly, 'I won't interrupt.'

As bid Hawkins continued smoothly with his explanation.

Apparently, more affected by his mother's recent funeral than he had let on, that night Hugh Dovedale had indeed been out on a bender. At first it had simply been a bit of carousing with the locals. But later after the pubs had closed he had wandered off on his own nursing a bottle of brandy. He had left the car parked on Constitution Hill, staggered down to Ferry Road and then up again, scrambling over the sand dunes lining the shore. Depressed and increasingly drunk he had blundered around in the fog chucking pebbles into the sea and swilling the brandy. Eventually he had veered off onto the path leading to the Casino. It was while supporting himself against its wall that he had seen the figure on the ground.

At this point in the narrative Hawkins broke off and said apologetically, 'I fear this is rather distasteful but it is what happened and you must remember that by this time Mr Dovedale really wasn't responsible for his actions.'

Rosy nodded, and he resumed the account. 'When he went to investigate he immediately recognised the man to be Mr de Lisle and realised he had sustained a fatal wound to the chest. Naturally he was exceedingly shocked . . . but you know, in that inebriated state your emotions are all haywire and you don't always register things in the normal way. Certain facts are magnified, others diminished. And some things strike you as unaccountably risible . . . Mr de Lisle's corpse being one such.'

Rosy was taken aback. 'I am not clear. What are you getting at?'

'Mr Dovedale and Mr de Lisle were not the best of friends – a mutual antagonism stemming from some schoolboy rift that had never healed . . . You may find this an unsuitable analogy, but there are certain dogs like that – they just don't fancy the shape of each other's snouts: what you might call an antipathy bred in the bone. Anyway, when he saw Mr de Lisle lying there like that he took it into his head to place him astride the cannon, apparently his words being, "With a blithering little tache like that you'll look a real hussar!" He told me he had said other things too, but I wouldn't care to repeat them, madam.'

Rosy was horrified. 'You mean to say that Mr Dovedale actually hauled the man off the ground and draped him over that gun? He must have been mad! And where on earth did he get the strength from? It must have been an awful struggle!'

'Not mad, just drunk. And, not that madam would know this, but when you are as tight as a tick it's amazing where the strength comes from.'

'If you say so,' she remarked dryly.

'And then you see, what with all that malarking about it is little wonder that he really did prang the drive wall when he arrived home; as I believe you learnt when you observed him under the weather the next day. So that particular crash was *not* my invention. Very little damage fortunately but it made the pugs bark.'

'I did hear something,' Rosy murmured.

She regarded her informant closely. With hands primly folded in his lap, he was gazing up into the sky seemingly engrossed in the progress of a flight of birds . . . either that or praying for heavenly guidance for his next fabrication.

'You are sure of this, Mr Hawkins?' she asked carefully. 'I mean you may have misheard what Mr Dovedale said or possibly he was pulling your leg.'

Hawkins looked affronted. 'I may be blind in one eye,' he replied frostily, 'but my hearing is impeccable – as is my judgement of Master Hugh. I have known him since he was a boy and have no difficulty in sifting his facts from his fictions. I can assure you this tale was the former.' It was his turn to scrutinise Rosy: 'I trust, madam, that none of this will go any further; it would be highly inconvenient,' he declared firmly.

She was startled. 'Well yes, doubtless it would be – but surely the police must be informed. I mean this is vital evidence!'

Hawkins shrugged. 'Not really. It is hardly germane to the actual killing. I gather from the press that the police have already established the approximate time of death and that the state of the wound suggests the bullet was from a Webley revolver – one of those left over from the war I shouldn't wonder. They also know that the deed occurred behind the Casino. The fact that Master Hugh chose subsequently to play silly beggars with the body is neither here nor there. From what I can see it has small bearing on the case. As one of the more enlightened of Laurel Lodge's guests you will I am sure appreciate that.'

He stood up, bowed his head briefly and added, 'I am

also sure that upon reflection you will agree that silence is by far the best policy. Meanwhile perhaps you would care for a tray of Darjeeling in the drawing room. We have some cream buns too,' he added gravely.

Somewhat dazed Rosy watched the dignified back as it slowly retreated to the house. The prospect of a cream bun was not uncongenial.

That evening there was a phone call for Rosy from Iris. She sounded flustered. 'Oh I'm so sorry to ask you this,' she said apologetically, 'but I wonder if I could possibly beg a favour of you – it's rather a big one, I'm afraid, and I will *fully* understand if you turn us down.'

'Er, who is "us"?' Rosy asked warily.

'The Blythburgh Friends. We are a sort of local charity that puts on talks and events, and the maddening thing is that our next scheduled speaker has fallen ill and there's no one to breach the gap. Unfortunately the hall is already booked. I don't suppose you would consider stepping in and saving us from humiliation and pecuniary embarrassment?' She gave a plaintive laugh. 'There are quite a lot coming and they will *all* demand their money back if we don't deliver the goods!'

'But what on earth would I talk about?' Rosy asked.

'Angela has told me that you were sterling at Dover in the war and operated all those searchlights and prepared the anti-aircraft guns and other frightfully vital things. That would be an ideal topic.'

After further compliments and cajoling Rosy found herself nervously agreeing.

'Oh what a brick! You've really saved our bacon. It will mean you having to prolong your stay, but I know Hugh won't mind a bit. He's more accommodating than you might think!'

With a relieved laugh she rang off.

Rosy gave a rueful sigh. 'Blundered into that one all right!'

CHAPTER EIGHTEEN

Still dazed by Hawkins' revelations of Hugh's bizarre behaviour and mindful of his earnest warnings to be discreet, Rosy said nothing to Lady Fawcett of her encounter by the bonfire. She knew, however, that the latter would still be eager to hold the 'consultative meeting' with Cedric and Felix, and rather reluctantly offered to telephone them.

'How thoughtful, dear Rosy! No, as a matter of fact, I have already done that. We are to rendezvous with them tomorrow morning at their hotel for coffee followed by lunch. If the weather is good a little stroll along the front in the afternoon might be nice – though naturally not too far. Exercise can be awfully overrated I always think.'

So can playing detective, Rosy thought gloomily. However, the prospect had reminded her of the folder at the bottom of the wardrobe drawer and her earlier intention of showing it to Angela. What with the business of Delia's funeral and now the extraordinary matter of the publisher's murder the thing had rather slipped her mind. However, with Angela determined to explore the mystery of her school friend's fate this might be the time to draw her attention to it. If nothing else she might be able to confirm whether it was the woman's handwriting: the two had corresponded when arranging the visit.

'How peculiar,' Lady Fawcett exclaimed, 'you would have expected it to be found in her desk. Still it's amazing how forgetful one can become. I remember once leaving my handbag in the potting shed – we didn't find it for days. I had gone there to pay the gardener and must have put it down by the lawnmower while he was explaining the complexities of the compost heap, his usual topic. Oh yes do bring it and we'll show it to Cedric and Felix. How intriguing if it does turn out to be a story she was writing!'

The next day they set off to Aldeburgh and Rosy handed her companion the pages. Lady Fawcett donned her glasses and proceeded to read. It had been a good move for it meant Rosy could drive undistracted by the usual running commentary. However, she assumed the silence would not last and was a little surprised when it did.

When they arrived at the hotel car park her companion returned the folder with the comment, 'Yes, very nice.' It wasn't exactly the response Rosy would have expected, but she was too busy easing the car into a narrow space to pay much attention.

In the reception area they were greeted by Cedric who

conducted them into the spacious lounge and to a corner commandeered by Felix.

'Did you attend my lecture?' were the latter's first words to Rosy.

Lying like a trooper she told him that, alas, she had been struck down by a migraine and had had to forgo the pleasure.

'Missed a treat,' he informed her, 'the audience loved it. I think I may revamp it for the *Tatler* – once we get back to London and away from this awful business.' He lowered his voice to a sepulchral whisper: 'Has Cedric told you that they actually suspect me of being involved in the Dovedale demise?'

Rosy giggled. 'Oh come off it Felix, nobody could suspect you of anything except gross exaggeration.'

He pouted. 'That was most uncalled for! I can assure you that the inspector person has been most officious in his enquiries and has been making all manner of innuendos. One hasn't had a moment's peace!'

Cedric smiled, amused that Felix, initially so fearful of being implicated, was now rather relishing the fantasy of being marked as 'Number One Suspect'. However, he doubted if his friend would be quite so ready to reveal his presence on Gun Hill during that fateful night . . .

They ordered coffee. And Rosy suddenly realised that Lady Fawcett had been unusually quiet; indeed not only quiet but abstracted. She was gazing out of the window oblivious both of Felix's chatter and of The Sandworth cat – which with a probing claw was busily plucking the strap of her handbag.

Rosy shooed it off and said brightly, 'You seem far away, Angela. Where are you – with Amy in the French campsite?'

She blinked. 'What . . .? Oh I am sorry, how rude of me! No, it was not the campsite fortunately, but I *was* in Paris. You see, those scribbles which you think may have been Delia's, they've rung a bell – quite a loud one in fact. It's strange really – though of course one *can* read too much into things. Amy does it all the time . . . Did I mention her latest postcard?'

'Yes,' Rosy said, 'you did.' (She had not.) 'But what about Delia? Why on earth should those rather lurid passages ring a bell?'

'Well it may sound ridiculous but they remind me of the intriguing scandal that was rocking the Paris salons in 1947 – not that there were many of those by that time; the war had seen to that.' She turned to Cedric. 'I expect you remember don't you? The French press couldn't get enough of it. And it certainly brightened up the table talk – one had become so bored with that dreary Vincent Auriol's election and his questionable plans for the economy. The men would so go *on* about it. So I have to admit that the sex and espionage business was rather refreshing – or as the French might say, *bien amusant!*' She beamed at Cedric clearly expecting him to share the memory.

'I have no idea what you are talking about,' he said. 'Unlike you and the Dovedales I was never in Paris after the war and I certainly don't recall the British newspapers featuring it – we had enough scandals of our own at that time, what with all the racketeers and Nazi sympathisers crawling out of the woodwork.'

'In any case you and Rosy have the advantage of us,' Felix added, 'you have read this Delia narrative – assuming it is hers; we haven't. It would be useful if one could see the thing – unless there are reams of it. In which case a study of the menu might be preferable, the lunch here isn't at all bad.'

'It won't take long,' Rosy reassured him, 'and while you are doing that we'll go and find the ladies.'

Thus leaving the men bent over the two extracts they went off in search of menus and to powder their noses.

'Does that thing really tie up with the scandal you were talking about?' Rosy asked as she applied her lipstick in the ladies. 'What a curious coincidence. What were the details?'

'That's what I am trying to remember. It all seems rather distant now, and of course with dear Gregory dead there is no one to jog my memory.' For a moment Lady Fawcett looked wistful, but then with a light chuckle she said, 'though I do recall it improved one's French considerably . . . I even started to read *France Soir*!'

They rejoined the others. Cedric was smiling. 'Quite amusing really, it would be interesting to read the rest wherever it is. Do you really think your friend wrote it?'

'It seems unlikely, I agree, but the handwriting is definitely hers.'

'Well if it is based on fact I wish I had spent more time with Delia,' Felix remarked. 'She obviously had sharper perceptions than one gave her credit for – could have been rather jolly on further acquaintance.' He turned to Lady Fawcett. 'Are you sure you can't get that chiming bell to strike louder?'

'Hmm, yes, it's coming back to me. There had been some girl accused of passing secrets to the Soviets – a purely commercial transaction I believe and unlike Mr George Blake et al little to do with ideology. Anyway the case collapsed for lack of evidence and she got off. I distinctly recall the expression of smug triumph on the face of the Russian ambassador; it stayed with him for days! But during the course of the trial it emerged that she was heavily involved in an exclusive vice ring catering for mixed genders and all tastes, with an eminent clientele and said to be operated by an Englishman – an idea naturally much favoured by the French.

'As you can imagine there was plenty of imaginative speculation, but no one was actually identified. I think some of the lesser operatives were arrested and sent down for a brief time, but the big noise remained obscure. It was rumoured that he had a white poodle, though where that tale came from I've no idea – probably the English trying to get back at the French.' She smiled. 'Actually it became rather a party game – trying to pin the donkey's tail on someone. Gregory was absurdly inventive and swore blind that it was Percy Flynn the embassy dogsbody, his argument being that one so monumentally dull was bound to have a sideline.'

For a moment Lady Fawcett's eyes clouded over and she sighed. 'Poor Percy – as a matter of fact he did have a sideline: he kept a beehive on his apartment balcony and died from a sting. One can't help thinking that if only he had cultivated prostitutes rather than bees his span might have been longer.'

'One of life's little ironies,' observed Cedric. 'So I take it this chap was never exposed and things continued merrily?'

'Yes, as far as one knew. The initial interest died down of course, but it would revive periodically whenever the press was at a loose end. Actually there was one rather nasty incident which set tongues wagging again. A young man was found floating in a tributary of the Seine. There had been a torrential storm and the river had burst its banks. The flood waters were really turbulent and it looked as if he may have fallen from a nearby bridge and swept downstream. However, as he was fairly notorious for being what I believe is termed a "rent boy", it was also surmised that he may have committed suicide or even been pushed by a client. One understands that some can be hideously vicious! From what I recall the police didn't do anything much and the whole thing rather blew over – or was covered up.'

She broke off and studied the remains of the coffee. 'I say I don't think I liked that terribly. Do you think we could replace it with a little champagne? I am feeling a trifle thirsty, and it *is* nearly lunchtime.' She looked around hopefully.

Her companions nodded vigorously and Felix jumped up to find a waiter.

In possession of the required glass, Lady Fawcett twiddled its stem and cast an appreciative eye on the bubbles. 'So refreshing at this time of day,' she murmured. 'I feel quite invigorated.'

'Good,' Cedric said, 'so now you can complete the tale

181

and tell us whether you think it accords with what is written here.' He tapped the folder.

Lady Fawcett took another sip from her glass, hesitated and then said, 'Well that's all there is really, except I seem to recall that the young man's name was Randolph – though whether he was English or foreign I have no idea. Very few details ever emerged, or at least not while Gregory and I were there. We returned to England shortly afterwards. As to whether it fits with Delia's story, it is difficult to say. But there do seem to be broad similarities, wouldn't you think?'

'One of them being that if one deletes the three middle letters of the name "Randolph" it becomes "Ralph" like the one in her story,' Cedric remarked. 'Coincidence?'

'Bound to be,' said Felix dismissively. 'Now do let's go and eat, I'm starving.'

In the dining room the speculation shifted from Paris to Southwold.

'But it is so dreadful about that poor publisher,' lamented Lady Fawcett, 'and what he was doing sitting upright on that gun one cannot imagine!'

'Oh he wasn't upright,' Felix said, 'sort of bent over like a jockey.'

'Really? How do you know that?' Rosy asked. 'That was how they described it on the wireless and in the local paper. Have you some inside knowledge?' she laughed.

Felix scowled. 'Intelligent supposition,' he said hastily. 'I mean if one were shot while reposing on a cannon I daresay one would slump somewhat.' He returned to his fish, filleting it with studied concentration.

'Perhaps our friend was there,' murmured Cedric slyly.

Felix looked up. 'Of course I wasn't,' he began angrily, and then stopped. 'Oh all right, all right – but I think that's most thoughtless of you, Cedric. You know perfectly well that I didn't want anything said!'

'Don't worry, dear boy – you're among friends here,' Cedric assured him. 'You know Angela and Rosy won't breathe a word.'

'*Do* I?' retorted Felix sullenly.

'Oh you can rely on us,' cried Lady Fawcett, 'one is the soul of discretion.' She craned forward eagerly: 'You weren't really there, were you?'

Felix gave a resigned shrug. 'Well as a matter of fact I did happen to be passing. I—'

'*Happened to be passing!*' Rosy exclaimed. 'Whatever do you mean? It was virtually the middle of the night – what were you doing sauntering about on the Southwold cliff in that fog! Searching for glow worms?'

'No, Miss Gilchrist, I was not searching for glow worms. I was endeavouring to get back to Aldeburgh having spent a most taxing time on the Walberswick marshes. Encountering that body was the last straw. Now if you don't mind I should like to continue my luncheon.'

'I think you had better tell them the whole story,' said Cedric gently, 'otherwise they may not do justice to the dessert.'

In the car returning to Southwold Rosy again noticed that her companion was unusually silent. Perhaps it was the champagne and the effects of the rather fulsome baked

Alaska. Angela had clearly been well disposed to both.

'That was rather startling, wasn't it,' she said, 'about Felix and his awful escapade – must have been terrifying suddenly coming across the poor man like that. Do you think he might have a sudden rush of blood to the head and decide to report it after all? One never knows with Felix: now that he has the Royal warrant over his shop door he might just elect to play the sober citizen!' she glanced at Lady Fawcett: 'What do you think?'

'What . . . Oh, report it? You mean to the police? I should think that's highly unlikely. His nerves aren't up to it. He already has this absurd *idée fixe* that the police suspect him of Delia's murder. The last thing he wants is to be associated with this latest drama . . . And besides, as Cedric said, such information wouldn't really add anything to the enquiry. One gathers the police already know the technical facts and I suspect that Felix's contribution might be – uhm – *gratuitous*. I think that's the term, isn't it? It is certainly what dear Gregory so often said about Amy's contributions . . .' She lapsed into silence again, gazing out of the window.

Rosy swerved slightly to avoid a pheasant. 'Idiot thing,' she muttered.

The action seemed to stir her companion, as turning from the window she said thoughtfully, 'It's very odd about that young man, he—'

'Very odd,' Rosy agreed, 'to be found in that situation!'

'It wasn't his situation I was thinking of, but what he was telling me at the funeral . . . I have to say it does rather confirm that the composition did indeed belong to Delia and that she had been in earnest about it.'

'What do you mean, what was he saying?'

Lady Fawcett proceeded to tell Rosy about her conversation with Floyd and his hopes for the Delia manuscript. 'He seemed to think it might make his fortune and was "literary dynamite" . . . One certainly recalls Delia *sounding* like dynamite, but one never expected her to write it!' She chuckled.

Rosy did not. Instead she stopped the car and gazed at Lady Fawcett. 'Are you saying that Floyd de Lisle knew about this stuff Delia was writing and that she was one of his clients? Why ever didn't you say so at lunch?'

'Well I've really only thought of it just now. He was very charming, but frankly I wasn't taking his words too seriously – you know how people exaggerate. Besides, I was trying to work out how to avoid being waylaid by Claude Huggins: he was hovering quite close and kept looking in my direction. It was most uncomfortable. Needless to say, he got me in the end because when Floyd had gone off he immediately zoomed in and started to make effusive comments about Delia. Rather tiresome really – one had already heard an excellent encomium from Lucas Brightwell, and any more, especially from Claude Huggins, was rather gilding the lily!'

'Still, I am surprised you didn't mention it when we got back.'

'Well frankly, my dear, I was rather tired and also had the vexing task of replying to Amy's latest postcard. When faced with that other things do tend to fade . . .' she gave a rueful sigh.

'Why was it vexing?'

'But I showed it to you.'

'Er, oh yes of course you did . . . But remind me.'

'It was perfectly all right until she reached the end where she wrote that "the French *jeunes hommes* think I am JOLLY GOOD! Isn't that nice?" Well naturally I spent the whole evening composing my reply, indicating that I did not consider Gallic applause was especially nice and asking if there weren't some decent English types on the campsite . . . Do you think it a good idea if I try to persuade her cousin Edward to go over there as a sort of chaperone?'

Rosy advised against it. 'It could be disastrous,' she opined.

'Hmm. I fear you are right. Dear Edward, he always means well . . .'

Rosy let in the clutch and moved off. Interesting though the dynamics of the Fawcett family were, at this particular moment it was the killings of Delia and Floyd that really intrigued her. Could Delia Dovedale's 'sensational' jottings really have a bearing on his death? How odd.

Rosy had been more than startled by Felix's revelation. But her surprise was less to do with his presence per se than the fact that he was the second witness to the event, or rather its immediate aftermath. How strange to think that both Hugh and Felix had been wandering in the vicinity at roughly the same time. Clearly, from Hawkins' account, Hugh had been the one closest to the murder itself (according to the press report the man had died somewhere between eleven and midnight). And presumably it could only have been shortly after the latter's shifting of the body to the gun that Felix had turned up – and had the living daylights scared out of him!

But then of course, *assuming* Hawkins' version was true and that Hugh had not done the deed, there must also have been a third party roaming around too: the killer . . . And then naturally a fourth man, the victim himself. Quite a little midnight party.

What were the killer and victim doing in that area prior to the attack – strolling arm in arm? She thought not. There could have been an assignation; fog and the lateness of the hour hardly suggested a random encounter in that spot. It was far more likely to have been something prearranged. So what was their business, or its pretext, before the murderer pulled the gun? In the course of their dealings had Floyd de Lisle said or threatened something to prompt the attack? Perhaps. But even if that were the case the other must have come prepared: not only did he carry the revolver, but according to the newspapers the thing was fitted with a silencer. Yes, the whole thing had surely been premeditated.

Despite her surprise at Felix's account over lunch, Rosy had kept quiet about what Hawkins had told her. This was something she would need to think about before doing, or saying, anything rash. After all, if Hawkins were correct about Hugh being a fool but no assassin, then telling the police, or anyone else, would seem to be of little benefit – indeed, it would only spread alarm and despondency where none was warranted. As with Felix, the fact that he had been there seemed of little relevance . . . unless of course Hawkins were wrong or lying, and their host the murderer after all. That would certainly put a different complexion on things.

She thought about the police. What purpose would it serve if she were to approach them with her tales? By now they doubtless had their own theories and knew far more about the details than she did. The forensic people must have realised almost from the beginning that the body had been dragged onto the gun after death. To report Felix's brief presence would be absurd, and unkind, and as for Hugh . . . well his having done the dragging might or might not have a bearing: that was his responsibility to admit and for the authorities to work out.

CHAPTER NINETEEN

While Rosy was justifying her non-interference in the matter, the authorities were indeed occupied with working things out.

'Are we to assume, sir,' Jennings said brightly, 'that the two events are linked – that the chap who poisoned Dovedale also did for de Lisle?'

'We assume nothing,' the inspector replied severely, 'you should know that by now.'

'Yes, but on the face of it—'

'I keep telling you, never put your trust in faces: an honest face will as soon as let you down as a villain's . . . However,' he conceded, 'it is a possibility that can't be ruled out. And when little Miss Morgan comes back tomorrow with her list of de Lisle's authors and visitors we may have something to go on. But in the meantime what bugs me is the disparity in the methods of disposal: cyanide and a slickly fired Webley MK V1. There's not a lot of consistency is there?'

'Perhaps the murderer is a medic who keeps a collection of old service revolvers but wanted to ring the changes.'

'Ho, ho. Very funny.'

Jennings looked slightly crestfallen. 'Actually, sir, it wasn't really a joke. I mean if he's a nutcase like we thought, he may have a whole arsenal of assorted means!'

'Perhaps. But where in particular would he get the cyanide? I doubt if your ordinary GP would have access – not as a general rule. You would need to be pretty high up the medical scale to get your hands on that I imagine. Of course some of these chemical boffins in laboratories could obtain the stuff – do you know anyone like that?'

'Not offhand, sir.'

'Thought not.' A sly grin came over the inspector's face: 'Tell you what – you could check out all the toxicology departments between Hull and Ipswich and examine their records for the past year. If there's any missing cyanide unaccounted for keep a note and then round up all Webley pistol owners. If one of them happens to keeps a store of the stuff in their gun cupboard then Bob's your uncle: we've got our man!'

There was a long silence while Jennings considered this instruction. 'Can I get you a cup of coffee, sir?' he asked.

As arranged Betty Morgan returned the next day with her list. She was relieved that the inspector wasn't there. She hadn't disliked him exactly but he had been a bit of a tartar and no mistake. It had taken her a long time to compile that list and the last thing she wanted was him picking holes. It was a generation thing – they were always so stern! Except for that Mr Brightwell, of course, he was a real gentleman. Really nice he was . . . very nice now she came to think of it; and he always seemed to listen most attentively to what she said. Which was more than Mr de Lisle used to do. In fact sometimes she thought her boss hadn't been listening at all. Like the time she had been telling him about that episode in *Mrs Dale's Diary* when that nice husband of hers, Jim, had had a heart attack. Mr de Lisle's auntie had had one of those so you would have thought he'd have been interested. Not a bit of it! 'Have you tidied the box files?' was all he had said.

Still, one shouldn't think ill of the dead; and after all he had been nice in parts. A bit like that senior policemen really: fine when it suited him, growly when it didn't.

Well at least DC Jennings wasn't growly – a bit of an old smoothie really, or better still a young smoothie! She had taken a lot of care over that list of the firm's visitors and had typed it out ever so neatly. It might be quite pleasant going through it with DC Jennings – yes very pleasant in fact.

The scent of Bonsoir Paris was not to Jennings' taste: sickly and cloying he considered it, his sister's Tweed being so much fresher. Still, on the whole at least it smelt better than the inspector's acrid pipe; and also on the whole the girl was prettier than the inspector.

They had been closeted for an hour in the back office and were making a rough kind of progress. That is to say a large number of names on her list had been eliminated being people known to him locally and whose literary submissions were present and correct. There had been a number of *nom de plumes* which had been puzzling such as Bagshaw Billinger and Clarice del Rio, but Betty had said she knew the authors well and that yes, their stuff too was intact. These and other names were regular visitors to the office, as were two of the mistresses from the nearby Saint Felix school. ('They write very nice stories about zombies and cut-throat wizards,' Betty had assured him.)

So where does that leave us? He had asked. Who else among her employer's recent visitors might have used the Merrivale pseudonym and been too shy to admit to it?

Betty had narrowed it down to a few possibles: 'Miss Martin from Reydon visited two or three times. She showed him her whole novel, but it wasn't to Mr de Lisle's taste (one of the God Awful ones) and I think she took it away in a huff, so it's not likely to have been her. Mr Champ comes in quite regularly but as far as I know it's only to have a chat and to moan about the government, I don't think he has ever written anything. Young Mr Snowdon from the ironmonger's dropped in a fortnight ago, but as his project is on spanners and drywall screws I don't think he would want to call himself Millicent Merrivale would he?

Jennings agreed that it was unlikely. 'What about that Mr Claude Huggins?' he asked. 'They say he's been writing some gardening book for years. Would he have been one of Mr de Lisle's clients?'

'Oh no, he's far too high and mighty for *this* firm. He's going to get a posh London firm to publish him, or so he says – and *when* it's finished!' She pulled a face.

'Hmm. Nobody else?'

She mentioned three more visitors' names, one of whom he recognised: the cyanide victim, Mrs Delia Dovedale. 'Oh? So what was she doing?'

'She was ever so cheerful and gave me a box of chocolates. A nice lady. It's awful really – her and now Mr de Lisle. I mean, you don't know what the world's coming to do you?' Betty observed brightly.

'I didn't ask what she was like but what she was *doing* in the office.'

The girl looked vague. 'I didn't notice specially, she always went into Mr de Lisle's private den. So I don't know whether she had given him a manuscript or anything. Or if she did he never mentioned it to me. After all I can't know everything that goes on in the office – kept too busy with typing and watering the plants! And then of course I have to go to the post twice a day so I'm not always there, am I?'

Like his boss earlier, Jennings detected a slight truculence in her tone but felt too despondent to care. He had envisaged unearthing a perfect and obvious match. None had appeared. The girl had been useful up to a point but only in a negative way, and there was nothing exciting he could show the inspector. He closed his notebook.

'Oh,' Betty said, poised at the door, 'I don't suppose the police station is looking for a new typist, is it?'

Definitely not in the foreseeable future, he had told her.

He sat down and stared at the last three names of random visitors, and then looked again at the *nom de plume* that had been attached to the sleeve of the empty file. Something struck him . . . something so tenuous that he almost dismissed it. But it was worth a try. After all as Agatha Christie so often demonstrated, a flimsy hunch could unravel all manner of things . . .

He reopened his notebook and wrote the three names on a fresh page. Then squaring his shoulders he went to knock on the inspector's door.

Jennings thrust the notebook under his superior's nose and pointed to the names. 'Does anything strike you, sir?'

'Yes, I note that Delia Dovedale is there. Are you suggesting that she might be the one? What about the other two?'

'Well,' Jennings said eagerly, 'Joan Brown and Keith Sims – they don't fit do they?'

'Fit what?'

'The *pseudonym*: Millicent Merrivale!'

The inspector frowned. 'Sorry, I'm not with you.'

'It's a question of rhythm,' he explained, 'that first pair have only two syllables each, whereas Millicent Merrivale has six and Delia Dovedale five. Numerically there is a closer approximation between the pseudonym and the name Delia Dovedale than there is with the other two. You will also note that both names are alliterative – DD and MM. Added to which the last syllable of Dovedale rhymes with the last of Merrivale, not to mention the shared internal echoes of 'v's and 'l's.' He paused; and then as afterthought added, 'And apart from the spondee of Dovedale I would suggest that for both of them the metre is basically dactylic, sir – or possibly anapaestic.'

The inspector regarded him thoughtfully. God it was

like being back in the classroom! 'Tell me, Jennings,' he said, 'where did you come in woodwork at school?'

'Er . . . bottom.'

The other nodded. 'I thought you might have.'

There was a silence while Jennings contemplated his boots and the inspector the light fixtures on the ceiling. Eventually he said, 'So what you are telling me is that because Delia Dovedale's name sounds a bit like Millicent Merrivale it is likely that the lady had devised that as her literary alias, and so it was her file that the intruder was after and took.'

Jennings looked up from his boots and beamed. 'That's about the measure of it, sir: it's the aural connection. I reckon it was either a deliberate choice – a sort of feeble pun you might say – or subconscious, i.e. a way of unwittingly retaining her identity while concealing it at the same time. In fact you could say that—'

The other cut him short. 'No, I wouldn't say; you've made the point. Remind me, what was that course you went on a month ago?'

'"Thought Processes and Patterns of Psychology: A Policeman's Guide".'

'Hmm, I remember. Well I am glad to see the public purse isn't being totally squandered: you may just have learnt something there,' he muttered grudgingly. 'There's an outside chance of a correlation . . . So what's next, Smarty-pants?'

'Search me, sir,' replied Jennings happily.

CHAPTER TWENTY

It was Friday and Rosy had gone into Southwold to meet Lucas Brightwell as arranged. As she approached The Crown she saw him coming towards her. He raised his hat and said, 'How good of you to come, and with the wretched case!' He took it from her smartly. 'So sorry for the inconvenience – the least I can do is to buy you a drink. What I suggest is that we go to the back bar, it's less noisy than the main one. At this time of day people suddenly have the urge to rest their weary limbs and have a little pick-me-up before lunch.'

He steered her towards the nether regions and into a small room which she assumed to be the 'Snug'. Given the choice she would have preferred the main bar . . . Did she want to be so closely closeted with Brightwell? The only other people there were two old ladies ensconced in a corner enjoying a tipple and a gossip – or at least, judging from the whispers and knowing facial expressions she assumed the latter was the case.

Still clasping the briefcase Brightwell went to the bar and ordered Rosy's requested dry sherry and a gin and tonic for himself.

He offered her a cigarette but seeing the Egyptian label she declined: 'I'm afraid I'm a plain Players girl,' she laughed. They exchanged pleasantries about the weather, highlights of the flower festival (though not its drama of Delia's death), and touched on the recent horror involving Floyd de Lisle, but with mutual tact did not pursue it. Brightwell mentioned a concert he and Freda were planning to attend in Aldeburgh. And Rosy was about to ask if he had any preferences regarding Britten's operas but before she could get further he had interrupted, exclaiming, 'If you don't mind I must just check that the Royal Garden Party invitation is safe, can't remember if I left it in this or on my desk. If that's lost my wife will never forgive me!'

She was on the verge of saying that it was there all right, but he had already opened the case and started to check the contents. 'Seems all in order,' he murmured.

Rosy felt slightly affronted. Did he imagine she had pillaged the thing? But then she felt a twinge of guilt, recalling her examination of the notepad and discovery of the photograph. Still, it wasn't as if anything had actually been removed.

Brightwell took out the cheques and slipped them into his wallet. 'Invitation safe and sound,' he announced, 'I have a reprieve! But I had better deliver these cheques pronto otherwise I shall be blackballed by all the firms in Southwold.' He laughed and rose to fetch more drinks.

Rosy would have been quite content with her single sherry but to be polite settled for an orange juice. She looked over at the two old ladies still heavily engrossed in their gossip. They were sitting by a mirror, and her glance caught Brightwell's reflection as he stood at the bar. He was half swivelled round, frowning and regarding her intently – or that was certainly her impression. Embarrassed, she quickly shifted her gaze.

When he returned he asked how she had enjoyed the Sailors' Reading Room. 'Such a fascinating place,' he enthused, 'Freda and I go there quite often when we are in the town: I like the pictures and she likes the quiet – it's what you might call a little oasis amid the hurly-burly of Southwold's Kasbah!'

Rosy smiled, while at the same time recalling Freda's surprise at the location of the lost case and her saying that she and Lucas hadn't visited the room for five years.

'Indeed as you know,' he continued, 'I introduced Miss Morgan there. Rather to my surprise she hadn't even heard of it, and since she was supposed to be handling a local history pamphlet that poor de Lisle was publishing it seemed a good idea to show her around.' He lowered his voice and in a confiding tone said, 'Actually my dear, it might be sensible not to mention this to Freda. She's going through rather a difficult time – I am sure you know what I mean – and is a touch sensitive these days. One has to tread a little carefully.'

Rosy took this as her cue for female sympathy and gave

an understanding nod. But she was peeved to think she was being made complicit in his wife's menopausal problems – if indeed that was what they were.

Feeling slightly uncomfortable she thought it time to make her excuses and leave. But at that moment a tall dishevelled figure appeared in the doorway and made for one of the bar stools. Rosy was rather startled, for the man was distinctly unkempt with long hair, straggling beard and frayed baggy trousers. Above these, somewhat incongruously, he wore a battered RAF flying jacket.

'Morning, Fab!' cried one of the corner ladies, 'how's tricks? We ain't seen you for a while.'

The man gave a slow smile: 'Well you've seen me now. Must be your lucky day.' He was about to turn back to the counter, but seeing Lucas and Rosy stopped.

To the latter's surprise he advanced towards her with proffered hand. 'I am the brother,' he announced.

'Oh . . . uhm, really? Er, whose brother?' Clearly a case of mistaken identity!

'Claude Huggins'. Your friend dined with us the other night. A nice little chap – Felix he was called. I showed him my collection of Suffolk Punch photographs. He was most appreciative.'

It was curious enough to think of the fastidious Felix hobnobbing with this rather ragged character, but Rosy had even greater difficulty in imagining him poring over pictures of galumphing shire horses. As far as she knew he had an aversion to any animal larger than a rabbit. Just went to show, everyone had their private passions!

Lucas cleared his throat: 'Yes, this is Fabius Huggins,

Claude's younger brother. He lives in Walberswick, though Southwold has the pleasure of his company from time to time. Always a gratifying experience,' he added dryly.

Fabius turned to Lucas. 'I hear you gave her a good send-off at the funeral, a neat little eulogy so they tell me. Very deft by all accounts.'

'I tried to do my best,' replied Brightwell a trifle stiffly. 'In the circumstances it was extremely painful.'

'Oh I agree, very painful. But I suppose you'll be gearing up for the next one now, will you?'

'What?'

'That Floyd de Lisle – assuming he has a funeral. He told me once that when he snuffed it he just wanted to be tossed into the sea with a bottle of gin. I told him I'd toss him into the sea all right but drink the gin myself. Poor bastard, I don't supposed he thought it would be so soon!' He looked at Rosy and apologised for his language: 'You must excuse me: I don't meet many nice young women these days.'

'Coo, he's got a cheek!' cried one of the corner ladies. 'Don't mind us!'

Ignoring the interruption Lucas replied, 'I very much doubt if I shall be called upon for that sad task again. I really only knew him by sight whereas the Dovedales and I go back some time . . . Now, we must be off,' he announced, 'things to do, people to see. You know how it is, Fabius, the giddy round!'

'Hmm,' the other grunted, 'but clearly that doesn't involve a round of drinks to include me. You owe me one from five years back.'

'What excellent memories you brothers have,' the other retorted lightly, and picking up his hat and briefcase guided Rosy out into the passage.

Once out of earshot, he murmured to her, 'I am sorry about that. Fabius can be tiresome, but he is relatively harmless; and you might not think it, but rather tough as well: he flew Spitfires in the war and was highly regarded. God knows what has happened since, some sort of breakdown I suspect. A peculiar cove.'

'Oh I quite liked him. But I wonder how he knew who I was?'

'Fabius gets to know most things . . . Contrary to appearances he is considerably brighter than his brother.' This was said with a touch of asperity. But recalling Hugh's and Mark's disparagement of Claude she was not especially surprised. Evidently Fabius was the local eccentric; Claude the local bore.

It was rather a pleasant day, the sun bright and for once little or no wind. Thus free of Brightwell's company Rosy decided to skip lunch and instead buy a couple of sausage rolls and in time-honoured tradition sit on the front, read the newspaper and admire the view. She chose a spot above the beach huts, and taking one of the deck chairs settled down to enjoy the sun.

Immersed in her newspaper and 'picnic' she was only vaguely aware of someone else having taken a chair next to hers. She had just turned to the crossword when a voice said politely, 'Ah, I trust you are enjoying our Southwold air. It must make quite a change from the London smog.'

Rosy was about to reply that actually the London smog was greatly exaggerated, when to her surprise she saw that her neighbour was Hawkins. Divested of his usual sombre suit he wore instead a pair of white flannel trousers, smart navy blazer and a rather raffish neck scarf. Was this his off-duty kit? If so for an old boy of near eighty he didn't look bad!

On his knees rested a small lunchbox, presumably of his own composing, and a book. She asked him what it was.

'It's a manual,' he replied, '*The Finer Points of Portraiture*. It's a little hobby of mine. I like to dabble occasionally.'

'What, you mean you paint?' she asked, a little surprised.

He nodded. 'But only in a small way, and only people. I used to do more before the eye problem but even so it is not impossible, just slower.'

'But do you always stick to portraits? Never landscapes or a seascape like this for instance?' she gestured at the sparkling waves and cavorting bathers.

He smiled. 'You mean like those clever French impressionists with their cliffs at Cannes or Trouville? No, my talents – such as they are – are confined to the contours of the human face; they represent much that intrigues. Seascapes aren't intriguing, just moving and beautiful.'

But what about a studio, she had asked. Didn't he need one of those?

Hawkins shrugged. 'An easel and a good window is enough. In Paris when I was there briefly with the Dovedales I had more sitters and was able to rent a small atelier, but now I work mainly from photographs. In fact the last time

I used a live sitter it was Mrs Dovedale herself. That was ten years ago when Mr Dovedale was still alive. He became very fond of that picture.' Hawkins gave a pensive smile.

'Oh! You don't mean that one hanging above the staircase do you? The one where she has the little dog on her lap?'

'Yes,' he replied simply.

'But it is splendid . . . I mean, naturally I never knew her, but there is a real person there! And someone rather nice,' she added.

The old man modestly acknowledged the compliment, and murmured, 'Madam was a very kind lady. People did not always realise that.'

Rosy felt awkward: her questions had unwittingly led to Delia – and inevitably to thoughts of the sitter's fate. However, in view of his last observation it would be unnatural not to express some sympathy. 'You must miss her,' she said gently.

'One does,' was the quiet reply. 'And Mr Dovedale too, a most enlivening gentleman – although one has to say his trumpet playing was not of the best but it was certainly *vigorous*.' He gave a rueful smile.

'So you enjoyed those long years with them.'

'It was a highly gratifying arrangement. Alas, not all employers are so agreeable.'

There was a silence as he nibbled a sandwich and contemplated the sea. Rosy's glance fell on the first clue of the crossword. *As the poet suggests, what those serving also might do. (4-5-3-4).* Only stand and wait, she surmised. Rosy waited.

Hawkins brushed the sandwich crumbs from the pristine trousers, cleared his throat and added: '*As*, I must say, is Master Hugh – agreeable. He has his little ways of course – always did have, even as a boy. What you might call a law unto himself – though his father used another term. But as I observed to you the other day, fundamentally he is sound. It would be a great shame, Miss Gilchrist, were it ever thought otherwise: a wrong and mischievous indictment and one liable to create a false scent. There are other trails.' Hawkins made a slight adjustment to his black patch, while the good eye regarded her unswervingly.

'Yes,' she agreed meekly.

He snapped shut the lunch box and stood up about to take his leave.

'But Mr Hawkins,' Rosy said boldly, 'quite apart from the case of poor Mr de Lisle, why on earth should your employer have been killed?'

There was a long pause while he seemed to reflect. And then he said sombrely: 'As they say in the films, because she knew too much . . . Now if you would excuse me I have some fresh brushes to collect. I am engaged on a new study.'

'From a photograph?'

'Yes, but I think I am catching the essence all right. Besides it is based on a memory.'

When he had gone Rosy lit a cigarette and brooded.

Clearly he was determined to defend his current employer from any whiff of blame regarding the publisher's death. Both in their conversation by the bonfire and even more explicitly now, he had virtually directed her to keep her mouth shut about the bloodied raincoat. In fact she rather suspected that he may have sat down beside her precisely to ram home that point. And as before, she wondered if such defence was prompted by misplaced loyalty or whether it was a sincerely held belief that Hugh was innocent. If the latter he could of course be deluded; but the more she thought about his manner and words the more she felt that he knew something which implied an alternative culprit.

Ironic, Rosy thought. She had selected this spot to bask languidly in the sun, toy with the crossword and indulge her taste for sausage rolls, but instead of such ease her mind had been put in a state of fretful activity. She would have done better to return to Laurel Lodge and have an afternoon nap like Angela!

As she wandered back down the High Street to where she had left the car she was taunted by Hawkins' cryptic reply to her question about Delia: *because she knew too much*.

What was it Delia had known and how had that knowledge been betrayed to whoever had administered the cyanide? She passed a bookshop and casually glanced at some of the titles displayed in the window: *Memoirs of a Spy, Dark Exposure, Gossip from the White House, The Fatal Fiction* . . . She recalled Angela's casual revelation that de Lisle had gloated about his good luck in having chapters from Delia's book.

Hell it was obvious surely! The knowledge for which Delia had been killed was without doubt portrayed in that novel she was writing. The extracts discussed at The Sandworth, while in themselves only mildly risqué, as part of a larger context and one factually based, could if published be sensational. What was it Floyd was supposed to have said? 'Literary dynamite' or some such. The titles in the window bellowed at Rosy, and suddenly what had been a mere hazy notion became a dazzling conviction. Had the narrative been explosive enough to require the death of its author *and* its intending publisher? It could just be. Motive enough, but as to the murderer's identity that was anyone's guess. Perhaps the police knew, she reflected doubtfully . . . Or Hawkins?

She opened the car door wondering what she should do. Absolutely nothing seemed the immediate course, except drive back to Laurel Lodge, put her feet up and have a long meditative bath before supper. She pushed the starter and eased the car into the road.

CHAPTER TWENTY-ONE

Felix had been invited to a wine and cheese function held by the festival organisers. He had been slightly reluctant to go as he had been rather relishing the prospect of parading his smart smoking jacket at the hotel that night. After all so far he had only worn it once: definitely time for another airing. However, it might have looked churlish to refuse . . . and besides he rather suspected the press might be there.

'You *will* come, won't you?' he had asked Cedric.

The other had replied that in view of Felix's misadventures when last driving alone at night it might indeed be wise. 'We can drop in at Laurel Lodge on the way back. Angela has a book of mine and I want to ensure I get it back, you know how vague she is.'

* * *

Thus as planned, they stopped off to collect the book and were inveigled into the drawing room for some coffee. Hugh Dovedale wasn't at home being apparently in London. In some ways Cedric was slightly relieved as he had found the young man's blend of charm and wayward gaucheness rather unsettling. Angela dutifully returned Cedric's book, but her comments were interrupted by Hawkins announcing that she was wanted on the telephone.

'Oh dear,' she murmured, 'I hope that's not Amy pestering me to increase her allowance. That girl will squander money anywhere, even on a campsite!' Looking unusually resolute she left the room.

Inevitably the conversation turned to matters sinister.

'Angela was right you know,' said Cedric thoughtfully, 'there are indeed broad similarities between her recollections of the Paris scene and how it is portrayed in Delia's account. In fact I am increasingly convinced that Delia deliberately intended to evoke Paris at the time she and her husband were there, basing her tale not only on the events, proven or otherwise, but also on people she had known there, for instance, people who are still around and have reason to fear being featured.'

'You mean people potentially imperilled by the lady's pen,' Felix giggled.

'Well one *could* put it like that, I suppose.'

Rosy was unsure. 'But according to Angela the Dovedales weren't in Paris all that long, a temporary sojourn before returning to London. I doubt if she would have been a close observer of what was going on.'

'She didn't need to be. What she didn't perceive herself

she would have absorbed through general gossip both at the time and later. As Angela indicated, the air was rife with speculation. That spy trial and what it exposed of vice in high circles would have been like a sort of cabaret brightening the grey days of post-war austerity. I'm guessing the identity of the principal *artiste* didn't strike Delia until much later . . . and it was only then, having pieced one or two things together and made certain connections, that she decided to produce this fictionalised version – except that an awful lot of it wasn't fiction but pure fact and not so pure at that.'

'Agreed,' Rosy said, 'but there's nothing in the text, or at least not the bits we've got, to suggest who she thought the anonymous character was. I mean she presents him as being rather suave and ruthless but there is no clue as to who he might have been.'

'Ah, there I think you have made an oversight,' Cedric observed in his best professorial voice, 'I rather think there is.'

'Look,' Felix said a trifle impatiently, 'it was sharp of you to see that she had probably substituted the name Ralph for the wretched Randolph victim in the river, but that doesn't take us very far. The chap is dead, and while he may have meant something at the time he certainly doesn't now, and not to us: a pathetic casualty of a squalid racket and literally sunk without trace one could say. Delia's compression of Randolph into Ralph is hardly a major factor and I cannot see anything else of note.'

'Perhaps you wouldn't dear boy, but *I* can. In fact it is really extremely obvious. Can't think why I didn't spot it when we lunched at The Sandworth. Probably too distracted by that rather good champagne they served.'

'What are you getting at?' Rosy exclaimed.

'I am getting at the name of *Lightspring*,' Cedric replied. He regarded them over the rim of his glasses. 'I take it you do see its meaning?'

'Not really,' Felix said carelessly. 'It's the sort of damn fool name novelists invent for their characters.'

Rosy said nothing at first but stared at Cedric incredulously. 'You don't really think that,' she whispered, 'it's ridiculous!'

Cedric shrugged. 'It strikes me as being a bit of a coincidence – particularly when appended to the forename of Lucian . . . Frankly it's not the most subtle of substitutes, which is why I am annoyed not to have seen it before. However, one—'

'Brightwell!' Felix yelped. 'They mean the same thing! It doesn't refer to the season but to a well of water!'

'Sharp as a whippet, isn't he?' Cedric remarked to Rosy.

Felix was too excited to take umbrage. 'I never liked him,' he muttered, 'one of those stiff-necked types.'

'But you've only seen him once – at Delia's funeral.'

'Quite enough on which to base a judgement,' he replied tartly. 'He asked me what I did in London, so naturally I informed him of Smythe's Bountiful Blooms, and in passing just happened to mention her Majesty's patronage. And do you know what he said? He *said*: "What, you mean the Queen Mother? You do surprise me. How very extraordinary!" I was about to ask him what was so extraordinary about my business having a royal connection but he had walked off. Rude wasn't in it!' Felix scowled at his companions seeking indignant sympathy.

But their minds were elsewhere: Cedric's calculating the odds for a coincidence regarding the names (rather long in his view); and Rosy's recollecting the contents of Brightwell's briefcase – specifically the photograph of the young man. In the light of what Cedric had just pointed out, the letter 'R' on the reverse of the photo now took on a distinctly sinister significance. If Angela had been right in saying that the victim fished from the river had been someone called Randolph, and thus the same as Delia's character Ralph, it was not inconceivable that the initial 'R' stood for the same person: the drowned rent boy. But *only* of course if Lucas Brightwell and Lucian Lightspring were indeed one and the same person. The whole hypothesis hung on that . . . a supposition for which there wasn't a shred of evidence.

She began to tell them about her discovery of the photo and her now tentative suspicions, but hadn't gone very far before being interrupted by Felix. 'I cannot imagine why you are even giving him the benefit of the doubt,' he exclaimed, 'a most unsavoury specimen in my view. You should have seen the disdainful look he gave me. Just because he is tall and thinks there's a gong in the offing I suppose he imagines he can look down on a *mere* florist! And what's more—'

'Felix, dear chap,' Cedric said hastily, foreseeing a rant, 'there is nothing mere about you! What was it Godfrey Winn wrote in his social column recently? Something like "no one but an idiot would dream of—"'

'"None but a philistine would dream of commissioning anyone but Felix Smythe to supervise their nuptial flowers.

213

His floral mastery lends charm and cachet wherever displayed. Undoubtedly London society would lose a little of its elegance without the fragrant presence of Bountiful Blooms and its discerning proprietor."' Felix lowered his eyes modestly.

'How clever of you to remember,' smiled Cedric.

Rosy thought it would be cleverer still if they could ignore Felix's sensitive ego and revert to the Dovedale murder. 'Look,' she said, 'if Brightwell really is the alter ego of Lucian Lightspring and Delia was hoping to capitalise on her character's lurid activities then he might certainly have something to worry about! I mean it's not just the sexual shenanigans that she features or even the hints of treason, but she clearly suggests murder as well . . . or at least judging from the extracts that we have she does. If that book had ever achieved publication and hit the headlines, as doubtless Floyd would have ensured, it would have caused quite a stir. And just possibly Brightwell would have had more than public respect and a knighthood to lose!'

'And serve him right,' Felix declared righteously.

At that moment Lady Fawcett reappeared looking both relieved and bemused. 'Not Amy, but Edward,' she explained. 'He is always so cheerful but I am never entirely sure what he is talking about. But still it was very nice to hear him and learn that all is safe in London – or at least that's what I *think* he said.'

Rosy smiled. Angela's communications with her daughter and nephew were invariably fraught with puzzled confusion. 'Perhaps you could do with some more coffee,' she said, 'I'll get Hawkins to—'

'No, not really – though a light sherry would be nice; I am sure Hugh wouldn't mind if we helped ourselves.' She subsided on to the sofa while Rosy dealt with the request. 'Now what have you all been talking about? This extraordinary business no doubt. Any progress?'

Cedric apprised her of what had been said and their reasons for suspecting Brightwell. 'You will probably think it is total nonsense,' he remarked, and was slightly taken aback when she shook her head firmly.

'Oh no,' she replied darkly, 'I remember thinking in Paris that he never *quite* added up. I don't know why really but one gets a "feel" about certain people and he was one of them.'

'Agreed!' Felix exclaimed, helping himself liberally to his absent host's whisky, 'my sentiments exactly!'

'In fact,' she continued, 'the real surprise is that dear Delia should have fiddled about with those names. I don't recall her showing such inventiveness at school. The benefit of time and age I suppose . . . I wonder what talent Amy might develop.' She gave a wistful sigh.

'What is unclear to me,' said Cedric thoughtfully, 'is that *if* Brightwell is our man how did he discover what Delia was doing? Certainly he could have picked something up from the grapevine to the effect that she was writing her Paris memoirs, but he couldn't have known he was being featured in that way unless he had tangible proof, such as he had read some of it.'

'Perhaps a nod was as good as a wink,' Felix suggested. 'Having learnt what she was up to he decided to nip it in the bud – like a twinging tooth: whip the thing out before it can get worse or cause collateral damage.'

'Rather an extreme reaction surely,' Rosy remarked. 'He was hazarding a hell of a lot for a mere guess . . . No, I agree with Cedric: he must have had access to the thing, but how?'

There was a faint movement from the sofa as its occupant replaced her sherry glass on the stool and cleared her throat. 'It seems to me,' Lady Fawcett said, 'that we are being a little precipitate.' She glanced at Cedric: 'That *is* the word isn't it . . .? You see while our suspicions may be fully justified we don't really *know*, do we? Personally I am not mad about the man and never was, but that would hardly stand up in a court of law. It would be frightful if we were barking up the wrong tree – just think of the waste of time and energy!' She closed her eyes. '"Watch and wait" is what my dear papa used to say. He was in the Intelligence Service during the Great War and caught an awful lot of spies that way by just hanging about propping up lamp posts, and I think that is what we should do now.'

'As it happens,' she continued, 'we shall have an opportunity of doing a little watching tomorrow evening. After I had spoken to Edward just now Freda Brightwell rang to say we should all be welcome to dinner at their house in Blythburgh. I gather she wants to discuss Rosy's forthcoming talk to their Literary Circle . . . or was it the Ramblers' Society? Something like that anyway.'

'The Blythburgh Friends,' said Rosy tersely.

'Oh yes of course, I knew it was something affable . . . So

you see, dining with the Brightwells will give us an excellent chance to look sharp and be on the *qui vive!*' She beamed and glanced vaguely towards the cocktail cabinet.

In the car going back to Aldeburgh Felix turned to Cedric and clearing his throat said, 'Actually if you *don't* mind I think I might give tomorrow evening a miss.'

'Why?'

'Ah . . . well I may have other plans.'

'What plans?'

Felix pursed his lips. 'Well they certainly don't involve being patronised and snubbed by that murderer!'

'But Felix, dear boy, we have no *proof* that he is a murderer! So far it is all supposition, albeit not ill-based. That is the whole point in accepting their invitation – to see if we might establish a *firmer* base. With the four of us there – propping up lamp posts as Angela put it – one of us is bound to notice any verbal slip or careless allusion. And even if we deduce nothing tangible at least we can form a better impression of the man, get his measure as it were. Naturally a closer inspection may yield nothing at all; indeed we may conclude that our target is entirely blameless – a man of utter probity as he purports to be. Thus in either case further acquaintance could be most beneficial.'

Felix sniffed. 'Not to me it wouldn't . . . Besides, I am bespoke.'

Startled, Cedric slipped his foot from the pedal. '"Bespoke"? What are you talking about?'

'I rather think I may have a prior engagement,' the other replied stiffly.

'Really? Since when?'

'Since this morning. I was walking on the promenade and happened to bump into one or two of the musicians – you know the group I mean, B.B. and people . . .'

'Including the tenor?'

'Oh yes, he was there of course,' Felix said casually, and catching his reflection in the wing mirror flicked his hair. 'They were most affable, and I rather inferred they would not be averse to my attending a little soirée being held at Crag House tomorrow.' He folded his hands and gazed out of the window. 'How enchanting the trees are at this time of year,' he murmured.

There was no contest, Cedric thought wryly. Given the choice of being socially snubbed by a putative murderer or clinking musical glasses with the attractive and eminent, his friend would naturally elect the latter. Besides perhaps it was only fair: hadn't he himself ratted on the Claude Huggins' invitation! A fair exchange he supposed.

CHAPTER TWENTY-TWO

Betty Morgan sat in the High Street café sipping her coffee and staring rather pensively at the door. The last time she had sat at this table Mr de Lisle had come in and she had handed him the typing she had done. He had been very complimentary and bought her a tea cake; even kissed her hand. He could be like that when he was in a good mood and things were going well with the business. He had said something about a run of luck and an arrangement to meet a chap who was going to fix him up with some foreign firm wanting an English publisher. When he was pleased with life he spoke at the rate of knots so she hadn't really been paying all that much attention – too busy planning her date with Algie . . . Huh! That had been a disaster and no mistake.

She frowned recalling her beau's morose silences and

stinginess over the cinema seats. He had bought the cheapest – the one and ninepennies if you please – and they had sat at the front staring at a screen so blurred you could hardly see a thing. She had a crick in her neck for days afterwards! Well one thing was for sure, she wouldn't go out with him again. No class – that was it. Not at all like that smart Mr Brightwell. Now he did know how to treat a lady.

She took another sip of her coffee being careful to crook her little finger like her mother always advised her to do. 'It looks more refined,' she would say. Actually Betty found it a rather awkward gesture and had twice burnt her knuckle and nearly lost hold of the cup. Still, practice made perfect as her mother was also fond of saying. Thus with finger carefully poised Betty thought about Mr Brightwell and his nice manners.

The first time she had met him she had been sitting on Gun Hill during the lunch hour checking her typing of a longhand script before taking it back to the office for Mr de Lisle's close perusal. God, he had been so pernickety! She had been in a hurry as she was planning to get away early to meet Algie. But then this tall man had sat down beside her and started to make conversation. At first she had been wary – a girl knew all about such overtures! But it became obvious he was not one of *them*, far too polite and classy and had shown a real interest in what she was saying. He said he had seen her a couple of times going into the office and asked if she enjoyed working for a publisher. She had told him it was quite nice but there was a lot of *pressure* due to the stacks of typing her boss slung at her and what with him being so picky. 'Although he is all right at the moment,' she had said. 'A client has offered some chapters about Paris after the war and he says he intends making it top priority. So that's put a smile on his face though I don't know why really.'

Mr Brightwell had laughed saying it must be something rather special. She had laughed too and said that as a matter of fact they happened to be the chapters she had typed that morning and was about to take back to the office. 'Are they exciting?' he had asked. She had shrugged and said that since she was only the typist and not an editor she wouldn't know, adding that there were other things on her mind. She had giggled, thinking of Algie. 'I bet it's a lucky chap!' he had joked. And then when she mentioned she was in a hurry to get the typescript to her boss before meeting Algie he had kindly offered to deliver it himself: 'I shall be passing there shortly and can easily drop it in; that'll give you extra time to prepare for that date.' So that's what she had done: given him the manuscript and gone home early. And much use that had been! Rotten Algie hadn't even complimented her on her new hair style, and she had taken ages pinning it up.

Well, she mused, no one could say Mr Brightwell was short on compliments. He was most charming. Like when he had shown her the Sailors' Reading Room the other day and asked her all about her work at Mr de Lisle's office. 'Don't you find it rather complicated dealing with so many different submissions?' he had asked. 'It would get me terribly confused. I'd be bound to mess the whole lot up!' She had explained that it was quite easy really as Mr de Lisle had a very exact filing system where everything was put in its proper place. Mr B. had seemed most interested in the organisation of the cabinets and what stuff went into which; and told her he was surprised that one so pretty was also so practical. 'You have to be bright to manage a system like that,' he had said. Beauty and Brains didn't always go together he had assured her. She had blushed a bit at that, but he seemed to have meant it because just as they got up to leave he had touched her hand and murmured that he wished *he* could have such a secretary as her . . .

She finished her coffee, and with an approving glance in the mirror decided that if the police station didn't want her efficient services (and her beauty!) then perhaps Mr Brightwell would. With luck she would see him again. She hoped so.

'How is the portrait coming on?' Rosy enquired politely. She was sitting in the morning room reading her book when Hawkins had come in to refresh the flowers.

'It is finished, madam,' the old man replied, 'or at least as far as it ever will be. There are always tiny nuances which one can rarely recapture especially if working only from memory and a photograph, indeed not a very good photograph – one gleaned from a newspaper. However, it is a fair resemblance and I think the recipient will be satisfied.' He bent to pick up a toy discarded by one of the pugs.

Rosy very nearly asked where he was sending it, but thought better of it. After all it was none of her business and presumably if Hawkins had wanted to tell her he would have. In all probability it was to the subject. But out of curiosity she enquired if she might see it. Judging from the one he had done of Delia it might be rather good.

Hawkins hesitated, and then with a slightly shy smile said, 'If madam is really interested I will fetch it. It is always useful to have a disinterested appraisal of one's efforts.'

When he returned she was surprised to see he was carrying a relatively small canvas of no more than a foot or so in diameter. What had she expected – some socking great thing like the one on the stairs? He propped it against the wall on a side table.

Rosy stood back absorbing the delicate colours, the subtle brushwork, the finely executed features, and the merest smile playing tauntingly around the subject's mouth. She judged it to be very good.

It was also familiar – astoundingly so. The pose was different and the eyes cast a fraction to the left whereas in the other they had confronted the viewer directly. But there was no mistaking the subject: the person in Hawkins' portrait was the same as the person in the photograph found in Lucas Brightwell's briefcase.

Despite her shock Rosy betrayed no recognition, and instead exclaimed, 'How alive you have made him – just like the one of Mrs Dovedale. And yet the characters are obviously so different . . . Did you know him well?' she asked casually.

Hawkins paused, and then murmured, 'Sufficiently well.'

It was an ambiguous response and Rosy was unclear as to whether he meant sufficient for the execution of the painting or sufficient to satisfy his acquaintance with its subject. It could have been either and since he didn't enlarge it would have been intrusive to ask.

However, it was as if Hawkins had sensed his own reticence, for as if to compensate he added vaguely that the man was someone briefly encountered in Paris just after the war. 'When I was there with Mr and Mrs Dovedale,' he explained. He gave no further details and Rosy tried another tack.

'Did you like Paris?' she asked. 'There must have been an awful lot going on at that time!'

'It was not entirely to my taste – too noisy and too French. I was glad to get back to England, as of course was my employer poor Mr Dovedale.'

'Why *poor* Mr Dovedale?' she couldn't resist asking. 'From what I have heard he rather liked noise especially the trumpet. You mentioned that yourself.'

'Oh yes. He liked the trumpet all right and used to visit some of the jazz clubs in Montparnasse. But he didn't like what happened as a result.'

'Why, do you mean he went deaf?' she enquired facetiously.

'There was rather an unpleasant incident. It is common enough knowledge so I am not speaking out of turn. It happened one evening when Mr Dovedale was returning home from one of those clubs, Sydney Bechet had been playing if memory serves me right, and he had the misfortune to witness a brawl, rather a vicious one in which one of the participants was knifed, albeit not fatally. The attacker – I gather a somewhat distasteful semi-degenerate – was apprehended and sent for trial and subsequently to gaol. Being the only witness Mr Dovedale was required to give evidence; in fact the French authorities recalled him to Paris for the purpose. Tiresome really, it was the start of the grouse season and he missed the opening week. It was a great inconvenience.'

'Yes, I suppose that was a bit of bad luck. Er, was the man in gaol for long?'

Hawkins cleared his throat and seemed to reflect. 'You could say that: he died there. He was found hanged in his cell. Suicide. Mr and Mrs Dovedale were most distressed when they heard.'

After he had gone Rosy sat down and stared into space her mind in a whirl. All very unfortunate about Dovedale and the suicide business, it must have been most unsettling for them. But far more unsettling was Hawkins' painting! Was it really of 'R'? If Brightwell's photo was indeed that of the river victim then so was Hawkins' portrait. Despite the latter's artistic embellishment the two were virtually identical.

She lit a cigarette and gazed at the ceiling reflecting on the old man's words. He said he had encountered him in Paris when he had been there with the Dovedales – a time which fitted with both Delia's and Angela's account; and of course when Brightwell had been at the Bourse. Yes, same face; same period. She thought of the portrait and Hawkins saying he had used a newspaper picture, so not the same as Brightwell's. Why should the young man have been in the paper? For winning some sports event in the Bois de Boulogne? Hardly. Far more likely for reasons of tragedy or notoriety.

But if it was the dead Randolph why on earth had Hawkins chosen to paint him now? And who was the intended recipient for God's sake, and why? Had it been specifically commissioned or was it an unsolicited gift?

She brooded. And then a thought struck her and she grinned. Perhaps Hawkins harboured a secret yen to be an exhibitor at the Royal Academy's Summer Exhibition and he was sending it to the selection panel for assessment. That would certainly solve part of the mystery! With that in mind she stood up and went to find the pugs. At least they were straightforward.

CHAPTER TWENTY-THREE

Like several of Blythburgh's houses the Brightwell residence looked charming. Set back from the road it was a rambling mixture of the seventeenth and eighteenth century, its walls covered in strands of Virginia creeper and the front door surrounded by frothy wisteria. The Brightwells greeted them warmly, and the day still being fine they were invited to take drinks on the terrace.

An agreeable half hour was spent admiring the garden and engaging in social chit-chat; the deaths of Delia and the publisher being studiously avoided. Cedric gloated over the splendour of their delphiniums and Lady Fawcett congratulated Freda on the peace and quiet – 'Knightsbridge is becoming so *loud* these days. Sometimes I think even louder than in the war.'

'I know exactly what you mean,' her hostess agreed,

'peacetime can be so raucous! That's why we retreat here whenever possible – a bolthole from London. If Lucas had fewer business engagements I think we would make this our permanent home.' She turned to Rosy: 'Miss Gilchrist, it's so good of you to agree about that talk, a number of our retired military have shown considerable interest. I think you can count on a full house.'

Rosy wasn't quite sure whether to be reassured or otherwise. Confronting Dr Stanley was one thing; addressing rows of veterans on the logistics of guns and searchlights might be even more of a challenge! However, she smiled and said how much she was looking forward to it.

'Actually,' Freda whispered, 'if you don't mind perhaps you and I could slip away before dinner and have a little pow-wow about the usual procedure. I always like to prime our speakers well in advance, and then you can also tell me if you want a lectern and whether you would require water or something stronger such as Lucozade.' (Lucozade? Rosy thought. Brandy more like!)

Thus ten minutes later Freda beckoned Rosy to follow her into her husband's study to discuss 'logistics'. She produced a list of the audience members, suggested a small fee – which Rosy waived – and began to explain how the event would be managed. Rosy listened attentively . . . And then something caught her eye which made her lose interest immediately.

On Lucas's desk lay a flat package partially unwrapped, a pair of scissors lying by its side. The crumpled brown paper was pulled back exposing the contents. As Freda chatted on busily Rosy's eyes were riveted on the desk. Although parts of the thing were obscured by the wrapping, she recognised it instantly: Hawkins' painting of the young man.

She stared blankly. What on earth . . . ? Freda followed her gaze and stopped in mid-sentence. 'Do you know,' she exclaimed, 'the most extraordinary thing has happened, it's really most peculiar. You see that over there?' she gestured towards the parcel. 'Well the postman brought it this morning. It's a watercolour portrait, and neither of us has a clue who the sitter is or why it's been sent. There's no name or address of the sender, no note – no nothing! An absolute mystery.'

'Er, wrong address?' suggested Rosy faintly.

'Well no not really – it's addressed to Lucas. But clearly there's been some mistake. I was going to ring up the Post Office and make enquiries though Lucas said it wasn't worth it. In fact when I came into the study he was on the verge of shoving it in the basket for the dustmen! But I said that was ridiculous as it's really quite a striking face and presumably someone must have taken trouble over it.' She lowered her voice. 'As a matter of fact I think I might show it to Mr Finchley, he lives in the village and is a bit of an expert. But I shan't mention that to Lucas – he was getting rather huffy about it though I've no idea why.' She paused, and then added, 'Actually between you and me he seems to have been rather on edge lately – probably worrying about that wretched knighthood. Honestly, as if one cared!'

Rosy smiled sympathetically and with a last glance at Brightwell's unsolicited gift followed Freda into the dining room to join the others.

* * *

The unexpected arrival of Mark and Iris was a bonus and the conversation flowed easily, though inwardly Rosy was bursting to tell Angela and Cedric what she had just seen.

Earlier she had been in two minds whether to mention Hawkins' picture. Extraordinary though the coincidence had been, it had somehow felt like a betrayal of the old man's trust and she had deliberately shelved the matter. Now, however, things were surely different. What had seemed a probable link between Brightwell's photograph and the painting had become a virtual certainty – and the clue had fallen into her lap quite unsought!

She glanced at Brightwell. If he was under pressure as Freda had hinted, he certainly wasn't showing it that evening. His manner was easy, disarming, genial – everything typical of the perfect host. But what lay beneath that smooth surface? From Freda's comments it would seem that the picture had been an unwelcome shock. So why had Hawkins sent it? Judging from the reception it had not been a kindly gesture (or if so the gesture had backfired). Could it have been some sort of taunt? A sly reminder of more dubious times? After all Hawkins' sojourn in Paris had overlapped with Brightwell's, so he was likely to have known something of the widely rumoured scandals. Perhaps he had guessed or suspected Brightwell's involvement . . .

'My goodness, Miss Gilchrist,' laughed her host, 'you *are* in a brown study, as one used to say. Clearly something very deep is going on behind those thoughtful eyes!'

Rosy gave him a dazzling smile. 'Actually I was just thinking how pleasant it is to be in such attractive surroundings and with such charming company.'

There was general laughter. 'Oh well done,' said Mark, 'just the sort of thing Lucas likes to hear. You are bound to be offered second helpings of this splendid soufflé.' He turned to Brightwell: 'You see it wasn't just the behaviour of enemy aircraft Miss Gilchrist was getting to know at Dover but also the essence of diplomacy!'

'Oh I am sure our guest knows a great number of useful things – she has a keen eye,' Brightwell replied lightly. Then changing the subject he turned to Cedric: 'Professor, I am dying to read your book on the Cappadocian caves. Tell me, did it take you ages to research?'

Rosy was relieved to be out of the spotlight, for Brightwell's last remark had unsettled her. Was it quite as casual as it sounded? Coming from anyone else it would have been totally innocuous. But from him? Had his word 'keen' been a euphemism for 'prying'? In her mind's eye she saw the briefcase he had been so quick to check at The Crown and the searching look he had given her in the bar mirror. Had he guessed then that she may have seen the photograph and indeed inspected the notepad? Perhaps she had replaced the items more carelessly than she meant – there had been a number of pockets in the thing so possibly she had slipped them back into the wrong one. Just typical!

Then another thought occurred and she nearly upset her glass . . . Oh my God, it had been Lucas who had welcomed Mark and Iris when they arrived. The study door had been ajar and she had heard the front door being opened the instant the bell had rung. Since the terrace was at the back of the house he must surely have been in the hall already, and thus could have overheard their conversation about the portrait – perhaps even noted herself looking at the thing. If he did suspect she had found the photo then presumably he wouldn't be too pleased to know she had also seen the picture! Is *that* what he had meant by 'a keen eye' . . . or was she just getting paranoid?

Fortunately such thoughts were diverted by Iris insisting she should try the *Pêche Melba*. 'Do you know, Freda makes this herself? It's her speciality, we all love it!'

It was in fact delicious and Rosy's fears were temporarily lost in the enjoyment of fruit and unguent ice cream. It was then that Lady Fawcett took the bull by the horns.

'I wonder if the police are making any progress,' she said conversationally to no one in particular. 'That inspector strikes me as being a little brighter than he appears – or at least one hopes he is. He may seem a trifle dour but I suspect he is the dedicated type, a sort of plodding bloodhound. No doubt he will unearth something before too long, they generally do.' Not, Rosy recalled, the view she had expressed earlier. Was this a gentle attempt to apply the Fawcett frighteners?

'I gather she was supposed to be writing a book,' Cedric said.

'Oh you mean that one on gardening?' Iris asked.

'No, not that. Wasn't it rumoured there was a novel floating about somewhere?'

Freda laughed. 'Oh yes it was *rumoured*. I heard of it myself from a couple of friends in London ages ago. They said it was supposed to be rather racy and even potentially slanderous. But like all good rumours not a shred of detail of course. I told Lucas and we had a bit of a laugh. Somehow the idea of Delia penning a novel seemed most unlikely: she was too impatient. Besides, as I said to Lucas, who on *earth* would she slander!' Freda turned to her husband: 'You remember, don't you?'

He gave a perfunctory nod and got up to deal with the cheese which the maid had left on the sideboard. Glancing out of the window he remarked: 'It's getting rather too dark for coffee outside. I'll ask Gillian to serve it in the drawing room.' Excusing himself he went out to the kitchen.

The conversation returned to broader topics and the rest of the evening passed pleasantly.

'Well at least we now know how Brightwell got wind of what Delia was up to even if it doesn't explain how he got access to the material,' Cedric remarked as they drove away. 'Obviously he had known about her project for some time having heard of it from Freda.'

'But only as the vaguest of rumours,' said Lady Fawcett.

'I imagine that if you had quite a lot to hide even the vaguest rumour would be worrying. It would certainly set you thinking; and possibly planning . . . Yes, at least that's one thing we've established.'

'Actually there is something else,' Rosy murmured and she proceeded to tell them about her discovery in the study.

When she had finished Cedric said to Angela: 'My goodness, our genial friend was absolutely right – she does have a keen eye! A keen nose too – perhaps we should rent her out to the local hunt as a pointer.'

* * *

As they neared Laurel Lodge Lady Fawcett emitted a deep sigh, one less of fatigue than perplexity.

'I do agree that the matter of Hawkins' painting is most peculiar,' she said, 'and his sending it to the Brightwells certainly seems to confirm Lucas's link with the wretched Randolph. But Rosy dear, I take it you are absolutely sure that the faces were the same? I mean mistakes can be—'

'Quite sure,' Rosy replied firmly. 'Besides, Hawkins said he had known the man in Paris: it's too much of a coincidence for it not to be the same.'

'Hmm. But even if Delia's proposed revelations did give him the idea of murder, how did he get hold of the cyanide and how on earth could he personally have administered it? I mean, like Hugh, I gather he wasn't *there* when it happened – chairing some charity meeting apparently.'

'Yes,' Cedric agreed, 'this has been bothering me too. Yet he certainly has the motive, and judging from Delia's depiction of him he also possesses the necessary ruthlessness. Your term "personally" is crucial . . . I suspect he had a minion or accomplice. He devised the plan, the other carried it out.'

There was a silence as they digested this. And then Rosy said thoughtfully, 'In that case do you think this A. N. Other was simply a hired lackey, a sort of professional hitman – or did he also share a vested interest in Delia's death?'

'Ah, a leading question! But I note you say *he*. Perhaps if there is a collaborator it is someone of your own fair sex: the lady who took the tickets at Felix's last lecture for example. She looked distinctly shady to me – I mean, an Alice band at seventy?' He laughed and switched off the engine. 'And talking of Felix I must make haste for Aldeburgh, he'll be avid to regale me of his musical evening. But before I go would it be too much trouble if you gave me Delia's notes? I'd really like to take a closer look. We shall be in Southwold tomorrow so we can drop them back then.'

'If it would help,' offered Lady Fawcett graciously, 'you could deliver them to me at the hairdresser. I have an appointment at eleven and it would save your coming here.'

'How thoughtful,' he replied, 'but won't you be incognito?'

'What *do* you mean?'

'Camouflaged as a hairdryer. One would hate to give them to the wrong person!'

When Cedric finally reached The Sandworth it was to find Felix sitting alone in the cocktail bar nursing something or other. It was very late and Cedric was surprised to find the bar still open.

'It's a wonder the staff aren't all in bed,' he said.

Felix beamed. 'They *were* about to batten down the hatches but I told them that I had spent such an enchanting evening and just *had* to relax for half an hour before retiring to the Land of Nod and would they mind granting the weeniest extension.'

'And presumably they didn't mind?'

'Well I wouldn't go so far as that but they were certainly very obliging.'

'Hmm. So I suppose you want to tell me all about your soirée.'

'Not *just* at this very moment,' the other replied. 'I need to mull things over and hone my report for tomorrow – after all one wouldn't want to miss anything out.'

'Oh heaven forbid!' murmured Cedric greatly relieved. 'A little shut-eye will do us both good.'

They exchanged solemn winks and made for their rooms.

The following day, rather to his surprise, Cedric woke early. The sun was already sidling under the curtains, and he knew there was no point in trying to return to sleep. Thus reaching for his spectacles he sat up in bed, and with pillows propped comfortably began to reread Delia's excerpts.

In fact there were four pages, not the original three that Rosy had first shown them. Yes, in addition to the narrative part and its brief memo list there was another one with additional notes and jottings. Being a writer himself, albeit not of the lurid fiction Delia seemed to espouse, he knew that such squiggles and desultory phrases could have meaning – sometimes indeed crucial to the theme of a whole chapter or section. Thus settling his glasses more firmly he began to make careful inspection.

As perhaps to be expected, the name of *Lucian Lightspring* had been doodled a couple of times in the margin, and on the page itself those of *Ralph* and *Randolph*. But there was another name too that Delia had presumably been toying with – *Klaus* the character in the bar, plus what looked like two surnames with question marks after them: *Hogarth* and *Huguenot*. The latter was circled – a sign of approval?

In brackets was written: *K selects & vets the 'employees'.*
Non-participant but voyeur.

There followed a list of scribbled words and jottings.
Under the heading Cigarettes she had jotted *Gauloises*,
and then crossed it through and in capitals written
ABDULLA. This was followed by the note: *Blue eyes –*
change to brown but retain the naevus on cheekbone
and manicured nails. If further confirmation were
needed, which it wasn't really, the allusion to the naevus
and manicured nails certainly fleshed out the persona
of Lucian – and indeed of his counterpart Lucas whose
features of naevus and neat nails Cedric remembered
noticing. He tried to recall the latter's eyes. They were
rather good – and yes, distinctively blue. A prudent
amendment. Delia had clearly been very definite about
the brand of cigarette. Did Lucas smoke? He didn't
know – only Mark and Freda had smoked with the coffee
that evening, but that didn't mean anything. He would
enquire of Rosy Gilchrist, she might know . . .

So far things fitted with what they had guessed. But what
about the German Klaus (or with the name of Huguenot
perhaps French)? Now that really was interesting. What
part did he play in this absurd drama? And was he fact or
pure fiction?

He was about to put the page aside but spotted a final
item: *NB. Ask Fl. about chapter headings.* So who was this
'Fl.' that she intended to consult?

Cedric removed his glasses, lay back on his pillows and
gazed at the ceiling . . . Perfectly obvious: Floyd de Lisle of
course. It was to him she must have taken the bulk of the

manuscript and that was why the dead man's premises had been broken into and ransacked – and very likely why he had been killed . . .

Cedric brooded; and then glanced at his watch. Yes, perhaps he could just manage half an hour's shut-eye before his newspaper was brought: after all, energy would be needed for breakfast. With Felix's report on his own evening's sortie it was bound to be rhapsodic!

CHAPTER TWENTY-FOUR

Cedric and Felix had spent a most congenial evening with three ladies whom they had met at the festival. The women were friends up from the metropolis and seeking sea air, bird life, golf, music and 'anything else that takes our fancy'. Whether Cedric and Felix were of that last category was not entirely clear, but they had evidently met with approval, for the ladies had invited them for a light supper of crab and cocktails in their rented cottage near St Edmund's.

They were a lively trio and rather to their surprise the two friends had found their company most convivial. Indeed Felix had gone so far as to say that should they ever be passing his Knightsbridge premises he would be delighted to present them with some of his choicest blooms. (Cedric felt a trifle sceptical of this.)

The evening over they took their leave amid fond farewells and mutual compliments.

'I think we made rather hit there, don't you?' Cedric said.

'Oh they found us charming,' Felix agreed. 'And I must say they were better company than Claude Huggins and that dreadful woman who keeps pestering you to recommend materials for her rockery!'

They had parked the car in Bartholomew Green, and as they strolled in that direction they saw a tall figure emerge from the King's Head. To say it was walking unsteadily would be a euphemism: the man reeled and staggered as if the victim of a shoot-out in a Wild West film. With much muttering and moaning he lurched towards them.

Cedric gripped Felix's elbow: 'Avoid,' he hissed.

They pressed themselves into a doorway hoping the drunk would pursue his tortuous way. He didn't, of course, but stopped a couple of yards from where they stood and leant against the wall breathing heavily. A street light threw into focus an unkempt beard and mane of hair.

'Oh my God,' breathed Felix, 'it's him!'

'Who?' whispered Cedric, 'not an associate I trust.'

'It's Huggins – the brother, the one at Walberswick where I dined the other night.'

They remained stock still in the shadows, and then to Felix's dismay heard the hiccupping sound of sobs. 'Oh God,' he muttered, 'that's awful.'

Huggins must have sensed their presence for the next moment he had raised his head and stared directly at them.

'It's Felix,' he declared tearfully. 'What are you doing there – having a pee?'

Felix assured him that was not the case and they had just paused to admire the contents of the shop window (ladies' vests and bloomers) before going to their car. 'Er, are you all right?' he enquired diffidently.

'Oh yes, chirpy as a cock sparrow,' was the slurred reply. He looked at Cedric. 'So who are you?'

Cedric explained he was a friend of Felix and visiting the area.

The other blew his nose, and leaning towards Cedric slapped him on the shoulder. 'Any friend of Felix is a friend of mine!' he boomed.

Regaining his balance Cedric smiled wanly. He could have done without the accolade. Politely he asked if Fabius was on his way home.

'Not with a punctured tyre I'm not,' the other replied morosely, 'besides, given my present state it might be *problematic*,' he hiccupped.

There was a long pause at the end of which Felix coughed, and avoiding Cedric's eye said, 'Perhaps we could give you a lift, we shall be passing the turn.' In view of the man's earlier hospitality it seemed churlish not to make the offer.

Cedric sighed inwardly. Yes, it had been inevitable, but he just hoped the chap wouldn't be sick in the car! 'Have you eaten?' he enquired warily.

For some reason the question seemed to elicit more sobs and a spate of muttering which consisted mainly of the words 'bastard' and 'sod'. Cedric liked to think they were not directed at him.

Thus slowly they weaved their way back to the car and bundled the lachrymose Fabius into the back seat, Cedric taking the precaution of spreading an old mackintosh over their passenger's knees.

Once on the main road Fabius seemed to recover himself; alarmingly so, as the muffled sobs were suddenly replaced by raucous singing. The folk song 'The Foggy, Foggy Dew' was rendered with ear-splitting verve.

On the whole Felix considered it lacked some of the refinement of the Pears/Britten version and he could see Cedric's jaw tightening. 'I say,' he said, in an attempt to quell the noise, 'do you know any lullabies?'

'Dozens,' he replied airily, 'I used to sing them on my missions. It steadied the nerves.'

'What missions?' Cedric asked.

'Flying against the Hun, of course. A bit hair-raising that was, especially when we dropped into France . . . Curtains if they caught you, *after* the interrogation, of course. Still, I was one of the lucky ones. It was the lullabies – brought me luck. I'll sing one if you like,' he offered graciously.

The first notes of 'Hush Baby Bunting' were struck, but Felix headed him off: 'You produced a magnificent supper the other night, and what a superb table-setting!'

The ploy may have been a diversion in one respect, but in another it was less successful. Fabius emitted a strangled howl of rage followed by a profusion of profanity. Mercifully this soon ceased and from amid the ensuing silence came a lingering snore.

Cedric drove on grimly. 'Clearly a madman as well as a

drunk,' he observed. 'Do try to be more selective over your dinner invitations in future dear boy.'

Felix closed his eyes and thought of bed.

When they arrived at the cottage Fabius was still asleep. 'We had better wake him up,' said Cedric, 'though it seems a shame, there's bound to be another outburst. If we can get him into the house we can just leave him there and then take off pronto.'

Felix agreed but warned the other of the mess they would encounter. 'He is not the neatest of householders.'

After a couple of prods Fabius opened his eyes. 'Here already?' he said brightly.

Manoeuvring him up the path was not as difficult as they had feared. His sleep had made him placid, and although taller than both of them they were able to ease him along with little resistance. However, at the front door he stopped and muttered, 'I don't really want to go in there, not sure if I can face it.'

Felix was puzzled: if he was referring to the mess, he must surely be used to it by now.

With a little coaxing they succeeded in getting him inside and then into the sitting room. At the threshold they stood aghast.

Apart from the ordinary shambles, which Felix had expected, there was something much worse. He gazed horrified at the centre of the room which on his previous visit had displayed the exquisitely adorned dining table. It was still there, but, as if by thunderbolt, virtually every piece of its splendid setting was destroyed . . . the shimmering crystal and Meissen porcelain dashed to smithereens and even the white napkins doused in lurid red wine, the decanters cast to the floor.

There was silence, during which Fabius stumbled to the sideboard and uncorking a bottle of brandy took a long spluttering swig. 'You see what the fucker has done?' he cried, 'I told you didn't I! Christ, I'll get him if it kills me!' Rage, pain and alcohol made him slump to the floor, while Cedric and Felix looked on stupefied and helpless.

At last, having gently disengaged him from the brandy they were able to calm him down and ease him into an armchair. They unearthed cushions and a rug, and urged him to drink some water. Then they watched irresolute as Fabius sprawled in the chair, his bony fingers kneading the rug while listless eyes stared into space.

Felix leant forward and said diffidently, 'I say, shall I see if I can find one of your cats?'

Fabius looked up. 'Most thoughtful,' he said, 'the darker one will do. It's called Tom.'

After Felix had slipped out, Fabius looked at Cedric and nodded approvingly. 'Bright little guy, your friend, isn't he? He shares my interest in shire horses, you know. Do you like them too?' he asked conversationally.

'Remarkable creatures,' Cedric replied blandly. At least the man had ceased effing and blinding, and if Felix could find the damned cat it might distract him further. He shot a glance at the table and wondered vaguely if they should try to clear some of the debris: it was hardly a cheerful spectacle for the poor chap.

Felix returned with a protesting cat in his arms. He placed it firmly on Fabius's lap where it settled down and began to purr. Mechanically Fabius started to stroke its back.

For a moment nothing was said. And then clearing his throat, Cedric took the bull by the horns: 'You seemed to imply that you know who was responsible. Are you going to press charges and report it the police? I take it there was a break-in.'

Fabius continued to stroke the cat. And then he said quietly, 'There was a break-in, yes, I do know who was responsible and no I am not going to report it to the police . . . or at least not just yet I am not. Got a bit of thinking to do first and then I shall act – you can be sure of that. The bastard's gone too far, too far . . .' He looked up at them and added simply, 'Those things were very precious to me.' He lapsed into silence and was clearly not going to be drawn further.

'Well,' said Cedric briskly, 'I think a little tidying up is needed and then we'll be off. You could do with a good sleep, I imagine.' He gestured to Felix and they set about transferring the bulk of the broken bits into an empty box found in one of the corners.

When they had finished things still looked a mess, but at least all the shattered pieces were out of sight. By this time it was clear Fabius was on the edge of sleep; but as they moved to the door, he said drowsily, 'I appreciate your help, but I should be grateful if you would mention this to no one. Do you understand? No one.'

They assured him they fully understood and with some relief let themselves out.

* * *

'Astounding,' exclaimed Cedric as they regained the car. 'What on earth was all that about? I must say that some of that tableware was very valuable – and beautiful. No wonder he was hopping mad!'

Felix shuddered in agreement thinking of his own collection of exquisite valuables in London. How frightful to come home and discover them in that state!

He lit a cigarette and pondered. 'Difficult to tell in a room like that but it didn't look as if anything had actually been stolen – just vandalised. Who could have done it? Some cretinous philistine with a grudge?'

'Well it was obviously malicious and there is no doubt that Fabius knows the person, or thinks he does. He made that abundantly clear.' Cedric gave a dry chuckle: 'If he does seek him out I shouldn't like to be in that chap's shoes. Fabius at full throttle would be like a one-man lynch mob!'

'Talking of throttle, do you think you could go just the teeniest bit faster – I am desperate for my bed. It has all been rather exhausting. I shall look utterly drained tomorrow.'

Cedric obliged and then said slyly, 'Well one thing is for certain, you have definitely made a hit with the chap; quite the bosom pal! I gather the pair of you bonded over cart horses, or so he believes. And I must say he was most impressed with your suggestion regarding the cat – as was I. What made you think of it?'

'We had one at home, a frightful fellow called Denis. Whenever my mother walloped me, which was not infrequent, the cat and I would curl up and go to sleep together. Most soothing, I can recommend it.'

*　*　*

As they drove through Snape on the road to Aldeburgh Felix stared out at the expanse of reed beds and darkened marshland, and for a disturbing moment was reminded of his encounter with the monster coypu – beastly thing! But then glimpsing the shape of an abandoned pillbox in the middle of a field he thought of something else: the war and the ever-present threat of enemy fire from the skies or invasion by hordes of parachutists. He closed his eyes. Well at least thank God that was all over and done with . . .

But the image of parachutes dangling from the heavens returned his thoughts to the man they had just left. 'Do you think Fabius really did fly dangerous missions in the war? He must have been a rather more stable character than he is now . . . Mind you, had he been captured I should think he would have confused the Germans all right. I cannot imagine Oberstleutnant Fritz having a happy time interrogating him!'

'Oberstleutnant Fritz would have had him for breakfast,' replied Cedric dryly, 'which is why he would have been supplied with a cyanide capsule. It was obligatory.'

CHAPTER TWENTY-FIVE

The inspector was none too pleased. There had been little progress with the two cases, the press was on his tail, his tooth ached, some tiresome woman from the flower festival had reported her purse stolen (why leave it in the lavatory for God's sake!), and worst of all the superintendent was leaning on him: 'Have another go at the Dovedale lot,' he had directed, there must be more to get from that quarter. I would do it myself except I'm up to my ears with the Beccles fraud case. We've got them on the run – won't be long now before *yours truly* can make an arrest.' He had given a cheery grin.

All right for some, the inspector thought gloomily, smug so-and-so.

At the door the superintendent had paused and said, 'My money's on the butler like in the novels; probably hid the cyanide behind that eye patch!' He laughed heartily at his own joke (poor in the inspector's estimation); and then growing serious, said curtly, 'Anyway see to it, we can't hang about – doesn't look good.'

Hang about? What did he think he did all day – file his nails? Besides he doubted if the butler had also dispatched the chap on the cannon. No, the more he thought about it the more he was convinced the deaths had been caused by separate people. Jennings' suggestion about the murderer having an arsenal of weapons was absurd of course. The publisher's death had been a quick snappy business, a single shot well aimed and immediately lethal. Why should someone with a pistol at his disposal have bothered with the poisoning charade when she could so easily have been gunned down swiftly in a back alley – or more likely from cover of the garden hedge when walking those piddling pugs! No, he brooded, different means, different mentality, different person.

Recalling the piddling pugs he sighed, thinking of the recent directive. Another interview with the 'grieving' son was not a cheerful prospect. Having clearly established that he had been elsewhere when it happened, the man seemed to assume that no further assistance was required. Like getting blood out of a stone it had been! Well at least he could push him more about his mother's past life: it might just yield the odd clue he supposed.

He turned his mind to the butler: he hadn't been easy either. All very aloof and correct; the soul of discretion. But then that was probably typical of that sort – too busy guarding their rumps to be useful. Still he had certainly been present at the prize-giving event, he had been roped in to help with the washing up . . . The inspector grinned. Perhaps he could pin it on the pair of them: the absent young master being the instigator, the poor old servant his poisoning lackey. That would make a handy package! But then of course they would still have to find the Third Man who had done the dirty work on de Lisle. He scowled. And then getting up he opened the door to the outer office. 'Jennings,' he called, 'what was that pseudonym you were burbling about?'

'Shall I telephone ahead and tell Mr Dovedale we are coming?' Jennings asked.

The inspector shook his head. 'No, we'll surprise them. Sometimes it's better that way, you get what one might call a more spontaneous response as they don't have time to prepare themselves – or their stories.'

Thus they arrived unannounced and initially their knocking yielded no reply although the distant sound of a dog's yap could just be heard. They went back down the steps and peered in at a downstairs window. This also yielded nothing. And then Jennings spotted a well-padded posterior bent among the begonias. 'It looks like the gardener, sir,' he whispered.

They approached and enquired the whereabouts of the owner.

'He's not here,' the man said, 'he's gone off. Who are you?'

On being told they were police officers he pushed his cap to the back of his head and sucked in his breath. 'Ah, s'pose you've come about the mistress. A bad business if you ask me, she were a nice lady. And she really liked her flowers, very keen she was. Now young Mr Dovedale, he ain't so keen – don't know a daisy from a daffodil. But he likes to see the garden neat and tidy, very particular in fact; so I expect he'll still be wanting me. Leastways let's hope so otherwise there'll be a hole in my wages!' He grinned ruefully.

Unconcerned with the gardener's job prospects, the inspector asked when Mr Dovedale was likely to be back. The man shrugged and said he didn't rightly know but Mr Hawkins could probably tell him.

'Oh, so he is here? There was no answer when we knocked.'

'That don't mean nothing. It's his afternoon off – doesn't like to be disturbed. Pretends he can't hear.' He grinned again and added, 'No flies on old Hawkins. Try knocking again. If the dogs set up a good racket he'll answer soon enough.'

They tried again and this time were greeted by Hawkins roused and distinctly disgruntled.

'I fear there is no one here,' he informed them stiffly. 'Our guests have gone over to Aldeburgh and Mr Dovedale is in London. It is good for him to get away, he has found this whole affair most distressing.' This was said in a tone of mild reproof. Clearly Hawkins felt their presence an imposition.

'I am sure he has, but if justice is to be done matters must be pursued. We simply wanted to ask him a few more questions about Mrs Dovedale's life before she came to Southwold.'

Hawkins paused fractionally, and then said, 'You mean when Mr Dovedale's father was posted abroad in the diplomatic service?'

'Yes, and I believe you were with them, were you not?'

'I was with them for a period before the war in Switzerland and subsequently afterwards in Paris when they were there for a brief spell prior to returning to England. Since then you could say I have been a permanent fixture,' he added dryly.

'Hmm. Well when Mr Dovedale returns we will explore that with him. But meanwhile, Mr Hawkins, perhaps you could be of help. For example can you think of any incident when you were with them in Europe that might have prompted someone to hold a grudge against the deceased or indeed anything of that period which might be linked with her murder?'

Hawkins sniffed and said tartly: 'My role in the Dovedale household is entirely professional. As such I was not privy to my employers' private lives or that of their associates.'

'Oh, come on sir,' Jennings protested, 'surely you might have picked up something. I mean – you know – straws in the wind, that sort of thing.'

The other gave a dry smile. 'I can assure you, Constable, had I observed such straws it was hardly my place to draw conclusions from them. I dislike rash assumptions and even more, inappropriate curiosity.'

'So in other words,' the inspector said sharply, 'during that period you didn't see or hear of anything that might have a bearing on her murder.'

'Not that I am aware of.' He cleared his throat and added, 'Now, sir, would you like me to inform Mr Dovedale of your enquiries when he gets back? I am sure he will be entirely at your disposal.'

'We will contact him as necessary,' replied the inspector shortly. He hesitated and then said, 'There is just one more thing, Mr Hawkins. Does the name Millicent Merrivale mean anything to you?'

The old man looked startled; but then shaking his head said thoughtfully, 'Merrivale? No, no I can't say it does . . . unless of course you refer to that Newmarket favourite Major Merrivale, he's tipped for a big win I gather.' He flashed a rare smile and then enquired if that would be all.

'Well he's not exactly a bloke to pass the time of day with!' Jennings exclaimed as they returned to the drive. 'A bit shifty if you ask me.'

'Put you in your place though, didn't he,' the inspector observed with a whiff of satisfaction. 'But yes, you're right – he's a rum bugger and I suspect he knows more than he's letting on. Did you notice that the one time he lost his balance was when I asked him about the name Millicent Merrivale? Caught him on the back foot there I fancy. What did that gardener say? No flies on old Hawkins? Well what's the betting that just at that moment one may have landed.'

'So what you are saying is that if my theory is right about Millicent Merrivale being an alias for Delia Dovedale, then Hawkins could have known she was writing the thing and under an assumed name. In fact,' Jennings added excitedly, 'maybe Hawkins was her amanuensis!'

'Her what?'

'You know – doing dictation and such, sort of literary assistant.'

'Unlikely I should think. The old boy probably had enough to do polishing the silver and playing guard dog at the front door without having to be her clerical whatsit as well . . . No, that's a bit of a no-ball I should say. But what I do think is that given our theory about the real author, then it *is* quite likely that Hawkins knows or at least guesses its contents. Wouldn't you say?'

Stung by the dismissal of his inspired suggestion, and having noted his boss's replacement of 'my theory' with 'our', Jennings merely grunted and looked at his watch.

CHAPTER TWENTY-SIX

Walking home that night down Pier Avenue the inspector brooded on the case.

Yes, he mused, the key to the whole affair surely lay with that ruddy novel. The woman had been killed because she was writing it; the man because he had intended to publish it. Quite clearly the object of the break-in had been to steal the manuscript – the open money box a clumsy effort to confuse the issue. Find the novel or its bits and all would be revealed . . . Except of course the thing wouldn't be found: the murderer was bound to have destroyed it by now. Conceivably a draft or rough scraps might exist somewhere but certainly nothing of that nature had emerged when they were checking the deceased's desk and private papers. At the time, of course, they had been looking for clues of a different kind: diary references, threatening letters etc., but any written pages would have been thoroughly checked; and the bank strongbox had yielded nothing except the usual pile of share certificates and other financial documents.

His thoughts were interrupted by a youth bicycling by whistling his heart out. Huh! It was all right for some! He scowled unreasonably at the boy and stopped to light his pipe.

His mind returned to the butler. Apart from that hesitation over the name of Millicent Merrivale the man had been coolly composed; but as he had said to Jennings, he felt pretty sure the old boy knew something. Unfortunately gut feeling alone would hardly licence them to grill the chap until he broke. (A device favoured in the Yankee films). A pity really – in his present mood he wouldn't mind doing just that. Anyone would do, it didn't need to be Hawkins.

By this time he had reached his front gate he had brightened. At least there was one certainty. The wife had promised him Sole Bay crab and cockles for his supper, his favourite. For a few hours the case could go hang.

It had been a happy suspension. But the following morning he was back in the office again compiling an interim report for the superintendent; an irksome chore at the best of times and this was not the best.

Jennings entered with a mug of cocoa. 'I have been thinking, sir,' he said.

'Good.'

'You know that Casino building where de Lisle was killed.

Well they say it's like the station clock at Waterloo – it's a popular local meeting place. I bet the deceased had arranged to meet the killer at that spot.'

'Yes, very likely, but it seems an odd place and time all the same. One can imagine an illicit tryst being held there, a couple in a covert liaison; but I doubt if that was the killer's pretext. But the meeting was obviously in de Lisle's interests, something sufficiently pressing to warrant his turning out at that time of night.'

'Of a more professional nature perhaps?'

'Possibly. Let's check his engagement diary again. It should be with the file.'

Jennings returned with the diary but also with an envelope. He grinned and held it out. 'The desk has sent this through – the postman brought it a few minutes ago.'

The inspector looked at it and groaned. In capital letters it bore the inscription:

TO WHOM IT MAY CONCERN,
THE POLICE STATION,
SOUTHWOLD.

'You can open it,' he said indifferently, 'it'll only be another of those *I think you ought to know* letters – some old girl complaining about the neighbour's cat peeing on her geraniums or a peeping Tom incensed about the "goings on" under the pier.'

Jennings slit it open and frowned. As with the envelope the contents was in capitals.

It simply said: 'Ask C. H.' There was nothing else.

He passed it to the inspector. 'That's a bit cryptic, isn't it sir? I mean who is C. H. and what is one supposed to ask him?'

'Ah,' replied the inspector darkly, 'that is all part of the conundrum. And to solve it I suggest you contact all the C. H.s in the Suffolk phone book and ask each of them what precisely it is they are hiding. It's called a process of elimination. A most instructive exercise.' He bent his head again to the superintendent's report.

Jennings continued to hover. 'But sir—'

The other looked up and said curtly: 'File it with the other bilge and get back to work.'

Jennings retired to the outer office taking de Lisle's diary with him. He flicked through its pages to the day before the body had been discovered. Yes, it was as he recalled. DENTIST stood out in bold letters followed by the four entries. They were office appointments each with a client's name, one in the morning, three in the afternoon. The script was large and untidy, and it was only as he was about to flick to the previous page that his eye was caught by a much smaller scribble squeezed into the margin. Unlike the rest it was in biro and at first sight seemed like a doodle. But on closer inspection he discerned the words: *B. re Paris publisher.* No time featured and it had the appearance of a hasty jotting.

The Paris bit was obvious enough: but the initial was the difficulty . . . and if the inspector made another crack about trawling through the telephone directory he would spike his cocoa!

Of course, he mused, it might have no relevance at all; merely a carelessly scribbled memo nothing to do with anything very much, least of all with a nocturnal rendezvous with a would-be killer. Funny though that it should have been put on the same page as the other engagements *and* under that fatal date . . . A coincidence? He wondered.

'Find anything?' enquired his boss over lunch.

Jennings showed him the page with its barely decipherable note. To his relief nothing was said about telephone directories.

'Hmm, could mean nothing, could mean a lot,' the inspector said thoughtfully. 'Like these modern paintings: *ambiguous* – you pays your money and you takes your pick. And talking of which, I think we might pick up Miss Morgan again. You never know, if she can keep her mind off shopping she might be able to shed some light though I don't exactly bank on it . . . Tell you what, instead of bringing her in here again it might save time and tears if you paid her a visit at home. You know, nice and casual like.' He gave a slow smile and added, 'A little treat for the sharp eyes.'

Since her last meeting with Mr Brightwell at the Sailors' Reading Room Betty had seen him only once and that was on the opposite side of the street with a middle aged woman whom she assumed to be his wife. The woman was examining something in the draper's window and Betty had taken the opportunity to give him a gay wave. The greeting had not been returned; in fact he had looked straight through her as if she didn't exist. Rotten so-and-so. He had seen her all right!

Thus feeling peeved she had rather welcomed the telephone call from that nice Detective Constable. Unlike miserly Algie with his moods and stupid winkle-pickers he seemed sensible; and unlike that Mr Brightwell he was young. She began to feel better and went to apply her most vibrant lipstick – Fool's Gold by Lalange. It was their newest and everyone was talking about it.

When Jennings arrived she greeted him with weak tea and a dazzling smile (rather jammy actually). He showed her the diary entry, took out his notebook and with patient probing succeeded in getting her to tell him what she knew. As the inspector had feared, this didn't amount to much but at least it was something.

No, she really couldn't say what or who the 'B.' stood for. If it was an initial she didn't recall him using it elsewhere. However, the Paris thing was easy: he had told her that he was due to see a man who had plenty of clout with a French publishing firm eager to obtain English novels of popular appeal, ideally crime and skulduggery. Apparently Mr de Lisle thought he could offer just the right thing and said with luck the man would help fix the deal. She had asked him about the title and author but he had laughed and said that would be telling. He had seemed very excited and she had the impression the meeting was imminent.

At this juncture Jennings wondered if he should say something about her lipstick. It was very assertive and seemed to make her mouth look very big. He didn't think he liked it much but suspected she did. However, as his psychology manual stressed, a judiciously placed compliment could pay dividends.

He cleared his throat. 'My sister wears a lipstick like that,' he lied, 'but it doesn't suit her nearly as well as it does you.'

Betty smiled graciously. 'Well it needs style I suppose, not everyone's got it.' She flicked back a blonde curl, and raising her tea cup was careful to stick out her little finger.

He nodded firmly. 'Yes, style, that's it.'

The ploy proved well-judged for she became increasingly attentive to his questions.

He checked back in his notebook to his previous interview with her when she had been sorting out the scattered files. 'This Millicent Merrivale script, the one you reckon disappeared, can you recall any of its contents? What was it about?'

The red mouth pouted and she gazed into the distance obviously thinking hard. Eventually she said, 'Well I don't really read much of their stuff – too busy typing it. And anyway a lot of it is boring. But I do remember one or two bits . . . It was definitely set in Paris because it mentioned the Eiffel Tower and the River Seine and there were a lot of French words used. I think it was just after the war because there was some stuff about the German occupation and how they were glad it was over.'

'What about the characters?'

She shrugged. 'I didn't notice . . . they seemed a bit boring really or stuck up. I think there was someone called Klaus who wasn't very nice and there was another man too who was a bit weird, a nasty piece of work from what I could make out. He had a poodle called Pipi. Now isn't that a stupid name for a dog! But it all seemed a bit daft – not my sort of book at all. I like Barbara Cartland. Her stories are really nice and the girl always gets her man in the end. Have you read any?' Jennings shook his head. 'But as I said, with Mr de Lisle's stuff I was always too busy getting my typing right to bother about plots and such.'

He thanked her for the tea and told her she had been most helpful.

'You're welcome any time!' she replied archly; and then added, 'Oh, by the way, that meeting he was going to have – he said it would have to be in the evening out of office hours as it was the only time the man could fit it in.'

He returned to the station moderately pleased. So that was it then: 'B.', whoever he was, had deliberately inveigled the publisher to the Casino under the pretext of fixing him up with a buyer, and then silently shot him dead. Task done, he would have whipped smartly over to the office and lifted the Dovedale/Merrivale chapters.

Jennings grinned. Presumably he must have been a bit startled to learn the next day that his victim – last seen dead on the grass – had somehow relocated himself to the barrel of the cannon!

Of course it still didn't explain how the killer had known where to look. It was obvious from the scattered manuscripts that he had had to search the contents of the cabinet to find the right one – but he must have had prior knowledge about *which* cupboard or cabinet to select.

How had he guessed that the better material was kept there and not in another one? It rather implied that he may have known de Lisle sufficiently well to be familiar with the way he had the place organised. Was he a friend or social contact? Or had someone else casually supplied the information?

Well one thing was clear: Delia Dovedale had certainly known 'B.' – why else was her novel so vital to him? And since, as Betty had said, the thing was set in Paris then very likely they had been in Paris at the same time. It just went to show, he mused, the Betty Morgans of this world did have their uses.

On returning to the station he was informed by the desk sergeant that the inspector had received an anonymous telephone call.

'It was some geezer saying it would be in our interests to interview that Claude Huggins over at Dunwich – you know the one, always in the local press complaining about how the visitors keep tossing their crisp packets into his garden. Anyway, according to the boss the caller was most insistent but rang off before he could ask questions.' The sergeant shrugged. 'Probably one of these nutcases who enjoy wasting police time; there's always one like that once a case gets into the newspapers.'

'So what's he done?'

'Sent a couple of chaps to make routine enquiries. You have to take these calls seriously, or appear to. Most of them are from lunatics but there has to be some sort of response – it's called covering your rear.' He grinned.

Jennings thought of the earlier note which had been filed as 'bilge'. Perhaps its writer had felt he had been too gnomic and wanted to flesh things out a little. At least now that old Huggins was revealed as its target there would be no bright talk about 'processes of elimination'!

CHAPTER TWENTY-SEVEN

Cedric and Felix stood on the shingle opposite the hotel admiring the evening sea. The tide was in and there was little sound except the soft rhythmic slap of wave on beach. The rays of the westering sun skimmed the sails of distant fishing smacks, and the air was redolent of warmth and the merest tang of salt.

'How peaceful,' Cedric murmured, 'and how utterly remote from our life in London. It's almost like another world – serene and strange.'

'I don't know about strange, damned sinister I should say given recent events!' Felix replied. 'But I agree, utterly beautiful. No wonder my musical acquaintance is reluctant to tear himself away.'

'Oh no wonder,' Cedric tactfully agreed.

'Rather a shame that one hasn't had a proper chance

to explore,' Felix observed. 'I mean what with my festival commitments and all the police palaver there has been so little time. I know you gadded off to Minsmere for ages leaving me marooned with Claude Huggins and his earnest cronies, but *I* have seen very little of the area.'

'Except of course the habitats of coypus and the odd gun emplacement,' Cedric reminded him.

'Oh yes, very funny I am sure! And talking of Huggins, a visit to Dunwich would have been nice. I don't mean to his house of course, but the coastal part. The history of that submerged town and its ghostly tolling bell sounds most intriguing. I wonder if Clarence House is familiar with it . . .' he sighed. 'Ah well, one day perhaps.'

Cedric consulted his watch. 'We are rested and fed,' he said, 'we could drive over now if you like. Rather a good time actually: no sightseers, and judging from the present scene it should be ideal at this time of day. Who knows, one might even catch the sound of a distant bell!'

'I don't mind what sound we catch as long it is not Claude Huggins prosing on about his confounded book. When I was at dinner I asked him if he was hoping to get Floyd de Lisle to handle it. That didn't go down at all well. He looked at me as if I had made a rude noise and said that perhaps I didn't realise how scholarly the thing was and that naturally it was intended for a proper London or Oxford publisher *when* the time was right.'

'Hmm. I am sure the publishing world is agog,' Cedric laughed.

'Exactly. As said, we should avoid at all costs.'

* * *

It had been an excellent idea of Cedric's. The drive itself was a pleasure: a benevolent sky, peaceful gorse land, and, despite the hum of the engine weaving through deserted lanes, a pervasive air of slumbering tranquillity. Arriving at the outskirts of the village they passed the ruins of the old abbey gaunt and spectral in the twilight.

After parking the car they decided to walk along the road to the church before inspecting the beach itself. The road was edged by a handful of houses beyond which stretching far into the distance lay a flat expanse of pasture and wild heathland. They lingered at a farm gate, lit cigarettes and gazed across into the encroaching dusk. Apart from the cry of a solitary curlew the silence was absolute.

'Pretty damn good,' Felix murmured, 'but we must keep our eyes skinned for old Claude. I have an idea his house is somewhere along here.'

'Has it got a name?'

'I think he said it was something like 'The Folly', not the most original.' He gave a faint titter: 'Like the book, doubtless a *folie de grandeur.*'

They walked on, skirted and admired the church and came upon its graveyard and the ruins of the ancient leper sanctuary.

'Extraordinary,' exclaimed Cedric, gazing at the crumbling walls and ivied arches, 'I wonder how often this has been painted. Grimshaw or Samuel Palmer would have gone potty about it.'

'Too spooky for my taste,' shivered Felix, 'just look at

those bats!' He lifted his hands to his head. 'They get in your hair you know.'

'Not yours, dear boy – it's the spikes, they wouldn't be comfortable.'

They turned round and set off towards the beach. Half way there Cedric nudged Felix and pointed to the other side of the road. 'I think that's it,' he whispered. 'There's a conservatory at the side and a long garden wall.' He put on his glasses. 'Yes, I can just make out the name on the post: you're right it is The Folly.'

They looked for lights but couldn't see any. 'Probably out gassing somewhere,' said Felix, 'or helping his brother sort out that broken glass and crockery.'

'I doubt the latter. I have the impression he is not the most altruistic of types.'

They continued to the beach and scrambled up onto the shingled ridge.

The scene that met their eye more than justified the drive. The silver-grey sea was awesomely vast and eerily calm; the great sweep of the bay seemed to stretch endlessly, its placid emptiness soothing yet vaguely mysterious. Standing alone on the silent shore they could have been on the edge of the world.

After a moment of silence, Felix observed, 'It's not exactly Brighton, is it? No breakwaters for a start.'

'Hmm. No ice cream sellers either.'

They continued to gaze. And then Cedric said, 'Just imagine that entire little town at the bottom of it all, swallowed up by the waves without a trace, and now no one the wiser.'

'Awful!'

'No, not really – a sort of metaphor for human life I suppose . . . *sic gloria transit* etc.'

'As I said, awful.'

Cedric smiled at his friend: 'You really need the bright lights don't you!'

'Yes,' Felix agreed, 'those and the odd professor, I suppose.' He lowered his left eyelid.

They started to stroll north along the beach; but then hesitated wondering whether to continue on or to retrace their steps and explore the sanded area below the sloping cliff. They decided on the latter.

They had only gone a few yards when Cedric said, 'Oh look, I think there's somebody up there.'

Felix followed his gaze to a figure standing on the higher ground. The stance and build were familiar and the sun's dying rays made the profile easy enough to discern. 'Oh my *God*,' he breathed, 'it's bloody Claude.'

He was right. Claude Huggins stood poised on the upper slope staring out to sea and dangling what appeared to be a pair of binoculars.

'What's he doing?' Cedric muttered, 'watching sea birds, I suppose. Do you think we can sneak off without his seeing us? I don't especially want to engage in social chit-chat just now, least of all with Claude Huggins.'

'Too late – the bugger's waving.'

Cedric groaned. 'Look the other way.'

'No good; we are caught all right. Look, he is coming down.'

Picking his way with careful purpose Huggins descended the cliff path and walked towards them. Used to seeing him in formal attire they were slightly surprised at the open-necked shirt, flapping boy-scout shorts and worn plimsolls. Felix eyed them quizzically: not the most flattering garb he couldn't help thinking. He glanced down with approval at his own neatly-pressed slacks and polished leather sandals; a rather classy pair carefully selected from Simpsons of Piccadilly.

'Well met!' Huggins exclaimed. 'I saw you through my binoculars and hoped you would come my way. It's always nice to have a good chinwag at this time of the evening, wouldn't you agree?'

They said nothing but smiled politely. 'I suggest we take that direction,' he continued, gesturing to the way they had come, 'there's a bit of the beach further on that affords an even better view than from here, and it's a real sun trap – or at least when the sun is out it is, not now of course.' He gave a loud laugh that made Cedric wince.

'Actually,' Felix began, 'we were about to go, so if you don't—'

But any such excuses were drowned by their companion's continuing babble as he steered them firmly along the strand. He was walking at a brisk pace and Felix's toes were being jabbed by random sharp pebbles. Really, it was too bad – his sandals were made for sauntering not striding!

Just as Cedric was about to call a firm halt to things, Claude pointed to a mound of scree and sandy tussocks. 'That's where we will sit,' he announced.

'It's getting rather late for sitting,' Cedric replied curtly. 'I am afraid we shall have to desert you.'

Claude's manner which up till then had been effusive and garrulous changed dramatically: 'Oh dear, *desert* me, will you?' he enquired with heavy sarcasm, 'now that *is* a coincidence – or should I rather say another piece of the tedious pattern?' He began to chuckle in a way that was far from genial.

'I don't know what you mean,' replied Cedric coldly.

'Then I suggest you let me enlighten you . . . Pray tarry awhile while I unburden my woes.' Claude emitted a caustic laugh.

Despite his distaste Cedric was curious. What the hell was the fellow getting at? He shot a glance at Felix who seemed similarly intrigued. 'What woes?' he asked.

Claude bent to adjust his plimsoll; then lifting his head, said: 'The woes of persecution.'

'*Woes of persecution!* What are you talking about?' Felix gasped. 'Who's persecuting you?'

'All of them,' Claude replied. He picked up a pebble and tossed it casually at a piece of driftwood.

'Ah,' Felix said earnestly, 'I know *just* what you mean: there are some days when other people can be too dreadful for words. I can't tell you how beastly the tax man has been to me recently. And as for that firm in Madeira which is *supposed* to be supplying my early blooms – well frankly I think they are being positively vindictive!' He ran his fingers through his hair which the salt air had made even spikier than usual.

Claude Huggins regarded him impatiently. 'Your paltry problems have little to do with me, Mr Smythe. Mine are on a rather grander scale.'

Felix bristled. 'Well really! One starts to show a fellow sympathy and—'

Cedric cut in. 'Tell us about this grand scale, Mr Huggins,' he said quietly.

The man studied him, paused and then said, 'Since you have the courtesy to show a proper interest I will tell you: I am the victim of an unjust pursuit which will end in my imminent and tragic disposal.'

'I see. And who exactly are these pursuers?'

Huggins sighed and settled himself more comfortably. 'The first is dead I am glad to say. I suppressed her with great dexterity and not a little drama.' He turned to Felix. 'Wouldn't you agree, Mr Smythe? I believe you were present at the time.'

Felix gaped and said nothing.

'Yes,' Huggins continued, 'Delia had been most tiresome with that stupid novel of hers. I think she thought it was rather clever – too clever by half as things turned out. Had she kept her mouth shut, or rather her pen sheathed, she might be alive now. As it is . . .' his voice trailed off and he gazed towards the sea. 'There were other reasons too but I really haven't time to go into those.'

'Why not?' Felix asked.

'Because my *dearest* brother has shopped me to the police and as a consequence they are doubtless pounding their way here at this very moment.' Theatrically he cupped his ear: 'Hark! Are those their dulcet footsteps scurrying nigh?'

They listened to the enshrouding silence broken only by the gentle slap of distant waves.

But then the stillness was broken by a harsher sound: Huggins emitting a wild laugh. 'Yes, one is a veritable fugitive from the law. But as they say in the films, there is another gunning for me too and whose clutches I must elude.'

'Whose clutches?' they demanded in unison.

He shrugged. 'Lucas Brightwell of course – or Lucian Lightspring, as our inventive Delia named him. He disposed of de Lisle and now he will try to dispose of me. I know too much and am an embarrassment to him, an encumbrance – just as Delia was to both of us.' He looked at Felix: 'You don't happen to have a cigarette on you by any chance?'

Felix hesitated. Did he really want to hand one of his best Sobranies to this raving lunatic? Even HM wouldn't be as gracious as that! On the other hand, since by his own admission the man was a fiendish murderer it might be prudent to do so . . . after all if he took offence anything might happen! Thus rather nervously Felix complied with the request and even supplied a light.

Cedric was not really surprised by the reference to Brightwell: it fitted with their suspicions but it was shock to learn that his co-murderer had been this unsavoury specimen. As depicted in the bits they had read, Delia's novel had stressed the protagonist's cool ruthlessness. Thus Huggins' assumption that he was a marked man was probably correct. But if so what was he doing lolling about on the shingle puffing one of Felix's cigarettes? Surely flight might be the more practical course.

'I expect you would like to know where I obtained the cyanide,' Claude said casually.

'Your brother?'

'Spot on. How did you guess?'

'Oh just something he said.'

'Yes, Fabius used to fly secret missions into France and Germany in the war. Like an idiot he kept the cyanide capsules they were issued with. He said he had a sentimental attachment to them. Naturally their retention contravened all regulations, but somehow he wangled it. I knew where they had been put so I stole them; cut them open, poured the stuff into a file and spiked her soup . . . It was easy enough,' he added nonchalantly.

Cedric was intrigued. 'So you say Fabius has informed against you. Why?'

'Because he is sneaky fellow. Pure malice! We had an altercation – rather heated I fear. And consequently I trashed his table.'

Felix gasped. 'My God so it was you! But he had some superb Meissen plates and Bohemian crystal!'

'Not any more he hasn't,' Claude said smugly.

'That was a bit excessive, wasn't it?' Cedric remarked. 'It must have been quite a row.'

The other gave an indifferent shrug. 'Entirely his

fault. A couple of years ago I had foolishly left my Paris journal lying around. It contained a number of indiscreet entries and unfortunately he read them. At the time he said nothing; but after he had discovered that I had filched his cyanide capsules he became most disagreeable and accused me of Delia's murder. He had the nerve to say that if I were not his brother he would report me to the authorities. Well you can understand my anger – hence the table. When the police came sniffing around making so-called "routine enquiries" I knew what he must have done. As said, pure vindictiveness . . . Mind you,' he added darkly, 'he has never been quite right since his breakdown after the war.'

There followed a dazed silence during which the narrator scratched a mosquito bite on his leg.

Felix cleared his throat and as a change of subject said politely, 'If you don't mind my asking, how is your book coming along these days? You were most enthusiastic about it at dinner the other night.'

There was a long pause. And then eventually Claude said quietly, 'I imagine the fish are reading it: I threw it into the sea two days ago.'

'You did what!' Felix exclaimed. He was almost as shocked by that as by the other revelations. Surely the man had been labouring at it for years! Having bored everyone else with the thing had it now bored him?

'What use is it?' Claude asked indifferently. 'In my present situation flowers and shrubs are of little account. The police are closing in; that visit was just the prelude. It is simply a matter of time, short time at that. And besides, as I have said, Brightwell will come for me. So one way or other, by noose or by gun, I am a dead man . . . always have been really. Except for the time in Paris – that was diverting. Yes, you could say that that was Klaus Huguenot's finest hour: a prime procurer and oh *so* discreet! The Russians found me useful too . . . Hmm, I wonder why Delia assigned me that ridiculous name: a rather laboured play on Claude Huggins I suppose.' He gave a mirthless laugh, stood up and began to remove his shirt.

'What are you doing?' said Felix faintly, still trying to absorb the man's words.

He made no answer but stooping down started to take off his plimsolls. 'Thank you for your time gentlemen,' he murmured, 'an unexpected and most pleasant way to spend my final evening.'

Before they could say anything he had turned, and now naked except for the drooping shorts began to pick his way over the pebbles towards the waiting sea.

'Cedric,' whispered Felix hoarsely, 'I don't think he is just going for a swim is he?'

'No, he isn't.'

They watched in silence as the portly figure reached the water's edge and without a pause began to wade into the surf.

'We could pull him back,' Felix urged. 'If we run we can still reach him!'

'There's no point,' Cedric replied grimly. 'What would we save him for? To stand trial and then the noose or at best Broadmoor? Besides if he's right about Lucas Brightwell he is destined to be shot anyway. As he said, whatever happens there is no future. He has made his choice – to go the same way as his book and the drowned village.'

Turning from the now darkly swelling sea they began to retrace their steps along the lonely beach. At one point Felix did look back but to his relief saw nothing.

CHAPTER TWENTY-EIGHT

Rosy stepped down from the platform to the sound of warm applause. It was the first time she had spoken at length in public and she had been horribly nervous. But once into her subject and reliving those extraordinary times with the other ATS girls on the south coast she had found herself enjoying the experience. The enthusiastic response was gratifying – and reassuring.

The only thing to distract her had been the presence of Lucas Brightwell. He and Freda had been sitting in the third row flanked by Mark and Iris. Their neighbour's normally bland face had seemed pale and strained and on two occasions she had seen him glance at his watch. It had been slightly unsettling. Were her reminiscences being so irksome? But she had also noted Hugh sitting at the back of the hall looking unusually alert and interested, so presumably her performance couldn't be that bad.

Once it was over and the audience dispersed, she and Lady Fawcett stayed behind drinking coffee with Iris, Hugh and Mark. And it was then that the most extraordinary thing happened.

The door of the hall was thrown open and Freda appeared looking visibly upset, in fact Rosy thought she was on the verge of tears.

'What is it?' Iris exclaimed. 'You don't look too good.'

'Oh I'm all right,' Freda said quickly. 'But it's Lucas, he's in an awful state. He can't get the car to start – my fault, I was going to get petrol this afternoon and forgot. He's fearfully angry!'

Iris laughed. 'Oh silly you! Come on, we'll give you a lift of course. Tell Lucas it's hardly the end of the world. When the garage opens in the morning they can send their pump man with a can; old Bill is awfully good like that.'

Freda looked slightly relieved and was about to return to the car park when her husband entered.

In his hand was a length of hose, and addressing Mark he said, 'Would it be a bore if I siphoned a gallon of petrol from your tank? It's rather urgent.'

Mark looked taken aback. 'Ah, er, yes, I suppose—'

'But that's hardly necessary,' Iris protested, 'we have just told Freda that we can drop you off. It's only a short way.'

'Thank you, but I am going rather further than the village. I have a business appointment and am late already.'

'In that case I suggest you order a taxi,' Hugh said,

'although ten o'clock at night does seem rather an odd time for a business meeting. Still, not everyone adheres to the social norm.'

Whether that last comment was intended as a barb Rosy couldn't be sure, but it certainly produced a reaction.

Lucas Brightwell's eyes swept over the younger man and with an icy sneer he retorted: 'Some of us lead busy lives – an experience presumably you wouldn't understand.' Something must have gone badly wrong inside the suave Brightwell. For when his wife caught his arm and cried, 'Oh Lucas, how can you say that – it's too much!' he swung round, and with a face contorted with fury called her a 'stupid fucking bitch'.

There was a stunned silence broken only by the striking of the church clock. And then Hugh stepped forward and hit him.

Brightwell staggered backwards, lost his balance and fell to the floor. Blood streamed from his nose.

His assailant glared down at him. 'You are such a feeble fraud, Brightwell,' he observed, 'and no wonder my mother always said you were a cad.'

'But not a feeble one,' the other snarled. And reaching into his coat pocket he pulled out a pistol . . . a Webley, but minus its silencer.

He levelled it at Hugh and flicked the safety catch. The bullet caught its target smack on the shoulder and with a gasp of shock Hugh sank to his knees.

Brightwell raised his arm to fire again, but was incommoded by Rosy's handbag. It was a large one containing her notes for the talk, and its impact on his head did the job. The bullet hit the side of the stage and the gun slipped from Brightwell's grasp – to fall at Angela Fawcett's feet.

'Oh dear,' she murmured, and bent to pick it up. And then waving it vaguely in Brightwell's direction, said firmly: 'And don't try any funny tricks!'

My God, thought Rosy, where did she get that from – Bob Hope?

Mercifully Mark stepped forward and discreetly relieved her of the weapon and the watchers could breathe again, not least the man on the floor.

Mark ordered Brightwell to lie flat on his stomach, and without taking his eye off him snapped, 'Someone call the police, we must get them here at once.'

'Is there a telephone?' Rosy asked. 'I didn't see one.'

'There's one over there,' said Lady Fawcett pointing to a corner, 'but I'll see to it; you had better help Freda, I fear she's about to faint.'

She lifted the receiver and dialled the local police station, its number boldly displayed above the phone.

'Ah,' she said, 'I have to report a rather disturbing incident that has just occurred in Blythburgh's village hall . . . Oh, my name? It's Angela Fawcett, Lady Fawcett. I am staying at Laurel Lodge as a guest of Mr Hugh Dovedale. My host has just been shot and maimed, and it would be helpful if you could attend to the matter . . . What's that? No, I am not the one responsible and I suggest you come quickly otherwise the actual culprit may foil us and make his escape. I also suggest that you use one of your speedier vehicles, we don't want any hiccups . . . Thank you *so* much. How very kind.'

She gave a gracious smile and replaced the receiver.

Listening to her Rosy thought it had sounded as if she were ordering wallpaper from Harrods. However, it certainly did the trick for ten minutes later there sounded the purr of an engine, and a flashing blue light illuminated the car park.

Freda did faint – which was perhaps just as well for she was spared the spectacle of her husband being hauled off the floor, handcuffed and propelled into the waiting police car. It had been an ignominious end to an illustrious career.

On his way out the captive had suddenly pulled back, and looking at Rosy said coldly: 'Neat work, Miss Gilchrist. I always suspected you were one of life's interferers – quite lethal in your quiet way!'

'Aren't you?' she had wanted to retort, but no sound came and she watched sickened as he was hustled out through the doors.

The sergeant turned to her. 'What was that he said, miss?'

She shrugged. 'I've no idea – I think he's mad.'

A little later when they had a moment together, Lady Fawcett whispered, 'Very wise Rosy, the less said the better. I cannot see that we have a bearing on any of this. Heads beneath parapet as my Gregory used to say.'

Rosy nodded, feeling too numbed to say anything to anybody.

As the guests were being driven back to Laurel Lodge – their host's shoulder being attended to at the cottage hospital –

Cedric and Felix were also driving away from their own ordeal.

After ten minutes of silent cogitation, Felix murmured tentatively, 'Uhm . . . do you think it is *absolutely* necessary that we should mention this? I mean *we* didn't push him into the water, he was planning to go in anyway. I cannot see that our being there has a bearing on anything really.'

'No bearing at all,' replied Cedric firmly. 'I think we adopt the parapet policy, that is to say we keep our heads below it. After all, what Claude Huggins chose to do in his spare time was his own affair.' He paused, and then said, 'And whatever may or may not emerge in the course of the police enquiries our being on that beach is neither here nor there. The body will be washed up somewhere, they will doubtless find his shirt and shoes and obvious conclusions will be drawn. But it will be nothing to do with *us*.'

Felix breathed a sigh of relief. What it was to have such a sensible friend! 'I am presenting my trophy tomorrow,' he said brightly.'

'Exactly; and we wouldn't want anything to interfere with that would we? Besides it is the Cambridge lecture soon: I have my notes to prepare.'

He depressed the accelerator.

CHAPTER TWENTY-NINE

Seated between the two officers in the back of the police car Lucas Brightwell began to contemplate his next move; and then feeling the pinch of the handcuffs realised that all moves were barred.

One way or another it would all come out; not just the Paris high jinks (and his London recreations) but the business of the wretched Randolph and that oily little prick of a publisher. Grasping fool! He had swallowed that tale of a French firm wanting his book like a fledgling grabbing a worm. The shooting had been easy – but in the event it had somewhat backfired. Brightwell gave a mirthless laugh which startled his captors.

'Glad you find it funny, sir,' said the sergeant woodenly.

'Oh it's going to get much funnier yet,' he replied bitterly.

An image of the watercolour danced before his eyes and

he flinched. There could be only one person who had sent that, the Dovedale's manservant. He had been in Paris with them and said to be a bit of an artist. Nasty chap – too smooth by half, and watchful with it. It was Freda's fault. If she had filled the car up as he had instructed he could have nipped over to Dunwich and done the job. Simple. Just as it had been with the other two. But with Claude alive he didn't stand a chance; there was no loyalty there, never had been – which was why the Soviets had found him such an easy tool in Paris.

He brooded on Claude, or 'Klaus' as Delia had dubbed him, and resolved that whatever happened, doubtless the worst, he would make sure that he swung too. What was the expression the underworld used – to sing like a canary? Well he would sing all right!

As if to prepare for his aria Brightwell began to whistle a couple of bars from an Ivor Novello musical.

'Shut up,' snapped the young constable.

He relapsed into silence. It was women really: they messed things up. Freda, lethal Delia, and then of course the prying Gilchrist girl – fancy being felled by a sodding handbag! If it hadn't been for them, particularly Delia with her literary delusions, his pleasurable life could have continued as smoothly and lucratively as ever. As it was . . .

At the station Brightwell was cautioned, given a cup of tea and asked if he would require a solicitor.

He sighed wearily. 'Absolutely no point, no point at all. Hurry up, let's get on with it.'

And so they did.

* * *

It had been Jennings' late shift and he had not been required at the station until later that morning. It had meant a nice lie-in and a long breakfast.

When he arrived at his desk he sensed an air of buoyancy, a muted excitement which he suspected had little to do with the sudden change in the weather from drizzle to dazzling sun. Evidently something had happened in his absence.

'There's been an arrest,' the desk duty sergeant told him 'and the inspector wants you to report immediately.'

Jennings did as directed and entered to find his boss on the telephone. 'Yes, yes sir,' the inspector was saying, 'I take your point about him being a bit of a bigwig and to go carefully, but I can assure you by his own admission he has broken every rule in the book including murder. He made a full confession last night and very colourful it was . . . No, we won't release details to the press . . . But one thing: I don't think the Chief Constable will be pleased – they play golf together.' He gave a sepulchral chuckle and put down the receiver.

Turning to Jennings he said, 'Ah, you've missed some fun and games, my lad. While you were languishing in your bed, some of us have been working. I was called in late last night to conduct an interrogation of Mr Lucas Brightwell. Worn out I am, but all very instructive – most instructive.' He grinned.

Jennings was taken aback. 'But we didn't have grounds.'

'Oh yes we did. Initially of the attempted murder of Mr Hugh Dovedale – but there's going to be a lot more than that I can tell you.'

'What happened?'

'Over in Blythburgh. He used a gun on Mr Dovedale: a Webley, the same model that killed de Lisle. A silencer was found under the dashboard in his car. When we enquired why he needed a pistol in his pocket when attending Miss Gilchrist's lecture he explained that he was on his way to Dunwich to have a little chat with his good friend Claude Huggins. Apparently he was anxious to get to Mr Huggins before we did.' The inspector shook his head sadly: 'Just goes to show what they say about best laid plans . . . seems his wife had forgotten to fill the petrol tank. Very put out about that he was.'

Jennings frowned. 'But I thought you said to the Super just now that he *had* murdered someone, not just attempted it. Surely just because the weapons are the same it doesn't conclusively prove that he had killed de Lisle . . . a bit circumstantial I should say.'

'Would you now. Well in normal circumstances you *might* be right, but in this particular instant you're not.' He paused and stretched for his pipe and then seemed to take an excessive time lighting it.

The operation complete, he leant back and said, 'You see our friend made a full confession – full, frank and lurid you might say. He was very explicit. Confirmed immediately why he had shot de Lisle – to prevent publication of Delia Dovedale's novel. He had been its central character and a very nasty one it seems, although I don't think he saw it that way himself. He seemed to think he had been rather clever.

'Your Miss Morgan was right: the thing was based on post-war Paris where he and his then crony Claude

Huggins had been engaging in all manner of unsavoury antics, including in his case the disposal of a call boy named Randolph. I won't bore you with the details now but it was a sordid little saga. And you know what gets my goat? The sod has been such a flaming hypocrite! I feel sorry for the wife. Apparently he only married her for cover – to give an aura of righteous respectability. He was a user, just as he used your Betty to get information about the publisher's filing system and a sighting of a bit of the typescript.'

Jennings wanted to make it clear that she was not 'his' Betty, but there was something more pressing. 'So how did he administer the cyanide?'

'What?'

He repeated the question.

'Oh no,' the inspector said, 'Brightwell didn't murder Mrs Dovedale – at least not directly – that was Huggins. I tell you, Brightwell has really shopped him. Told us lot of interesting stuff. Apparently he was furious when Huggins killed her – felt he had jumped the gun and that if they had sat tight things might have blown over or been handled more subtly. It was only when he learnt that Delia's death was not the end of things and that de Lisle already had the manuscript and was hell-bent on publishing that he too felt compelled to act.'

'Huh! A charming pair. But what I don't understand was why Huggins had acted so rashly. I mean even if he had heard from Brightwell that it was rumoured she was writing this book it was only hearsay, he couldn't be sure that he featured, or at least not in a crucial way.'

'Precisely what Brightwell thought which was why he

had been so miffed. But he reckons there was more too it. According to him Huggins had developed an obsessive dislike of poor old Delia. Apart from the threat of exposure there were other things that offended him, the main one being that she had been married to the man he had come to hate. By chance Dovedale had witnessed a knifing incident in Paris involving Huggins' then boyfriend. He had been required to give evidence and as a result the attacker, Huggins' boyfriend, was sent to gaol where he later hanged himself. Huggins has born a grudge ever since . . . But according to Brightwell there was something else too, something which he thought was very funny. I thought so too but I wasn't going to share my mirth with that basket.'

'So what was that then?'

'Well from what I could make out she had disparaged his precious flower project. Indiscretion and a loud voice is not the best of combinations and unfortunately poor old Delia had both. She made a remark to a friend which he happened to overhear – something to the effect that she couldn't imagine how one so dull and prissy as Claude could possibly pen a book that would appeal to the plant-loving public. "Think of the turgid prose!" she had cried. Brightwell thinks that was what tipped the balance – she had signed her death warrant. Barmy really.'

Jennings nodded gravely. 'Oh yes, that's very common; you often come across it.'

The inspector, who had been in the middle of relighting his pipe, paused surprised. 'Do I? Come across what?'

'Well perhaps not you *personally*, sir,' Jennings explained patiently, 'but just in a manner of speaking.

It's an established psychological fact – it's the little things that tilt them over the edge, especially when it affects their vanity. They take umbrage you see.'

'Hmm. Do they now. So what have you been reading – your textbooks or Agatha Christie again?'

Jennings looked nettled. 'Actually, sir, she's jolly good. You ought to try her, she's—' He broke off, struck by a thought. 'But what about Claude Huggins? What's he saying?'

'He's not saying anything because we haven't got him. The bird has flown, done a runner. When they went to pick him up last night to bring him in for more questioning he wasn't there, not a sign – though his car was still in the drive.'

'Run out of petrol?' Jennings murmured.

'Oh yes very funny!' The inspector scowled.

At that moment the telephone rang. He picked it up and listened in silence before saying curtly, 'Thank you. That's most helpful.' Replacing the receiver he removed his pipe and stared morosely at the ceiling. 'That's all we need,' he sighed.

'What's he done – caught the Harwich ferry?'

'No. He has *been caught* in a fishing net south of Thorpness. The skipper was most indignant. He had been banking on a good catch and all he got was Huggins' body.'

Jennings nodded. 'As you said sir, the best laid plans . . .'

CHAPTER THIRTY

Shocked and exhausted Rosy and Lady Fawcett returned to Laurel Lodge driven in a police car. It was three o'clock. And yet as they mounted the steps Rosy was surprised to see Hawkins standing at the open front door fully dressed in his usual daytime attire. He gave a formal bow and informed them that the hospital had rung advising him of his master's accident, and he had thus taken the liberty of placing hot water bottles in their beds.

'Not seasonal I grant you,' he murmured, 'but in the circumstances I thought appropriate. Shock induces cold.'

They were about to thank him for his thoughtfulness when he added, 'I have left some biscuits and cocoa on a tray in the drawing room. However, if you don't mind my saying I feel you may be in need of something a little more fortifying. Thus in addition to the cocoa I have supplied two large glasses of Mr Hugh's best cognac.' He permitted himself a brief smile: 'Better than a sleeping draught any day.'

He took their coats and ushered them into the drawing room, where again despite the warm weather there was a fire burning brightly. He turned to Angela: 'Will that be all, my lady?'

'Oh indeed, and thank you so much,' she said appreciatively.

As he turned to the door Rosy stopped him. 'Actually Mr Hawkins that won't be all – there's something I want to ask you.'

He looked at her quizzically.

'Tell me, what made you send that painting to Mr Brightwell? What did you hope to achieve?'

He regarded her steadily.

'Nothing except my own satisfaction: I wanted to make him sweat a little.' The old man paused, and then added ruminatively: 'He was a bastard of the first water.'

Rosy was startled and slightly amused; not so much by the use of the term 'bastard' but his choice of idiom. What century was he living in for goodness' sake? But verbal oddities aside, and despite the quiet tone, his anger was obvious.

'Yes, you are certainly right there,' she agreed, 'but what made you think that? And in any case why send the picture to him now?'

Hawkins gave a dry smile. 'I am about to retire shortly and reside with my sister in Frinton. I wanted to cause a stir, to do something wild before the onset of dotage. A servant lives in the shadow of others and defers discreetly to their whims. One is required to be bland and biddable: rarely initiating, merely complying. As it happens this mode of life has suited me well, especially after I was taken on by the Dovedales. Tact is my forte – and indeed my livelihood. But now I am nearly free of such constraints and can make a gesture of my own, ruffle some waters – and who better to disturb than Mr Brightwell?'

'You mean you are breaking the mould.'

'Exactly, madam, how well you put it.'

Hmm, Rosy thought wryly, the mould wasn't entirely broken.

'Yes, I understand that,' she replied, 'but why Lucas Brightwell – what did you know of him?'

'I knew little but suspected much. The subject of my painting, Randolph Lister, had been attached to a friend of mine in Paris. They had been close until Brightwell took over and then everything was smashed up. My friend was upset – even more so when Randolph's tragedy became known. He was convinced that Brightwell was responsible. There was no proof of course and it would have been injudicious to pursue matters. Given my position I naturally tried to keep out of things but I have always suspected that my friend was right: Randolph had become irksome, a liability which had to be discarded.'

'And what about Randolph – did you like him?'

Hawkins seemed to ponder. 'No,' he said finally, 'I did not. But he was superficially attractive and had a very striking memorable face . . . I rather enjoyed painting it.'

'And then you sent it to Brightwell to needle him.'

The old man nodded. 'Yes. It was most gratifying.'

Rosy hesitated and then said frankly: 'Actually, Mr Hawkins, I think your action may have needled him more than you expected. Although he wasn't an obvious police suspect he must have been under an awful strain. That picture coming out of the blue must have caused a sort of blind panic and sent him over the edge. His shooting of Mr Dovedale was a crazy attack which, one could say, fatally backfired . . . hoisted by his own something or other.'

'Petard,' Hawkins said gravely.

When he had gone and they were left alone Lady Fawcett remarked, 'Well they always say that a change is as good as a rest. I cannot say that I have ever subscribed to that view and in the circumstances one feels far from rested. But it has certainly been a *change*. Not at all what one had envisaged! London will feel quite humdrum after this.'

Rosy thought she detected the merest tinge of regret.

Angela's face clouded. 'It's desperately sad of course and I feel so sorry for Hugh. I wonder what he will do. We must visit him tomorrow if he isn't discharged by then. That shoulder wound looked rather nasty to me so they may keep him in for a while. But naturally we must say our goodbyes.'

Rosy agreed and reminded her that they should also say goodbye to Cedric and Felix. 'They won't know about all this yet. I'll telephone them in the morning. I have an idea that Felix is doing his trophy presentation in the afternoon, so they'll be coming over to Southwold anyway . . . Oh and remember we are required at the police station to make statements. It won't entail much I gather, just a brief résumé of what we witnessed.'

Lady Fawcett looked suddenly anxious. 'I take it that they only want the details of what we saw last night . . . It would surely be quite unnecessary to refer to anything *beyond* that, don't you agree? I mean if Lucas has made a full confession all manner of things may have come out about his Paris activities and his connection with Mr de Lisle. And talking of whom, I rather fear the Huggins creature may have overheard what the young man was telling me at the funeral; he was lurking about in a most intrusive way. If so our words may have stirred his imagination! I shouldn't care for that conversation to be included in any police report.' She gave a delicate cough. 'Yes, other than the facts of last night's little drama I don't think we should know anything, do you? It would be most unfortunate if they thought we had been withholding evidence. Although it's not as if we have had anything actually tangible to offer, is it? Merely hypothesis and speculation. And after all one doesn't like to push oneself forward.'

Rosy nodded. 'You mean we keep our traps shut.'

Her companion looked affronted. And then she giggled: 'Do you know that's exactly what dear Delia used to say at school! And she was so right then . . . as I think you are now.'

Rosy sighed. 'Well that's a relief. I'm worn out and that cognac is taking effect. Time we went to bed – another full schedule tomorrow.'

* * *

The following day they went to give their statements at the police station where they encountered Mark. The latter had already been there some time and had been informed of the fourfold charges being brought against Brightwell: for attempted murder of his cousin Hugh, as accessory to the murder of Hugh's mother Delia Dovedale, for the intended murder of Claude Huggins and the actual murder of Floyd de Lisle.

While they were there news also came through of the would-be victim's body being found in a fishing net that morning. 'At least he was thwarted in that respect,' the inspector was heard to mutter to his assistant, 'what you might call a case of being foiled by time and tide – or an empty petrol tank.'

As they walked to the car Rosy asked Mark how Freda was. 'It must be terrible for her!'

'Yes,' he agreed, 'she was pretty stunned as you can imagine. Iris stayed with her last night and she tells me that after the initial collapse she has rallied remarkably well. In fact if anything she seems strangely composed, relieved almost. Iris knows more about this than I do but I rather gather that she had been on the verge of filing for divorce and was just delaying until he had got his gong – a knighthood I think, not a baronetcy. Still, neither is relevant where he is going,' he said grimly.

'Why the divorce?' enquired Lady Fawcett ever interested.

Mark shrugged. 'Oh the usual thing, adultery of one kind and another. They had never been close. She is talking of going to stay with cousins in Kenya for a few months to recuperate and get away from the gossip. A good idea I should think.'

'Very sensible. A change is as good as rest,' was the sage response.

Rosy smiled. Not quite the view of a few hours previously!

They said goodbye to Mark and went to visit Hugh in the cottage hospital.

Yes, the matron told them, Mr Dovedale would be remaining a little longer. His shoulder had been quite badly damaged but nothing too drastic.

'She means,' a voice shouted form a side ward, 'that they won't have to saw the ruddy thing off!'

They followed the direction of the voice and found the patient lying in bed eating chocolates and reading an Edgar Wallace.

Despite the traumas of the night and the sling and bandages he looked surprisingly cheerful. He greeted them warmly, apologised for their less than tranquil sojourn and thanked them for their patience with the pugs. 'Nice little things if you don't mind short legs and snuffling noses. But they mean well – unlike that snappy little poodle Brightwell had for a time.' He frowned but then brightened: 'As it happens, I am feeling rather pleased with myself. The police were here earlier asking more questions about last night, so I thought I would take the opportunity to make a full confession; it's the sort of thing they like.'

'What sort of confession?' Rosy asked a trifle warily.

On the whole she felt she had had enough surprises.

'About poor old Floyd: shoving him up on the cannon that way. I have been feeling rather bad about that, it's been getting me down in fact. So I mentioned it to the inspector.'

'Was that wise?' Angela asked anxiously. 'Don't they call it tampering with the evidence or interfering with the scene of the crime?'

'Oh they are bound to have some term for it!'

'What did the inspector say?' Rosy asked.

'Not much. He looked a bit dour and said he'd have to look into it and that I would be hearing from them. He also mumbled something about mitigating circumstances, but at that point the nurse arrived and practically had apoplexy because of his pipe, so I didn't hear any more.' He closed his eyes.

'You must be tired,' Lady Fawcett said sympathetically, 'we're just going. But tell me Hugh, what are you going to do once this is all over? What do you think Delia would have wanted?'

'She would have wanted me to be happy,' he said simply. 'And that being the case I am going to New Orleans.'

'New Orleans!' they gasped. 'Whatever for?'

'To learn to play the trumpet. Besides, it's warm there – I can't stand this east wind.'

They gazed at him nonplussed. And then Lady Fawcett said thoughtfully, 'I seem to remember that your father was fond of the trumpet.'

He grinned. 'What you might call a zealous blower . . . which is why I want to learn the technique properly. Hence New Orleans.'

A thought struck Rosy and she asked him about Peep and Bo: 'They are not going to become orphans, are they?'

'They were Mother's not mine, so Hawkins is having them. I have given him a rather hefty golden handshake so he is kindly taking them to Frinton with him. His sister likes dogs and has grandchildren, so they will get all the attention they could wish.'

A nurse appeared and announced loudly: 'Now Mr Dovedale, it's time for your blanket bath.'

'Christ!' he groaned.

The ladies took their leave.

Later, as arranged on the telephone, they met Cedric and Felix for a light lunch at The Swan. Ready for the trophy presentation and Felix's speech, each was elegantly attired: Cedric looking suave in a light grey suit, Felix a little more raffish in cream jacket and floral cravat. His en brosse hair was sleeked with brilliantine (not entirely resilient to the spikes) and his polished shoes shone like beacons.

The two women filled them in on the events of the night and what they had learnt from Mark, plus the news of Huggins' drowning. The former prompted swift and animated comment. But for some reason their response to the latter was distinctly tepid, and the subject was quickly dropped in favour of more pressing concerns, such as the forthcoming ceremony. It was only six weeks later that Rosy learnt from Cedric of their unsettling encounter on the Dunwich beach.

Over coffee, feeling that his friend was becoming a

trifle too fulsome about his role in the trophy presentation, Cedric felt a small damper was in order.

Thus leaning across to Felix he said quietly, 'Let us hope that this time your performance on the platform will not be interrupted as it was at the last. It would be unfortunate were there to be a repeat *dose*.' He gave a sly smile.

To his disappointment Felix merely turned the other way and sighed disdainfully. 'Such bad taste!' he remarked.

Which of course it was; and for once Cedric felt duly chastened. He resolved to redress the gaffe by leading the applause in the auditorium.

Fortunately, as things turned out the ceremony proceeded without a hitch and Felix's address was a veritable triumph. Amid plaudits prompted by Cedric he beamed with gracious modesty and congratulated the runners-up on their valiant efforts. Rosy couldn't help thinking that the actual trophy recipient had been more than upstaged by its presenter. However, since the lady had also acquired a fat cheque she didn't look unduly perturbed.

As the two guests took their leave of Laurel Lodge and its pugs, and wished their host's loyal retainer well in his retirement, Rosy said 'Oh one thing Mr Hawkins before we go: you didn't by any chance leave some stationary in the blue room's wardrobe, did you?'

The old man hesitated and then with a sigh said, 'An oversight I fear. I intended to remove it before you arrived but forgot. And then once you were here it was too late . . . had you noticed it being there one day and gone the next its absence might have caused offence.'

'Most tactful I am sure, but what was it doing there in the first place?'

'It was part of an early draft of my employer's novel *Violets and Vicissitudes*. I believe she intended making a sinister feature of the former. She had shown it to me seeking my view. I told her that it seemed very promising but advised putting it in a safe place, that is to say, not her desk. As a temporary measure she slipped it into that drawer. More material was later produced which evidently she took to the publisher. Naturally I asked no questions and never pursued the matter.'

'Most correct,' Lady Fawcett observed approvingly. 'People are too explicit these days; a little reticence is always welcome.' She shot a meaningful glance at Rosy.

In the car she observed that Mr Hawkins was really an exemplary servant and were he younger she would employ him herself. 'Such an asset for my parties!' she exclaimed.

As Rosy and Angela were speeding their way back to London the two police officers were mulling things over in the office.

'Why did Huggins choose cyanide?' Jennings asked.

'That's what we would all like to know, but since he's dead I suppose we never shall. Even Brightwell seemed clueless on the subject. And when we asked the brother he just looked blank and scratched his head.'

'Hmm. So when did the brother turn up?'

'Straight after the suicide became known. Strolled into the station and casually admitted to giving us those tip-offs. When I accused him of withholding prior evidence he mumbled something about not having any and that it was just a hunch which had suddenly caught him unawares. Said he hadn't liked to be more direct for fear of confusing matters and misleading our enquiries, and he hoped we didn't mind. I ask you!'

'Dearth of imagination,' Jennings pronounced solemnly, 'it makes them odd. Still it's a pity about that cyanide – I'd still like to know how Huggins got hold of it. Presumably he thought he was being clever using that method in those circumstances.'

'Oh yes he thought that all right, as did Brightwell – the slippery hypocrite. But then there was someone else who thought he was being clever too, that Hugh Dovedale. *Very* bright shoving that poor beggar on top of the gun. What you might call a jolly jape, I suppose.' The inspector looked grim.

'Tight as a tick, wasn't he? But I bet we could still get him for obstructing the police in their enquiries.'

'Hmm. We could but is it worth it? It didn't obstruct us all that much and unlike the other jokers this one is harmless, just a bit skew-whiff that's all. And I suppose the death of his mother in that way can't have helped. No, we'll give him a caution and leave him be, the silly clod. The press will hound him for a bit of course – the public enjoys escapades of that sort. But that's as far as it'll go.'

Jennings looked disappointed, his sense of protocol offended. 'But what about the Super? Surely he'll want us to press charges, won't he?'

'Highly unlikely I should say. His Nibs rarely does more than is strictly necessary. And he's so cock-a-hoop over nailing Brightwell and that we can account for Mrs Dovedale's killer that he'll probably think anything else would be paltry in comparison and detract from the main effect. Always has a nice sense of theatre, has Mr Smithers.' A leer crossed his face. 'I tell you who won't be much pleased about all this and that's the Chief Constable. Brightwell was his golfing partner.'

The inspector knocked out his pipe, and opening his desk drawer drew out a bottle of whisky. I think after all our hard work we deserve a little treat – or at least I do. I suppose you would rather drink Tizer or some such.'

Jennings looked affronted. 'Certainly not sir! I'll have the same as you if you don't mind.' He pushed a plastic mug across the desk.

'Good lad,' said his superior.

CODA

After they had been back in London for a week Felix received a letter postmarked Southwold. It read as following:

Dear Felix,

I write to say how much I enjoyed your company at supper with us recently, and am delighted that you share my love of shire horses – something I fear my brother Claude could never do. I also wish to thank you and your friend for helping me when I was under the weather over that little upset about the dining table.

Fortunately, following recent events and a certain action I took, I am now feeling much better. Indeed life has taken on a rosy prospect.

*In celebration I have had a haircut (en brosse
like yours) and trimmed my beard. To redress the
wanton destruction of my valuables I have decided
to start a whole new collection and will thus be in
London shortly to see what Sotheby's has to offer.
Perhaps you and your friend would care to meet
me in Regent's Park to feed the ducks – or at the
zoo perhaps to inspect the monkeys.*

Yours gratefully,
Fabius Huggins

Felix set the letter aside, and gazing at the signed
photograph of his patron ran his fingers through his spiky
hair.

Rosy wondered how Angela was faring, and apart from
genuine interest felt it would at least be courteous to
telephone. She dialled and waited for some while. When
at last she heard the familiar voice it sounded slightly
muffled. 'I can't hear you terribly well,' Rosy said, 'are
you all right?'

'Not especially,' Lady Fawcett replied, 'I have taken to
my bed.'

'Oh dear! Are you ill?'

'Not as yet but I am likely to be.' There was a sigh.

'Ah . . . do you mean you are sickening for something? I
do hope that east coast wind hasn't—'

'No, it has nothing to do with the wind. It is
Amy: she has returned from the camping absurdity in
France.'

Rosy was puzzled. 'Er, I see . . . well that's rather nice, isn't it?'

'Far from it. She is accompanied by a Frenchman in a beret who assures me he is about to become my son-in-law . . .' the voice faded and the line went dead.

ALSO BY SUZETTE A. HILL

'WITTILY WRITTEN, TIGHTLY PLOTTED AND FUN TO READ . . . A SPARKLING GALLERY OF CHARACTERS'
SIMON BRETT

A Little Murder

SUZETTE A. HILL

London, early 1950s. Marcia Beasley of St John's Wood is discovered dead in her home, naked and covered with a coal scuttle and it's up to Detective Sergeant Greenleaf to solve the crime. The members of the deceased's social circle all have secrets to hide and grudges to bear. A host of colourful and comic characters hurry to identify the murderer, unravel the mystery of Marcia's life, and discover the importance of all that coal.

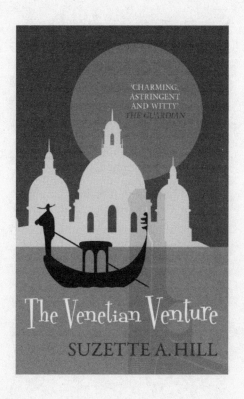

'CHARMING,
ASTRINGENT
AND WITTY'
THE GUARDIAN

The Venetian Venture

SUZETTE A. HILL

Rosy Gilchrist is sent to Venice to find a rare signed translation of Horace's *Odes* by the late Dr Bodger. Rosy jumps at the chance to fit some sightseeing around work, but the holiday plans are put on hold when she learns there is a significant bounty prize for anyone who discovers this valuable text. Finding herself in the midst of a cat-and-mouse chase, Rosy's rivals will stop at nothing, not even murder, to get their hands on the book . . .

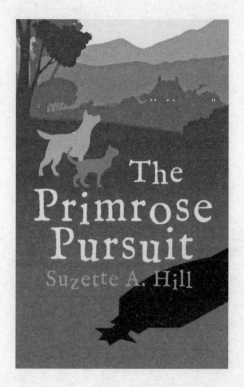

Following the tragic, though honourable, death of her brother, Francis, Primrose Oughterard has taken responsibility for her late brother's discerning cat and dog, Maurice and Bouncer. Hubert Topping, a new master at the local school is a man of seemingly impeccable conduct. Primrose, however, takes an instant dislike to him and is convinced that there is more to him than meets the eye. The arrival of the suave Nicholas Ingaza fuels her suspicions.

When a body is found on top of the downs, Primrose becomes caught up in a series of calamities and when the truth unravels it isn't long before things come to a head . . .